GIELGUD

Also by Dan DeWeese

You Don't Love This Man
Disorder
Soft Rock
Double Standard

GIELGUD

A NOVEL

DAN DEWEESE

PROPELLER BOOKS
PORTLAND, OREGON

PROPELLER BOOKS

SECOND EDITION
Propeller Books 2025
First published by Propeller Books 2017

Published by Propeller Books, Portland, Oregon.
For further information, email publicity@propellerbooks.com.

Gielgud by Dan DeWeese
ISBN 978-1-955593-13-7

Cover and interior design by No Hipness.
Illustration detail of "Cherry laurel (*Prunus laurocerasus*)" from *Medical Botany* (1836) by John Stephenson and James Morss Churchill. Public domain.

www.propellerbooks.com

GIELGUD

One

1 | The morning light appears in silence. The house, a hundred years old, absorbs the warmth, shifting with a creak.

A girl steps carefully down the basement stairs and walks to the empty side of the bed. She wears a sleeper that zips from ankle to neck and carries an old blue blanket she keeps from when she was a baby. Her brown hair is mashed and curlicued, her eyes bright. Geary flips the covers back and she climbs in. "What time is it?" he asks.

"I don't know," she says.

"Then why are you waking me up?"

He tickles her neck and she laughs. He raises his hand over her, wiggling his fingers. The hand is a spider that drops suddenly to her forehead and then scrambles wildly over her ear until she smashes it amid more laughter. The hand floats in the air again but this time the fingers kick in unison—it's a jellyfish that darts from her attempts to grab it. When it drops to her ribs, she shrieks.

"Let's play 'Neighbor,'" she says.

She turns away from him, pretending to sleep. He breathes noisily into her hair.

"Hey!" she says.

"Hi, neighbor!" he says in a lunatic voice. "Just thought I'd say hello, welcome you to the—"

"What are you doing in my house?"

"Do you have any flour I can borrow or a lawn mower, can I swim in the pool, I would like to borrow your pets and I would take them for walks and—"

"I'm calling the police!"

"Oh, I already know them, they come to see me all the time, like to tell me not to ask to borrow things or not to go into other people's houses or—oh. Is that what I'm doing?"

"Yes!"

The sketch dissolves in laughter.

He opens windows onto cool, damp mornings. Crows scream at dawn and then disappear, their cries replaced by the trill of smaller birds. Early rising neighbors chat in their bathrooms, anticipatory tones drowned in the sigh of showers or the roar of hair dryers.

A squirrel darts across the backyard grass and freezes, head tilted, listening.

Their winter days of stumbling into and talking over one another, trapped indoors, have given way to outdoor evenings, cool breezes. He walks his children to school in sunlight. They describe classroom intrigues and playground dramas, argue about which teacher will be taking over a different grade next year, which kids got in trouble at recess, who the principal likes or dislikes. They lower their voices when they cross the street to the school, safeguarding the gossip. When Geary asks in an intentionally loud voice why they are whispering, they glare at him. The boy is eight and the girl is five, but it is Geary who likes to play at being the naive child.

He decides to plant a garden in the three cedar-framed squares of dirt he has ignored in the backyard the last two summers. He pulls weeds for hours, plunging the long metal fork into the ground to get them by the root. The kids wander in and out of the house, playing, pouring cups of milk or apple juice for themselves, carrying fruit or popcorn in little plastic bowls. They come and go on imagined errands, private schedules. When watching television they sit elbow to elbow on the couch, ignoring its width. Each complains how loudly the other chews, breathes, hiccups.

Emily teaches school. She has a chalkboard on an easel in her room and addresses a phantom group of students—Geary can never tell how many. Some of them have names, though, and do well or get in trouble. She asks him to come and talk to them. He is the principal. He assumes a posture of authority and begins with the speech she wants, lecturing the students on the importance of attention and behavior. The principal becomes enflamed by his own enthusiasms, however. He begins to weep over the disrespect the students have shown Ms. G and threatens them, finger pointed, with the direst consequences. Emily tells him to stop, do it right. Though angry her father pushes her realist theater into farce, she always invites him back. He plays the role again and again, hands on his hips, staring down the invisible students.

Saturdays are exhausting. When they wake up he makes

them eggs, bacon, toast, and fruit smoothies while they watch cartoons or rented DVDs of *The Dick Van Dyke Show* or *The Brady Bunch*. There are piano lessons later in the morning, then the weekly trip to the library. Nathan only checks out movies or comic books about zombies. Emily is now old enough to explore the children's room alone. Geary checks every few minutes and is touched to see her seated at the long, low table, her head over a book, other titles stacked nearby. After the library it's home for lunch and then the Geary-imposed "quiet time." The children go into their rooms, where he brings them cookies and milk. They are allowed to read, draw, play, anything, as long as the door is closed and they are quiet. In the living room he turns music on at a low volume, lies on the couch, and drifts off for fifteen minutes.

In the afternoon there are soccer games for both of them. Sometimes the games overlap, and Geary and his ex-wife, Andrea, coordinate transportation from one game to the other. They watch together from the sidelines, trading information. They laugh about Nathan's obsession with Nerf guns—he can't resist the impulse to shoot his sister—or Emily's fascination with clothes, the way she evaluates every component of her outfits. Sometimes Andrea's new husband, Tom, is there, too. Emily has criticized his own outfits, he says. When he asked her what was wrong with shorts and a t-shirt, she told him he just wore it too often. They all agree Nathan would wear the same jeans and t-shirt every day of his life if they didn't force him to change.

At dinnertime on Saturday the kids go to Andrea's house. Geary returns home to the odd block of time that has appeared in his life now on Saturday evenings. He picks up the kids' scattered belongings, drinks a beer while paging through a magazine. The house is silent, the only sounds those that float in through the screen door. A cat picks its way from one yard to the next, collar bell jingling. Someone down the street practices piano, a classical piece Geary can't place. A man and woman laugh as they ride past on bicycles.

In the backyard, the squirrel leaps to the trunk of a tree. It hesitates a moment and then disappears upward, transformed into a quivering branch, rustling leaves.

2 | He was a freelancer. An alert freelancer, analytical, with a gaze that conveyed the ability to grasp the terms of a project quickly. He negotiated space with a kind of courtesy, keeping track, without any particular intention, of where people were in a room. His lean length and close-cropped hair, bald now at the crown, seemed an extension of these qualities. He found the way people hesitated in doorways or paused in grocery store aisles frustrating, nonsensical. A sense of geometry infiltrated even the abstract dimensions of his life. He thought of his various projects in spatial relation to one another, of his children as creatures navigating stations on a journey. He experienced life as movement through space, not time. One had been there, and there, and now here.

He sat at a long white table, looking over color mock-ups. It was 8:30 in the morning. The desks in the office were empty, the monitors blank.

"Have you designed for them before?" Larsen asked him.

"Yes, but it was a different..."

"Tentacle of the octopus?"

"It was internal communications. A sales guide."

"Arden said you understood their mix of earnestness and over-the-top obnoxiousness. He said you nailed it."

"I decided I was designing for a fraternity in which everyone really believed in the importance of the hazing rituals."

"That's it exactly. How is Arden?"

"He's well. Busy, I think."

"Yes. I'm sure he's always busy."

A long bank of windows faced the west hills, miles of green foliage tucked beneath the gray marine layer. Larsen rented this large office, had purchased all of the long white tables and desks, the computers and their oversized screens. The three men and one woman who worked for him would arrive later. He wore cargo shorts and a heathered polo shirt, light blue. He was soft-spoken, evenly tanned. This was his shop. He padded through it barefoot, at ease.

"What we're looking at is one of their non-profit programs, so you may have to drop the hazing rituals angle. Or maybe not. Maybe this program is just the fraternity documenting its good deeds."

"What do they call it when a fraternity and sorority have a party together?"

"Whatever we come up with still has to have an aggressive element, though. It's always about power. They call it *bold*. Every meeting I've ever had with them is about being bold." He placed a thin hardback book on the table and opened it. "This is about one of their other non-profits. We didn't make this—this is the thing they showed me that I think is a train wreck."

There were images of children running and smiling beneath words in all-caps: FREEDOM, CONFIDENCE. Text appeared in boxes that were purple, yellow, and green. Decorative scrolls and bullets and Victorian daggers dotted the pages.

"What's this copy font?"

"Exactly," Larsen said. "They're not made to be read, but still. Making something this inelegant is actually more work than making it nice."

"What are they doing with this page?"

"You get it. This is the let's-not-do-this."

They were happy, each pleased the other agreed. Larsen's dismissal of another firm's work didn't seem arrogant, just an observation. He ran his firm and it was natural to evaluate others.

They walked to one of the monitors and Larsen clicked through some spreads. "These are the mock-ups we gave them the other day."

"The icons are interesting."

"They're placeholders, just thrown together. You're free to design entirely for the visuals here. The copy is just a design element. No one reads it."

"I've often assumed that when writing copy."

"You write, too?"

"I used to."

"No offense, then. Here's a decent one, they liked this."

"Even simpler."

"*Bolder*. You have to say *bolder*." He tapped the screen with his pen. "This is maybe too much. At a certain point it starts to look eighties."

"It's the purple. They had purple triangles on Vidal Sassoon products in the eighties."

"You're right. I forgot. Let me print these out. Change

anything—these were just to get the job. They can be thrown out now." He clicked through more files and screens. "We've had projects I can't even…We had an outdoor gear company, one of the big ones. The founder was in love with their logo. They'd used the same logo and typeface on their catalogs and website for twenty years, completely outdated. We pitched him redesigns and he rejected them, over and over again. Then I was at an event and his daughter was there. She was in college, studying design, and she mentioned something about 'Daddy's logo.' He'd designed the logo himself but he wouldn't say so, he just rejected all changes. We also had a client—it's hard to tell the stories and keep people anonymous—but it was one of these artisan soda companies?"

"Sure."

"I don't drink soda, I don't need artisan soda, but they were the best clients."

"They let you change their logo?"

"Total freedom. They were enthusiastic about what we brought them, they seemed really happy to be working with us, it was fantastic. Their company had this three-on-three basketball tournament and they even invited us to enter. Me and Arden and one of our other designers played."

"Ten-foot rims, or did they lower them so you could dunk?"

"Ten-foot. They'd have to lower it pretty far for me to dunk. Anyway, I've been working in Portland for fifteen years now, I've done stuff I'm proud of and I've done stuff that sucked, and there's no way to know. You can turn in something that's beautiful and people will be unhappy, and then you turn in something awful and they think it's great."

He handed Geary a sheaf of printouts, pulled some booklets from a shelf, and handed those over, too. A man with a salt and pepper beard walked his bike, gears clicking, into the office.

"Mike, I was just talking about that three-on-three tournament we played in with Arden."

"Bubble Brothers?"

"Yeah. This is Don Geary, he's doing some freelance for us."

"Which project?"

"Vikram's non-profit."

The man grimaced. "Tough one. Nice to meet you." He propped his bike in the corner and walked toward the espresso machine at the back of the room.

"So maybe by Tuesday?" Larsen said. "Think you can have a rough layout?"

"What about the copy?"

"Oh, shit. I'll email it to you tomorrow. It's not much. And think about that previous one, the train wreck—they actually used that, so you really can't lose here. We might have some more work after this, too." He shook Geary's hand. His grip was firm, formal. "Good to meet you."

Geary rode home. Lines of cars and bikes flowed downtown, the streets filled with the bustling energy of people headed where they were needed. A sense of purpose rose from the tumult, as if the workday were a single great feat, wholly improvised. Geary rode the opposite direction, down beneath Grand and then up to where he could cross the freeway and enter neighborhoods where entirely different days were beginning. People lingered in coffeehouses, walked dogs, laughed at stories of the previous evening. Geary coasted past, black bag on his back, strap across his chest. He knew most of the coffeehouses, the restaurants with dark windows and the previous evening's menu still pinned by the door.

Weeds sprouted from the bark chips in front of his house. Dry moss lined the shingles. He carried his bike into the backyard, propped it against the pear tree, and dialed a number on his phone.

"Hello, Don," Arden said.

"Hey, Lem. I just met with Peter Larsen at Polymath. I wanted to say thanks for sending me his way."

"Are you still there?"

"No, I'm home now."

"He didn't invite you to work in the office? He has room. I think it's rude not to invite you."

"It's fine, I have what I need. I'm sure they're busy."

"Not so busy he doesn't have time to make out with Marcy at lunch."

"I didn't see her."

"I'm sure he keeps her in a locked office."

Geary unlocked the back door, stepped into his kitchen, and put the kettle on. "He said there might be more work after this, too."

"You mean he might want to continue exploiting free-lancers instead of hiring someone in an ethical way? Did you remind yourself he's a scumbag?"

"I forgot." He pulled his laptop from his bag, grabbed the printouts Larsen had given him. They were large, full color, on high quality paper.

"I told you to repeat to yourself, *This man has no principles*," Arden said. "He really didn't invite you to work in the office?"

3 | Sheckley lived in a brick duplex in Northeast Portland. He was the editor of an irregularly published journal about bicycling that, though it made no money, had a small but loyal readership scattered across several cities. His girlfriend, Brooke, was younger. She'd spent the last six years working her way through college. When she was done she sold her textbooks, threw her term papers out, and put her diploma in a drawer. Finally she could put aside the burden of school. It was time to start life.

Sheckley was short, fair, with a neat beard and vintage glasses. He'd tried a few jobs in his twenties—working in a bakery, writing ad copy, getting a grad degree in literature and teaching college composition classes—and had lived with different girlfriends in different cities, but things hadn't worked out. After the last breakup, he'd decided to start over. He dropped the classes he was scheduled to teach in Amherst and showed up in Portland a month later. He had no money and significant debt. He rented a room from a friend of a friend of Geary's and rode a bike everywhere. He was rained on often but unbothered by it, sometimes even pleased.

He met Brooke at a party. He'd been invited by a roommate and knew no one. Brooke had come with a friend. She had perfect, brilliantly white teeth and a winsome way of tilting her head when offering her sad-eyed smile. They dated, but he was strict with her—he could go out no more than twice a week. She had her studies and he had no money, though he omitted mention of the latter. He also knew it wouldn't last. She was too attractive. When she offered herself, he was shocked, apprehensive. When she touched him he reminded himself it was temporary, she would move on. Somehow she did not. He did not know how or why she stayed with him and tried not to think about it.

She found a duplex—two bedrooms, hardwood floors, over a garage accessed via a steep drive—and they moved in together. The garage held a few racks of dresses Brooke had inherited from her grandmother, four bicycles Sheckley had picked up over the time he'd been in Portland, and some old bookshelves they'd bought at a garage sale but had no place for. She got a job as a receptionist at a tech company downtown. These were just first moves, she felt.

"What is it?" Sheckley asked. "Is it a prize?"

He was at a work luncheon in a banquet room called The Cleaners, part of a fashionable downtown restaurant with concrete floors and an exposed kitchen. The non-profit he worked for, the Cascadia Arts Council, was entertaining donors with lunch and a speaker.

"I think it's origami," a woman at his table said. "It's darling." She was in her eighties and had dressed exquisitely for the event, including pearls. Sheckley understood she'd been giving money to the organization for nearly two decades.

He looked closely at the little paper basket everyone at the table was studying and recognized it from childhood: a prophecy game. The basket had four wings that, when placed over fingertips, could be opened one direction, closed, then opened the other direction. Each section's interior had tabs that told the operator how many times to flutter the basket open and closed. When the count was complete, you lifted a tab. In grade school you would find the scrawled name of your future husband or wife, the city you would live in, or secret truth about you.

"My grandkids make these," one of the other women at the table said. "They call them 'fortune tellers.'"

The featured speaker at the luncheon, an advertising guru named David Hulme, had placed one basket on each table. Sheckley looked at the four tabs in the basket on their table. The words *Hope, Dream, Vision,* and *Goal* were printed on them. When he opened the basket the other direction he found *Planet, Stars, Space,* and *Time.*

"We are made of stars," Hulme was saying. He stood at the front of the room in blue jeans and a black t-shirt and paced slowly back and forth, as if teaching school. "It's easy to forget, but we live on a planet that moves through space and time. Those are our parameters. Parameters are like the rules of a game. They are not the game itself, though. They create the potential for a range of possibilities. It's up to us to use the parameters to explore the field—the field of possibility. And the field of possibility is vast."

Sheckley had met people his first year in town, many through Geary, and had accepted any and all work offered. People liked him, and often saw him as a kind of younger brother. Now he typed the Cascadia Arts Council's social media announcements. He wrote their email newsletter, their solicitation letters on CAC letterhead, and the thank-you notes to donors that were printed on linen-quality paper and signed by the executive director. He wrote grant applications, ad copy, and updated the website. He'd been at CAC almost nine months, but still had a difficult time believing he'd landed a full-time job that seemed to require little more than the skill of writing clear, grammatically correct sentences. When the executive director or one of the program directors sent him drafts of things they'd written, though, he was reassured of his value.

"We are dreaming creatures," Hulme said. He was tall and thin, with dark hair and a snub nose that made him appear to be looking slightly downward. "We have dreams while we sleep, but we also have visions while we're awake. We try to make these visions real by turning them into goals. A goal is a dream. The feeling we have about a goal is what we call hope. Our minds drift through dream states while, at the same time, we live within the parameters of our physical existence. We can think of those parameters as the limits that keep us from achieving our dreams, but we can also think of them as helpful constraints. They're constraints that offer us potentials—the potentials to succeed in achieving our goals."

The CAC's eight full-time staff members were divided one each among the tables. Sheckley's table held five women, none younger than sixty, the oldest possibly ninety. They wore perfume, were polite over their meal, asked him about the organization and what events it would be hosting that year. They told him about events they had enjoyed in the past, complained about speakers they'd found rude. They remarked upon his youth. When conversation revealed Sheckley rode his bicycle to work, they congratulated him. It was impressive, they said.

Hulme told them it was time to use and discuss the paper baskets. The room filled with conversation. Sheckley wasn't sure whether he, too, should try the device or if he should serve merely as a facilitator.

Hulme stopped at their table and knelt between two of the women. He asked what they thought.

"Have you ever read Adam Phillips?" one of them said.

"No," Hulme said. "What has he written?"

"He's a psychoanalyst. It's nonfiction. Some of the things you were talking about today reminded me of him."

"Which things?"

"When you were talking about parameters and said they could either be limitations or potentials. Trying to think of something in one direction or the other—Adam Phillips does that. He does it at length, of course, in detail, but some of what you were saying was similar."

"I hope that's good."

"It is, but I had a question. You were talking about parameters as potentials. What if we accepted the idea of them as limitations? There are obviously parameters that make certain things impossible. I can't play professional football, for instance."

"But you can definitely play football. I can't answer to the psychoanalysis stuff—I'm just not that smart. I'm interested in that first move, though, of thinking about potentials."

"But certainly you would agree that some of us had strict limitations. I'm talking about being born a woman or a minority, things like that."

"It sounds like you're talking about sociology now. I was just thinking at the level of community."

"But that is sociology, isn't it?"

"I'm sure you're right," Hulme said, standing. "I'm not smart enough to go too deep with you in that direction. What I'm thinking about here is more in the moment, as a way of seeing solutions we don't see now, or of finding connections—potential connections."

"I understand."

"Thank you," he said. He moved to the next table. The woman folded her hands in her lap. Her lips were set in a line. She had the kind of closely cropped hair one sees on teenage boys and elderly women.

"Was his answer not good?" Sheckley asked.

"He said I was too smart for him, but that's not true."

"He's very tall," another woman at the table said. "I wonder how tall he is."

"Have you read Adam Phillips?" she asked.

"No," Sheckley said.

"Well, you should. If only so I won't be the only person here who has."

Sheckley looked across the room. He saw motes of dust suspended in the sunlight. Hulme described the power of positive thinking. He listened carefully to attendees' questions and responded with possible redefinitions of their terms. Beyond the room, the sidewalks were filled with people moving quickly past. Food carts lined the other side of the street. They advertised gyros, Hawaiian plate lunch, pad thai. One cart offered nothing but varieties of grilled cheese. Through the windows the carts appeared pale, blue-tinted.

Something settled in Sheckley. He was a part of things now—he felt it. He was not from Portland, had shown up almost on impulse, but a place had been made for him. The women at his table were talking about space, stars, other planets. They all agreed they wished they could go.

4 | Geary and Andrea sat in the waiting room. The wall of windows opposite them framed a view of fir-blanketed hills that descended into the distance until they became city streets and the silver cord of river. Cars sped

across the bridges, toy-like from this distance, though the vantage also lent their progress a solemn quality.

Nathan and Emily studied the fish that populated a tank in the middle of the room, then moved toward the corner where a cartoon was playing on a small television. They were too old for the toys or the wooden beads on wires, ignoring those as thoroughly as they ignored the board books or the babies in strollers.

"She's very good," Andrea was saying. "She took them on as a favor. Otherwise she's not taking new patients."

"Didn't they see her last year?"

"Last year was the first time. She already knows about the tic and the stomachaches."

The hospital was Andrea's workplace, the doctors, nurses, and staff her coworkers. The dietitians' offices were on the main floor, in a hallway hidden behind the registration desk. Her job was the reason she and Geary had moved to Portland after their wedding. He remembered her nervousness, her anxious belief her position could be cut any day. She'd worked Christmas Day, New Year's Day, the Fourth of July. Now she walked confidently through the hospital, knew every hallway, what was behind every door.

When they were shown to a room and the doctor came in, she spoke to the children first. She had long, straight hair and angular glasses and talked about the importance of wearing a helmet when riding a bike, of never petting strange dogs, of eating healthy food and not watching too much television. She turned to Nathan and said she'd heard he had a certain movement he did a lot, the kind of movement he sometimes knew he was doing and sometimes didn't. She wondered if it bothered him.

"It only bothers me when people talk about it," he said.

"I see. Would you like us to stop talking about it?"

"Yes." His gaze flitted to Andrea, to Geary, and then to the floor. He had the same hazel eyes as his father.

"I think that's right," the doctor said. "I think maybe we could take a break from talking about it."

"See?" he said. "I told you!"

His response surprised Geary. The tic had not been a constant topic. Geary and Andrea had agreed they shouldn't mention it to Nathan too often, only once in a while. The doctor's office was a site of authority, though, and Nathan clearly felt vindicated.

"Sometimes when kids get a little nervous or excited, especially when they're speaking or having a lot of thoughts or ideas, they have some habits," the doctor said. "Do you know what a habit is?"

"No."

"A habit is something you do and you kind of know you do it, but you aren't always aware you're doing it. Like with you touching your chin to your shoulder—that's a habit. But I think you're right about what we should do. Sometimes if you mention someone's habit it just makes them self-conscious and they actually do it more. So let's try this—let's try, for a month, maybe having everyone not mention your habit at all."

"That's what I want."

"So that's what we'll do at home. But what about school? Do the kids there talk about it?"

"A couple of them do."

She had moved him into a zone of disclosure. He answered her without any of the pauses or shrugs he employed with his parents.

"Does it bother you?"

"Yes, because they say, 'Why do you do that?' And I just feel like it's not…I tell them not to talk about it."

"Because it's not something you want to talk about."

"Right."

The doctor set her clipboard aside. "Here's something you can say to them," she said. "If they ask about it again, you can tell them your doctor said it's okay for you to do it. You talked to your doctor about it, and she said it's okay. And if they keep asking, your parents can tell the teacher about our visit today, and the teacher can tell the kids I said it's normal, and they don't need to worry about it."

"Okay."

"Good. I think we have a plan."

Nathan nodded seriously, as he'd been entrusted with a sum of money or the care of an animal. He hopped from the exam table.

The doctor pulled a fresh sheet of paper over the table in time for Emily to scramble up. She breathed upon request, rolled over and coughed. She lay on her back and lifted her shirt while the doctor pressed her palms to Emily's stomach. The doctor said she believed Emily was constipated. When she explained what this meant, Emily's eyes widened and she asked how the doctor could know this. A discussion about doctors, hands, and bodies followed, everyone offering thoughts. Emily frowned—her exam had not gone like her brother's. There were things to consider. The doctor explained how to mix some powder into a drink and that Emily should drink this twice a day. Geary already owned a bottle of the powder—the doctor had recommended the laxative informally to Andrea at work a few weeks ago—but Emily had refused to drink it, or she and Geary forgot about it, or they remembered only when she was already in bed. They all resolved to make sure Emily drank the medicine twice a day so her stomachaches would go away. The doctor typed some notes into a computer in the corner of the room. She repeated the advice about bike helmets and strange dogs and said she had to go, but a nurse would be in soon. The door closed behind her with a heavy, two-note click.

"You heard the doctor," Andrea said. "We're going to need to be good about the medicine."

"It makes the juice taste funny."

"We can find something else to mix it into. Maybe chocolate milk."

"I want chocolate milk," Nathan complained.

"You don't need this chocolate milk."

"Why?"

"Do you need to poop?"

"No. Why?"

"The medicine helps you poop."

"Oh. I didn't know that."

The nurse came in. Emily had to take two shots, one in each thigh. She winced but did not cry. Geary admired her toughness.

5 | When the rain shifted to a downpour they headed for the massive firs that stood beyond the margins of the field. The layers of branches that began fifteen feet overhead and continued seventy, eighty, ninety feet up

sheltered the ground so that the roots and soil surrounding the trunks remained dry. Parents beneath the trees flicked phones in complete confidence just steps from the wall of rain. Some peered alone into their screens, others while chatting about restaurants, schools, or the site of the next game. Their daughters played through the weather, running across grass and mud while their coaches, two fathers shouting encouragement and straightening small yellow soccer goals, walked back and forth through the scrum. The fathers accepted as their duty that they would be soaked while the other parents took shelter.

Geary stood against one of the trunks. He studied a magazine, looking up occasionally to watch Emily take her turn in a drill before returning his eyes to the page. He listened to the other parents. Their enthusiasm for trading information about food, schools, and sports seemed benign, a desire to thrive. He had absorbed in college the standard gloss of Freud, in which the professor had taught that all motivations were fundamentally sexual. Geary could sense the sexual overtones in parental competition, but he was also old enough to question the thoroughness of his education. With every passing year, in fact, he wondered more and more how many of his struggles might be linked to the thoroughness, or lack thereof, of his education.

Bouros had been the one who'd scrolled to the bottom of an image-driven website for a farm-to-plate produce delivery service to find, in small type in the bottom corner, the name of the site's designer. Weeks later, he'd read a humor piece on a website that covered local art and music. The piece was titled "A Brief List of Foods That

Never Appear in My CSA Box." The seventh item had read "Twinkies. I know farmers have them in their kitchens and barns. Why do they never put any in the box? I am tired of kale." This had tickled Bouros. The byline on the list was "Don Geary." When Bouros typed the first few letters into his phone, it autofilled the rest of the name before he could finish. He could not think of why he would have searched the name before. When he went to Geary's website, though, there in the "Portfolio" section was an image of the farm-to-plate website Bouros had liked. So Don Geary was a designer who also wrote jokes.

This, at least, was the story Bouros had told before describing the project he was pitching Geary. They'd met at a neighborhood whiskey bar—Geary, Bouros, and Bouros's business partner, Ed Norman. Bouros was young and slim. He had a meticulous goatee, wore a baseball hat and checked blue shirt, and spoke in the subdued tone of someone sharing a modest joke. Norman was older, clean-shaven. His glasses and paunch, combined with an officious detachment, lent him an owlish air. Together they described some of the projects they'd done recently and what their budget might be on the project for which they felt Geary would be a fit. This was what they did, they said: they incubated and developed projects. They seemed to Geary to be well-connected. He had a weakness for connection, it impressed him. If he signed on to the project they were describing, he realized he would be able to bill significant hours, maybe for a whole year. It was almost too good to be true.

They asked what kind of rate he thought he would charge. When he told them, Norman crossed his arms. Was that his standard rate? Geary steeled himself and said yes, it was.

"I understand we'll be employing you as a freelancer," Norman said. He traded a glance with Bouros. "I know you'll have other clients and you'll have to make your own decisions about how to manage your time. It's been our experience, though, that if we pay someone his standard rate, our project just becomes one of many to him."

Geary parsed this. Someone across the room was whistling a tune he vaguely knew. Was it a pop song? A movie score? "Are you saying you want to pay a higher rate so I'll make this a priority?"

"I'm asking you what that rate would be," Norman said.

Geary made up a number. Norman agreed.

I should have made up a higher number, Geary thought.

Bouros flagged the waiter and ordered a second round for everyone. "Another thing," Bouros said. "Please don't tell anyone you're working with us."

"In fact, remove the word *please* from that sentence," Norman said. "The politeness is misleading. We're not actually being polite."

"It's part of the confidentiality agreement you'll have to sign," Bouros said. "There's a certain community of people who, if they find out a project is funded by us—they ruin it. They're not enemies."

"They think they're our friends, but they're not. They're just bloggers," Norman said.

"They write about things before they're done, and it ruins things, in an entering-the-market way."

"In a very real, entering-the-market way. And the way something enters the market? The way it's introduced? It's everything."

"Well, it's not everything," Bouros said.

"It's everything," Norman said.

The room had grown warm. The buzz of conversation

from other tables formed a pleasant backdrop, a nest within which their own conversation grew.

"What am I not asking that I should?" Geary asked.

Bouros and Norman looked at each other. Norman shrugged.

"Have you ever seen the movie *Arthur*?" Bouros asked. Norman was clearly in his fifties, but Bouros, with his baseball hat pulled low, remained indefinite—Geary had been trying to figure his age. He had to be at least Geary's age to be asking this. "They're making a new one with Russell Brand, but that will be bullshit. I'm talking about the original *Arthur*."

"The new one could be good," Norman said. "You have to bring things back, reinvigorate them."

"Reinvigorate them?" Bouros said.

"Reboot them. Whatever it is they say. But we were talking about the Dudley Moore version."

"I saw it a few times when I was a kid," Geary said. "On VHS. Not since then, though."

Bouros said he'd seen *Arthur* the same way. He found *Arthur* an inspired film, he said, not only for Dudley Moore's portrayal of drunkenness, but also because of the dynamic created by the presence of John Gielgud. Bouros and Norman went on to discuss Gielgud at length. Another round of drinks was ordered. Geary couldn't tell if Norman and Bouros were rehashing an earlier conversation or covering new ground. Bouros felt there was an analogy to be found between the movie *Arthur* and the approach Bouros and Norman took to business. Norman questioned the accuracy of the analogy. He wondered where Liza Minelli fit in it.

"How many cast members do I have to incorporate before you'll accept it?" Bouros complained. "The entire cast? My point is that at some level what we want, Don, is for you to be our Gielgud. We can only keep operating as our Dudley Moore selves if we're protected by a Gielgud."

"His characterization, not mine," Norman said.

"It's totally accurate," Bouros said. "It's easy to find designers in this town, but we need someone who can not only design, but who can also be a Gielgud—to us and to the project. And you strike me as that, in all the best senses of what I mean. If and when we start behaving like Arthur, we'll need to be able to count on you to maintain a sober and productive direction for the project. Does that make sense?"

Bouros was comparing him to a butler? It was insensitive at best. "I think so," he said.

"Even though you'll sign the non-disclosure agreement, you'll of course have to answer your friends' questions about what kind of work you're up to," Bouros said. "So from this point forward let's just refer to the project as 'Gielgud.' If people ask what you're working on, just say you're working on a Gielgud project. Or a Gielgud website."

"And that you can't say more because of privacy issues, or negotiations with the John Gielgud estate. Something like that," Norman said.

"Or if you want to vary the reason, say because of the estate of Dudley Moore. More people need to remember Dudley Moore."

"Or say you can't talk about it because of professional courtesy regarding the projects of Liza Minelli. Or the estate of Judy Garland."

"Or negotiations with Peter Greenaway," Geary said.

"Who is that?" Norman said.

"He's a director," Bouros said.

"He made *Prospero's Books*," Geary said. "It was an adaptation of *The Tempest*. Gielgud played Prospero."

Norman frowned. "Maybe don't say stuff that fancy. Keep it simple," he said.

The cover of the magazine Geary held during the soccer practice featured a color sketch of Rodin's *The Thinker*, except the thinker had a bushy beard and wore a mesh baseball cap. Geary had the magazine open to the first page of a short story whose opening lines read:

> Around ten o'clock, sweating, elated, and carrying a Spalding basketball under his arm, the boy stepped from the driveway into the garage. A particleboard shelving unit filled with ceramic pots, bungee cords, tarps, plastic sprinklers, brass and aluminum nozzles for hoses, and other ephemera stood at the back of the garage next to the door to the house. The shelves sagged under the weight of the items they held and the years they'd held them, their fused particles—sawdust, wood chips, other mill detritus—visible to the eye. Sometimes the boy ran his fingers along a shelf, testing the contours of the board. Lumber, lumber scraps, sawdust, glues, clamps, shims, goggles, and tools lined the margins of his life.

Geary wasn't reading the story, though—he was studying the pages. The magazine was printed on high quality paper. The body font was Garamond. A hard rule ran across the top of each page. On even-numbered pages the story's title ran in small-caps above the rule, on odd-numbered pages the author's name appeared there. The story's title was "THE GREATEST GAME EVER PLAYED." The author's name was "DON GEARY."

He flipped a few pages. He'd written the story four years ago, not long after he and Andrea had split up. He'd revised it three years ago, sent it to a handful of literary magazines, and received their rejections. He made more revisions—mostly cuts. *People are not interested in your thoughts, they're interested in life*, he'd told himself while working on the story. It became a mantra he repeated when working: *No thoughts, no thoughts.* When he was done cutting he sent the story to more magazines. It was accepted by a small but respected journal in Brooklyn called *Harbinger*. They scheduled it to appear in an issue the following year, but a few months later he received an apologetic email from the editors telling him they had accepted too many pieces—they would push his story to a later issue. Then some kind of financial uncertainty arose. There was a change of editorial staff. The new editors announced the journal and its website would be redesigned, which meant further delays. Two years passed—years that for Geary were a blur of days spent finding clients and completing jobs while the kids were at school or at Andrea's house, of picking the them up from school and delivering them to practices and lessons, feeding them and putting them to bed and working until he fell asleep and then starting over again the next day. *Harbinger* was not relevant to anything in his life and he forgot about it. On the rare occasions he recalled the magazine's existence and his story's supposed publication, it was only as an item of outdated trivia, humorous and bizarre.

Today, though, a manila envelope had arrived in the

mail. When Geary opened it, two copies of *Harbinger* fell into his hand. A sticky note was affixed to one of them: *Thanks for being patient with us! Yours, Sarah.* He didn't know who Sarah was. He found his story in the table of contents. He could remember the time he'd spent working on it, remembered sending it out, and remembered getting the email from *Harbinger* telling him they'd accepted it. He could not recall the tone or character of the story itself, though, nor why he had felt the need to write it. What had he been trying to do? Scanning the story now was like looking at the overly earnest work of a stranger. He had no desire to read it.

The idea Bouros and Norman had pitched Geary struck him, at first, as laughable. They wanted to create the equivalent of the Internet Movie Database, but for books. Literature, however, wasn't an actual passion for either of them. Their description of the project concerned only the ways in which this was an unclaimed position in the field of internet culture and the ways in which they might claim it. Geary sensed a large number of potential billable hours in designing a site for them, as well as work that would be more interesting than designing restaurant websites. It didn't matter that he thought it was foolish. There was no question. He was in.

They'd asked him to keep it simple, so he'd kept it simple. He worked on Gielgud for months, developing a project more extensive and ambitious than anything he'd ever done. The project taught him things—code tricks, Photoshop techniques, Illustrator skills, technical things, yes—but it also began to change him. Gielgud became the film he'd never made in film school, the novel he'd never written in grad school. In the beginning he'd been interested in the billable hours. It was not long, though, before he began trying to make it good. It was not a conscious decision—he was simply living with the project. It was his primary work, so of course he tried to make it good.

Bouros and Norman wanted a site in which users would provide the content—users could list what year a book had first been published and who had published it. Users could upload an image of the first edition cover, as well as images of subsequent covers. Users would collectively write and rewrite and correct and edit the author's biography, as well as summaries of individual books. All that was necessary was a structure that was clean, user friendly, and visually distinctive. Geary suggested that if the goal was data, they should include the kind of data not currently available. The name of the person who designed the original cover, for instance. Or the book's primary editor. In fact, he said, they could offer information on the vast but hidden number of people involved in the birth of any book. He talked about the difference between a publisher, a managing editor, an acquiring editor, and a developmental editor. They discussed the difference between a cover designer and an interior designer, the degree to which print runs or sales figures of a book could or could not be gleaned. It was Geary who sensed how truly comprehensive—how *unprecedentedly* comprehensive—an individual page in the Gielgud site could be. Bouros and Norman had nodded at this. It was exactly what they were talking about, they'd said.

Gielgud became the first real design challenge Geary had faced. He looked at the little sites he'd built for friends and local businesses and saw they had been nothing. Gielgud wasn't just a website. It was a concept, a way of thinking.

Users were supposed to provide the majority of the site's content, but someone had to seed it, of course. So Geary started writing some entries himself. He aimed for racial and gender diversity in his examples. He'd recently read *Bullet Park*. His used hardback copy was a first edition, so he wrote an entry on the book, took a photo of the cover, and uploaded the image. He had, in his old files, a college essay he'd written on *To the Lighthouse*. He cannibalized the essay for an entry on the book. He pulled titles from his bookshelves and wrote more entries: *Invisible Man*, *The Counterlife*, *Clear Light of Day*, *Ficciones*. To establish the "Related" category for Borges, Geary added entries for *The Invention of Morel* and *The Hour of the Star*. To do the same for *Invisible Man*, he wrote an entry for *Cane*. He looked at his entry on *The Counterlife* and without hesitation created an entry for the character of Nathan Zuckerman. If it had occurred to him that the site should have character pages, it would also occur to other users, he decided. The site designer, he realized, was really the first user.

He became unhappy with his work. The pages were drafts, concepts. Visually they were mundane, almost mechanical. He redesigned everything, establishing different typefaces and proportions. He found a way to run all posted photos through an automated filter so that every image on the site had a consistent look. He incorporated ad spaces, then designed placeholder ads for them. He added a reference section at the bottom of each entry and spent a few days trying to decide what sites he should link to as the most reliable references on literature, until he realized that Gielgud itself should be the most reliable reference on literature. He was trying, in earnest, to execute the idea he had at first thought foolish: he was trying to create an internet database of literature that was superior to every other source of literary information currently in existence. Gielgud would have more information than other websites. Its information would be more reliable. The site would be better designed, more beautiful. It would, for people who loved literature, be home.

He had to take on other jobs—Bouros and Norman had budgeted him for no more than twenty-five hours a week. He worked on Gielgud more than that, of course, but considered the unpaid hours *pro bono*. He was reading, looking at books, researching publishers and editors and agents. He wrote an entry on his favorite bookstore growing up, The Tattered Cover. Bouros and Norman had never suggested making entries for bookstores, so Geary didn't bill for that time. The site he created, though intended as just a framework, became immense. He had to design a primary home page, then different category home pages: an authors home page, a covers home page, a publishers home page. It was far more work than either of his college degrees had required. At all times he felt behind. He was constantly refining Gielgud, improving it.

The year had slipped past. Gielgud was now scheduled to go live in six weeks. Geary had stayed quiet about it, had spoken to no one. It lived in his laptop and on servers, a web of elegantly designed and interconnected pages. He knew it would become a nationally or even internationally used site. It would require constant design support and further development—a full-time job, or multiple full-time jobs. When others saw it, they would stop what they were doing. They would see the beauty of the design, visually and architecturally. It would lead to new clients and new opportunities for him—the end of living month to month. The end of anxiety. It would lead to a career.

More importantly, though, he had, through Gielgud, finally communicated what he loved, what he cared for, and who he was.

This did not change immediate realities. He did the math often. Rent, food, utilities and clothing, child support and expenses for upcoming summer camps—those numbers formed a column. Money owed him, outstanding invoices, and time yet to be billed formed another column. The columns didn't match, but he had planned for this, had strategized. He just had to make it through six more weeks.

After flipping through *Harbinger*, he listened to the other parents again, to their conversations about the best restaurants, schools, and soccer clubs. Everyone shared the animal drive for dominance, for food and shelter and sex. Some grafted other issues onto the drive, though. In battle it was the warrior who, when he raised his sword or lifted the monster's head, expected everyone to sing his praises. In bed it was the man who told a woman to say his name, who afterward expected her to tell him it was amazing.

He looked up. The girls ran through the rain and mud and kicked the ball one way and then the other. Already one could see the few who understood the game and wanted to win. Geary identified Emily amid the scrum, soaked and laughing, her hair plastered to her forehead. Practice was scheduled to last another twenty minutes. The coaches seemed committed.

Nathan was waiting in the car, playing video games on

his little electronic device. Geary will have to lay towels across the back seat and peel Emily's muddy shoes and socks and shin guards off and throw them in the trunk. At home he will tell her to throw her clothes in the basement sink while he starts the shower for her. He'll make the kids macaroni and cheese, microwave some broccoli. They'll want ice cream or pudding for dessert. After dinner they'll do their homework: twenty minutes of reading for Emily, multiplication tables for Nathan. Geary will tell them to get their pajamas on, will ask once, twice, a third time for them to brush their teeth. Emily will ask him to lie next to her and read her a story before turning out the light. When he goes into Nathan's room, Nathan will ask questions about movies, guns, and World War II. After lights out, Geary will put dishes in the dishwasher, pick up shirts and pants and socks and underwear and carry them to the washing machine in the basement. When the washer and dryer and dishwasher fill the house with their machine hums, he'll make a cup of coffee, sit at his desk, and work on Gielgud.

Emily ran up to him. She was covered in mud—practice was over. "Daddy, Daddy, did you see me score that goal?"

6 | When the weather was good—when there was no threat of rain—he carried his dining table into the backyard. He'd purchased the table for the apartment he rented after he and Andrea split up, where Nathan had a

bed in one bedroom, Emily a crib in the other, and Geary slept on a futon in the living room. There had been a dining area, so Geary had allowed himself one new piece of furniture: the dark-stained oak dining table. He'd moved out of the apartment two years later to rent a house in the neighborhood of an elementary school that was well-regarded because it had a full-time art teacher and a part-time dance teacher. Though these positions didn't seem like much to Geary, they were enough to earn the school the distinction of being an "art school." The house he rented down the street didn't have a dining room, though—just a breakfast nook too small for his table. The table ended up against a wall in the basement.

Now it held a mountain of clean, unfolded laundry. Geary gathered the clothes, carried them across the room, and dumped them on the bed. Returning to the table, he gripped the opposing ends and tipped it toward himself. When the long edge settled against his thighs, he leaned back, cantilevering the table off the ground. No professional mover or physical therapist would ever condone the method. He shuffled forward, breathing hard, and made his way out the basement's French doors. Two concrete steps led from the basement into the backyard. He grunted up the first step. The table edge dug into his thighs. His stomach and back were tight, his palms on fire. He'd done this many times. One more move and he'd be on the grass. When he lurched upward, though, one of the table's legs clipped the step and the table jolted forward out of his grip. The edge flew from his thigh, struck him squarely beneath the ribs, and he fell back into the basement, curled and cursing on the fake wood floor.

When he opened his eyes he saw that one of the table's

legs hung unsupported over the steps, but the other three were on the grass. He raised his shirt. A sharp red mark ran the width of his torso. White peels of skin lined the mark and blood rose in pinpoints. He pressed his ribs—tender, but nothing broken. An accident. A moment of adversity.

He stood and paced a small circle, swinging his arms, breathing deeply. He hopped up the steps and scooted one end of the table and then the other, back and forth, until he had the thing beneath the pear tree. Done.

Later the table held a beer on a cardboard coaster, a can of peanuts, two books, an open laptop computer, and sheets of notebook paper on which Geary was writing sums. He had a column labeled "Debt," others labeled "May," "June," "July," "August," and a last, separate column labeled "Expenses." He added a number to the final column before again lifting his shirt to test his ribs. He looked up into the tree, studying the branches. He wrote another number.

He knew the way he operated was incorrect. His life was broken, improvised. He'd gone to film school for his undergraduate degree. At twenty-five he started a grad degree in creative writing. The degrees were clichés. In the nineties, newspapers and magazines ran trend pieces about how all the new college kids were going to film school. The same articles appeared ten years later with creative writing in the place of film. In both decades, his professors shook their heads. In both decades, he was a member of a predictable group. The more he has tried to escape—to become someone different, to become somehow himself—the more entangled he has become. Now he is a designer. And everyone, now, is a designer.

But he had felt it—the need to make things. And, cruelly, still feels it. Cruel because it eats at him. He finds all of life ridiculous and wants to make fun of it. He stares out windows, thoughts spinning. There is an energy in him that cannot find expression, a skip in his pulse. Toward the end of his graduate program, when he thought the energy had finally been killed, a friend gave him a copy of some design software. Within weeks, the urge was back. He'd sworn it off, but here it was, trying this new path. He made a few websites for fun, to teach himself. The best was an online pencil store, every pencil obviously the same pencil photographed from a different angle, but with a different name, description, and price. He invented makes and models: "Matchlight," "Firestarter," "Tinder," "Thunderstick." He photographed the last with such a long lens that the depth of field held only the *NDE* of *Ticonderoga* in focus, the rest of the letters a blur. He listed Thunderstick for $39.99. His friends laughed, forwarded the site to other friends. There were a handful of actual orders, and Geary fulfilled them, mailing individual pencils in comically large envelopes.

A friend asked if Geary could design and print some theater programs. That led to school fundraiser cards and flyers. He borrowed books on design from the library, watched documentaries on printmakers and the gig poster community. He found a design industry magazine in a recycling bin at the library. An article in it listed average hourly rates in different regions of the United States, and another article discussed best practices for billing. He adopted these rates and practices. He still had the magazine—it was the Magna Carta of his design life. Pages in it had been missing when he found it, and he sometimes wondered what information those pages had held. Had there been crucial addendums or disclaimers? He made sure never to track down a complete copy. It was perhaps best those pages had been missing.

When he was a child there had been a man down the road who had built his family's house himself. The man was an electrical engineer who had worked at Hewlett-Packard with Geary's father. His father had gone down the road to help the man move some lumber one afternoon and came back laughing. The family had been living in the house for two years but still didn't have doors inside, he said—not even on the bathroom. They just hung sheets over the doorframes. It wasn't even an issue of money, Geary's father had said, just time and priorities. It had been thirty years since Geary's father had mentioned this, twenty years since Geary had lived at home, but that neighbor with his crew cut and horn-rimmed glasses, his mousy wife, their two quiet daughters who walked home from the school bus in long skirts and knee socks—where were they? Time had spun them into some other world or life. Their square yellow house lived on in Geary's mind, though, clear as day.

Forging a path, had he lost his way?

Sheckley appeared at the corner of the house. He carried his bike down the steps from the drive to the yard, leaned it against the house, and unhooked the bungee cord that secured his satchel to the rack over the back tire.

"This is pastoral. You're working out here?"

"Something like that," Geary said. "There's a beer in the fridge with your name on it."

"Well, if my name is on it..."

He went back up the stairs and disappeared into the house. Geary gathered the sheets of notebook paper and placed the laptop over them.

"So you've read Adam Phillips?" Scheckley asked when he returned. In addition to the beer, he carried two books he'd pulled from Geary's shelves.

"Yes. Those two, at least. Why?"

"A woman at work was talking about him." Scheckley studied the covers. "*On Flirtation* and *On Balance*."

"*On Flirtation* was grad school reading," Geary said. "*On Balance* came out last year. You can take those if you want."

"What kind of class did you read *On Flirtation* in?"

"I don't remember. I remember the books but not the classes."

"That's funny, I remember the classes but not the books. Where are the kids? Did Nathan talk to the doctor yet?"

The kids knew Scheckley—they called him Uncle Kevin. Emily's favorite stuffed animal, a big brown horse she slept next to every night, had been a Christmas gift from him. When Geary told him the story of the appointment, Sheckley nodded. "You know, I have some things I do that I think of as just thinking habits," he said.

"I know," Geary said. He'd never gotten the full story on what Sheckley had left behind when he moved to Portland. It was clear something had gone wrong, though. The Sheckley he'd known in Colorado a dozen years ago had been a man of many possessions—books, bicycles, camping gear, skis, an old Volkswagen, and more. The Sheckley who'd shown up in Portland carried just a duffel bag with some clothes and a few books.

"Sometimes when I'm writing, I twist my belt loops," Sheckley said. "Even until they break. Then I have to snip them off with scissors. I have some pairs of pants that hardly have any belt loops left."

"Everyone has nervous habits. I sometimes tug little

strands of hair from my sideburns. I don't know why," Geary said.

Sheckley studied the red label on his beer. He tilted the bottle one way, then the other. "I kind of like twisting my belt loops," he said.

"I know," Geary said.

"It doesn't hurt anyone."

"No. It doesn't."

7 | He pressed the black button and the carousel sprang to life: Fleetwood Mac, Spoon, Elvis Presley, Journey, Cat Power, the Velvet Underground. The covers emerged from the right, rattled past and disappeared to the left. How many would go by if he continued holding the button? How many had he owned? He watched, transfixed, awaiting each lurching appearance's invitation to the past.

He sensed a group behind him moving away from the bar, waited for them to pass, and pivoted into their space. The bartender wore a black t-shirt and a week's worth of stubble. A bulb below the bar lit him a jaundiced demon happily at work.

"What can I get you?"

"Old German, please."

The man set a red and white can on the bar. "Two dollars."

The room was narrow and deep and divided by a central aisle. Dimly lit seascapes hung on the wood-paneled walls, each painting depicting the frothy height of a wave in its final moment before crashing on an empty beach.

Geary's friends were Kevin Sheckley, Jason Park, and Lem Arden. Sheckley he had known for fifteen years—before he was married, while he was married, and now afterward. They shared the understanding of those who have known each other in previous incarnations. With Park he shared a fundamental skepticism that presented as an ability to find humor in almost any situation—they both believed all was vanity. He knew Lem Arden less well, was connected to him because Arden possessed a personality the inverse of Geary's. Geary was confident in his ability to solve each day's problems and happiest when working out the solutions, but struggled beyond the confines of his desk, frustrated by lack of money and security. Arden was entirely proficient and connected in the design community, but found little satisfaction in it. He enjoyed his money and was pleased to be respected, but at the end of the day he rose from his desk feeling the work had been boring, pointless.

Geary returned to his table in time to hear Arden say the long fall had been grotesque, just grotesque.

"But from what height?" Park asked. "Was there ever any height in the first place?"

The table held a candle in a glass votive and, against the wall, a small lamp with a black shade. Arden wore his faded Supersonics shirt, Park wore a polo with a stripe set at the height and width of a previous decade. The stripe's color would have revealed which decade, but the dim light kept things indistinct, reducing the men to laughing, shouting faces surrounded by darkness.

"Don't be ridiculous," Arden said. "Sabbath was huge."

"They were niche. No one ever saw them, except on corny album covers or as figures on a distant stage."

Arden slumped as if absorbing a blow. He was a talented designer who moved from one agency to another every year or two, staying until he detected the repetition of projects, the recycling of strategies, or until he got to know the creative directors well enough to recognize their limitations. When he became disenchanted, he moved on. He was freelancing now, doing projects for some of the same firms where he had once been an employee.

The ice in his whiskey glinted in the candlelight. He looked around, searching for anyone who may have overheard, who shared his outrage. "Maybe I don't understand the point you're trying to make, Professor," he said. "Figures on a distant stage. Figures on a distant stage *who were huge.*"

"It hasn't been a fall is what I'm saying." Park devoured a French fry from a paper cone in a wire rack. "He was always that bad, or worse. We were finally given access is all. And you can't call me 'Professor.' I'm an Adjunct Instructor. Human Resources would be upset."

"But would Ozzy be upset? This is the question."

"Ozzy hasn't been seen in a while. He may be institutionalized."

"He's too rich to be institutionalized. He's at home, resting comfortably."

"Home can be an institution."

Four women sat at the table across the aisle. Two talked excitedly and a third leaned forward, listening. The fourth sat tall and straight. The vantage this gave her, combined with the tight ponytail that spilled over the back of her collared dress shirt, suggested someone merely observing. They were young. They had their first serious jobs and the money that made long evenings at the bar possible, Geary thought. A Stooges song was playing. He wondered how many images had rattled past in the jukebox before The Stooges appeared. The women would have been in elementary school when Kurt Cobain died. Geary had been a boy lying on the floor watching Monday Night Football when Howard Cosell announced John Lennon had been shot. The women would not know who Howard Cosell was.

"Are you not going to back me up on this? Sabbath was huge. Should we get our check? Back me up."

"I'm not the one to ask. I barely knew of them," Geary said.

"This is my whole point," Park said.

Arden was astounded. "How could you not have known who Black Sabbath was? The Blizzard of Oz and his Satanic eyeliner and press-on nails and greasy hair never came through? Where did you grow up?"

Colorado, he told them—an hour north of Denver, in the foothills. Cable TV didn't go out to where his family lived. They had five channels of television. The neighbors had a black satellite dish the size of a car in their backyard. What programs it delivered, Geary didn't know. He knew network television and the radio stations, but that was it. There were kids in school who drew weird creatures in their notebooks or on the palms of their hands. He thought they were just concoctions of boredom until he was at a friend's house one day and there among his friend's father's records were the creatures from the kids' notebooks—they were on the album cover of a band named Black Sabbath. "I'd never been to a rock concert. We only went to Denver a few times a year, and that was just to go to the zoo or the natural history museum or the big bookstore that was a crucial stop before the internet destroyed everything."

"Careful," Arden said. "That's my employer you're talking about. Also, with the figures on the albums, I think you're talking about Iron Maiden."

"See? I'm still not clear on it," Geary said. "We had an afternoon newspaper I read every day. And we got *Reader's Digest* and *National Geographic* and *Newsweek*. They never mentioned either Black Sabbath or Iron Maiden. I guarantee you no one on our road was a Black Sabbath fan."

"Nobody bit the heads off bats?" Arden said. "There were no bat-decapitators on your road?"

"There were probably bat decapitators, but only because if there was a bat that started living in your attic, you maybe killed it."

"You chopped its head off?"

"No, you usually poison animals like that."

"People in Colorado probably killed more bats than Ozzy ever did. But everyone blames Ozzy."

"Well—nobody on my road toured. Metalheads, skaters, K-Mart, fast food—that was all stuff that was down in town. That was where the world was. We didn't live down there. We lived outside the world."

The woman with the ponytail was gazing toward the front window as if bored with her friends' conversation. Geary found the capacity to be bored attractive in a woman. He knew this was typical, that men believed a woman's boredom signaled a desire to be enlivened—ultimately, by a man's cock. Everything was ahead of this woman: marriage, money, houses, kids. David Bowie was an old man to her. When her gaze shifted toward Geary he looked away.

"You had yet to be informed that your little country home was actually an outpost of the British Empire?" Arden said. "That by labeling those kids metalheads or skaters or whatever, you were othering them, as if you were normal and they were aberrations? Has anyone seen our guy? Do they not allow you to pay here?"

"According to my education, the skaters and metalheads and K-Mart employees were all colonizers," Park said.

"I wasn't aware the skaters and metalheads came over on the boats," Arden said. "Were they on the Niña, the Pinta, or the Santa Maria?"

"The skaters were on the Peralta," Geary said.

"That's right, I forgot. And the metalheads were on the Dio. I wonder which was the tighter ship."

"The Dio, for sure. Think of the discipline."

"The Peralta was probably a mess—guys just grinding the railings and falling overboard all the time. Did the waiter go to some other bar?" Arden pulled a pack of cigarettes from his pocket and surveyed the room. He wasn't married, had no children. He would freelance until someone he knew started a new agency or a shakeup somewhere else led to a place asking him to join. Freelancing was a layover between trains.

Outside, he lit a cigarette and stood next to a ten-speed locked to a no parking sign. He exhaled away from Geary and Park and the smoke disappeared into the night. The waiter appeared from around the side of the building. He wore the same jeans and black t-shirt combination as the bartender. When he asked if they were alright, Arden laughed and the waiter retreated into the building. Geary's phone buzzed. He opened it and saw a text message from a number he knew:

You have my heart, you know that.

He closed the phone, put it in his pocket, and studied the pavement. Two of the women from the neighboring table stepped outside—the woman who had been speaking so intently and the woman with the ponytail. The woman with the ponytail wore khaki slacks and high-heeled leather sandals with multiple straps. She had come to the bar straight from work, Geary thought.

"Is it okay?" she asked, raising a cigarette.

"Of course," Geary said.

She leaned forward to let her friend light her cigarette, then turned back to him. "You look like someone. An actor. He was in one of those comic book movies."

"It's just the dim light out here."

"It's a guy who's always a little mean or crazy—I'm just blanking on his name right now. He's in a lot of things. You know who I'm talking about."

She had a pale oval face and thin lips and stood a head taller than her friend. Her eyes reminded Geary of a girl he'd pined for in high school. The girl had been on the basketball team and Geary had considered this significant, as if people should pair by sport. When he got up the courage to ask her out, though, she told him she wasn't allowed to date. This seemed plausible—he'd never heard of her dating anyone else. When he asked her to the junior prom she turned him down for that, too, but went with another boy. She'd been so polite to him as to be impossible to read. Pestering a girl was pathetic and the last thing he'd wanted to do, but that was probably exactly what she'd felt. He'd been mortified. Other teams use different strategies, he'd discovered. He didn't go to the dance, he decided it was dumb.

"People must have told you before. I don't know why you're not just telling me," the woman with the ponytail said.

"Maybe if you think of something else it will come to you," he said.

"Here ees looking at you, kid," Arden was saying. "But vot does ze kid sink as vee are looking at her? Ze mystery of ze kid travels down sroo time to reach us here, from vare vee look."

"I held de light saber and sought of de force," Park said. "Vat vas de force? Vat could it mean to a culture like de Javas? Vee must respect zeir beliefs, for do vee not all sell our own robuts, in our own vays?"

"What are you doing?" Geary asked.

"Werner Herzog," they said.

The woman with the ponytail was fishing a phone out of her purse. Her friend was shaking her head. "I wish I could, but I can't," the friend said. "I've been here all evening."

"It's okay," the woman with the ponytail said. "I'll call a cab. I just don't know the number."

"Do you guys know the number for Radio Cab?" the friend asked.

"555-RIDE."

The friend repeated the number. The woman thanked them and dialed. No one spoke. Her impending conversation had taken center stage, was more important even than Werner Herzog impressions. She lowered the phone, touched the screen, and listened.

"What are they saying?" the friend asked.

"I'm seventeenth in line."

"It would be ten times faster for you to just get a ride with someone. Are any of you guys going to the Northeast?"

Arden pointed at Geary.

"Look—this guy is going that way," the friend said.

"It's okay, I'm already down to sixteenth. Thanks for offering, though," the woman said. She turned away, phone firmly to her ear.

Geary wondered what they had been drinking. Had there been wine glasses on their table, or cocktails? The friend had clearly spent the evening with the option of walking home already in mind. The woman with the ponytail moved to the door of the bar but paused at the threshold, searching for a place to abandon her cigarette. A black plastic ashtray sat on the brick windowsill. She stretched toward it to stub the cigarette out and disappeared into the bar.

"I don't know why she doesn't want to keep things simple," the friend said.

"She doesn't know us," Geary said. "It's smart to be safe."

"But we've talked long enough. I can tell you're not some kind of rapist or weirdo. You're perfectly safe and normal, aren't you?"

"I don't know. He grew up with people who killed bats," Arden said.

"I can tell about people," the friend said. "Anna just doesn't trust people. She needs to learn to trust people."

"If she manages to find a waiter who will deliver the check, she'll be ahead of all of us," Arden said.

8 | His card was rejected. The waiter was apologetic, he said he tried it a few times. Geary knew the balance was high, but was it really at its limit, or had the card just been damaged? He was at a loss. Park picked up Geary's part of the tab, waving off Geary's thanks. Their beers and fries hadn't added to much.

Arden and Park headed away on foot. Geary crossed the street, headed toward his car, and discovered Anna walking toward him, back to the bar. She looked up from her phone, chewed her lip. "I'm still in line on here, it's taking forever. Does your offer still stand? Normally I could walk, but these shoes."

"Of course. You don't want to walk alone late at night."

"Getting a ride with a stranger isn't very smart, either."

"What would make you feel safer?"

"Probably nothing. Probably only if I knew you."

He could not tell what it was about her sandals or their intricate straps that rendered them *these shoes*, and found himself again surprised by something he would not even have considered. Women could not walk alone at night for reasons of safety, but the fact that women's shoes were often not even made for walking never stayed with him. At some point in the next six months a woman would again not be able to do something because of her shoes, and it would again surprise him.

"My name's Don," he said. "I have two kids, a nine-year-old boy and a six-year-old girl."

"You're married?"

"Divorced."

"Okay. That doesn't really mean I know you, but thank you. I'm Anna."

In the darkness above the streetlights the highest

branches of a maple tree swayed, leaves rustling. The air smelled of lilac. When they reached his car he opened the passenger door for her. Her silhouette remained motionless as he walked to the driver's side. His movements felt formal, mechanical. He pulled away from the curb with the same care he'd used when he'd taken his driver's test at sixteen.

The streets were empty save for a couple cyclists, each of whom wobbled toward the middle of the street and then back toward the curb in an indeterminate manner. Geary moved into the oncoming lane when passing them.

"Thank you again," she said. "They said it would just be a couple drinks—I thought I'd be home for dinner. When they ordered food, I thought, Okay, I'll be home *after* dinner. But it just went on and on."

"You were trapped in a Beckett play."

"I don't know what that is."

"He wrote a famous play called *Waiting for Godot*. It's about two guys waiting for someone who never shows up."

"I was waiting to go home."

"I just mean the tone. Waiting."

She nodded, studying the passing city. In the car he could see her no better than when they had stood on the sidewalk outside the bar. She was maybe in her mid-twenties.

"My place is off Glisan," she said. "Not far."

"Did you grow up here?"

"No. Montana. I moved here last year." She straightened as if awakening from a daze. "Can we make a quick stop at the store? I just remembered I need to get a couple things—it will only take a minute. I'll buy you some water or something if you want."

"That's not necessary."

"Do you want to just wait in the car or..."

"I'll come in."

When they walked into the store she looked up at the video monitor hanging from the ceiling. He looked up too, in time to see a delayed black and white image of the two of them walking into the store, and of himself looking up. He couldn't tell what she was doing. Had she really asked a stranger to take her to the grocery store at one in the morning? Had she stopped specifically to have their images recorded on a security camera? Was she worried he was dangerous? It would almost be insulting if she weren't. It would mean she'd sized him up and decided he was a man she could have drive her around on errands.

She disappeared into an aisle. He wandered toward a rack of DVDs. The titles and cover images struck him as so lazy they seemed fake, the kind of pseudo-movies that appeared in the backgrounds of television commercials. The only other customers were a young couple waiting at the lone open checkstand. They wore black jeans and black shirts and seemed on their way home from a bar or concert. There were no employees around, but the couple waited patiently. The man murmured something and the woman nodded, brushing her hair from her eyes as she lay her head on his shoulder. Geary was there and not there. It wasn't the store or the people that seemed unreal, but Geary himself who had gone hollow. He didn't belong there, wanted to go in search of the place he did belong. But Anna was walking toward the checkout cradling a loaf of bread, a jug of orange juice, and a package of toilet paper.

Her place was only a few blocks from the store, one unit in a series of single-story red brick apartments around a small courtyard. Geary was a functionary, politely driving a girl home. He tried to imagine her looking back at him, or her head lowered in pleasure, but the image evaporated. She was buying orange juice and toilet paper. There weren't any parking spaces, so he stopped in the street. She put her purse in her bag of groceries, got out, and leaned down to speak through the open door.

"Would you want to come in for a cup of coffee or tea? Wait, I don't think I have coffee. I just have tea."

Who behaved this way? Who had no way home from the bar, then asked to stop and buy toilet paper? His inability to understand what she was doing astounded him.

"At one in the morning, asking a man in for coffee after getting a ride home from a bar means you want to sleep with him. You know that, right?"

Her face fell. "I'm not stupid. I just thought maybe we weren't playing that game. I thought maybe you were nice."

"You thought I would take you to do errands and then sit in your kitchen listening to you tell me about your problems while I sipped tea? While you play Zooey Deschanel fake-singing some fake, old-timey song?"

"Forget it. You're all the same, really, aren't you?"

"Yes. We all take strangers grocery shopping in the middle of the night and then take them home safe and sound. You're not a victim here."

"I didn't say I was a victim."

"You're acting like it. So disappointed in me, in a tone I'm sure you've stolen from your mom. Maybe you got away with shit like this in college in Montana, but you're being naïve."

"Thanks for the advice," she said. She slammed the door and turned up the walk to her apartment. He waited for her to unlock her door, go in, and close it behind her before he drove away.

9 | They'd gone places together, they'd done things. Mostly he thought of New York. They'd boarded a plane at midnight, arrived at JFK the next morning, and took the subway into Manhattan. When they climbed out in SoHo she hesitated, leaning forward against the weight of her backpack as she studied the buildings and signs. It had been five years since she'd lived there. Everything looked and felt familiar, she said, but she couldn't exactly remember the way. "This way, I think," she said, shrugging her pack into a more comfortable position.

He followed. She had places she wanted to visit, a list too long to complete during their two days. Through a circuitous route she brought them to Balthazar, where they bought coffee and rolls. She said she wanted to walk through the neighborhood a bit longer, to look at a few places, if he didn't mind. She stopped next to a parking lot and said she liked the look of the high brick wall across the lot—she remembered that wall. She wanted to take a picture of it to show her son. As she opened her backpack to get her camera, he took a pen from his bag and on the back of the paper with their flight information wrote:

Three broad stories earth-colored brick. Window of green-glass blocks that flash in the sunlight.

He folded the paper and put it in his pocket.
"What are you writing?" she said.
"Just something I thought of."
"Are you bored? Is there somewhere else you want to go?"
"No. Not at all."

They took the subway to Times Square and found their way to an address she had written down, a theater whose box office, they discovered upon entering the lobby, was currently patronized by a single customer: a young woman with a long green coat, her straw-colored hair in a twist atop her head. The ticket-seller was framed in the box office window, his glasses, gray goatee, and attentive posture forming an image of benign middle-aged power.

"How long will the tickets be available?" the young woman asked.

The man smiled. "Until I sell them."

"But do you have a lot left?"

"I do not."

"If I step outside to make a quick call, do you think there will still be tickets available in, like, three minutes?"

"I only see two people behind you. And I do have more than two tickets at this moment."

"I'll be right back." She dialed her phone as she shouldered open the door to the sidewalk.

Geary stepped forward. "We're wondering if there might be two tickets available for this evening's performance," he said.

"Two together, I bet," the ticket-seller said.

"That would be ideal."

The man typed rapidly while studying his computer screen. A paper sign next to the window featured a barred circle over a clip-art image of a cell phone. "NO. STEP OUTSIDE TO MAKE YOUR CALLS," it read.

"I do have two tickets together," he said. "They're stage right, all the way to the right. Some of the set might be slightly out of view, but the sets in this show are minimal—you'll be able to see just about everything."

"How much?" Geary asked.

"Fifty-two."

He turned to her.

"Fifty-two each or fifty-two total?" she asked.

"For you, darling, fifty-two total. A steal," the man said.

They bought the tickets.

They took the subway uptown to the studio apartment they'd rented. Geary's name was on a piece of paper taped to the door of an unlocked third-floor room. The keys lay on a table inside. There was a bed, a sink with a stove next to it, and a bathroom. They'd made it. They didn't know whether to undress themselves or each other. They knew each other's bodies, but not this way, not thousands of miles from jobs and children and responsibilities. They were free here. There were no rules. They wanted to do everything.

"I can't believe I'm here," she said later, as they lay staring at the ceiling.

"It's fun," he said.

"It's more than fun," she said. "It's amazing."

They went out. It was October, but warm. They bought sandwiches at a deli and took the train to the Brooklyn Bridge. The East River was wrinkled gray beneath a clear sky on which the sun sat like white glass. Pedestrians filled the bridge, darting past, jostling for position. In the distance out toward Governors Island they saw a waterfall in the middle of the river, cottony white, nearly invisible in the sun's reflection on the water. There were three other waterfalls at different points in the river. They'd read about them before arriving. An artist had built the waterfalls from scaffolding and pumps. Geary zipped his jacket. She asked if he was okay and he said he was fine, just cold. They crossed the bridge and walked into the park on the Brook-lyn side. Beneath the bridge's massive stone struts they found one of the other waterfalls, a building-size brick of scaffolding from which sprayed an unending sheet of water that fell quietly against the river's surface. Despite the immense metal tangle, the construction looked small huddled beneath the bridge. People lay on the grass in shorts and t-shirts. Geary took photos of the waterfall and then put his camera in his pocket and zipped his jacket to his neck. He needed food and sleep.

They took the train back across the river and bought some pasta, bread, salad, and wine. By the time they made it back to their building, Geary was shivering, putting one foot mechanically in front of the other. He was embar-rassed, tried to act normal. She seemed fine—energized, even.

"You're not feeling well," she said. "I can tell."

"I wish I'd slept on the plane. I can never sleep on planes."

"We'll take a nap when we get back."

"Do we have time?"

"A short one."

When they returned to their room he fell asleep as soon as he lay down. He awoke disoriented and covered in sweat. It was dark. The lone light in the room was the bulb above the stove, where she stood cooking.

"I let you sleep a little longer. How do you feel?" she said.

"Too hot."

"You can take a shower if you want."

He started the shower, undressed, and stood beneath the scalding water. This room in New York for a night and a morning, it was the thing they'd never had. Her son stayed with her ex-husband Wednesday nights only. Geary didn't understand how a man saw his son only once a week—it seemed a schedule from some other decade. He didn't say anything, though. It was none of his business. She was the one who had suggested the trip to New York. When he'd asked if her son would stay with his father, she'd said no, she would take him to stay with her sister in Seattle. She drove to Seattle Friday morning, had lunch with her sister while dropping off her son, and drove back that afternoon. It was more than seven hours of driving. She returned in time to pack and head to the airport for their flight. Their return flight was Sunday evening. She'd told him she would get her son Monday morning by making the same drive. He couldn't tell if she was going to exorbitant lengths to take care of her son, to spend time with Geary, or both. He didn't know what was normal, and neither did he want to owe her some particular debt, so he said nothing. How she took care of things was how she took care of things.

When he stepped out of the shower, the bathroom was so filled with steam that the lights were fuzzed. When he stood before the mirror over the sink he saw only a flat pane of silver.

"The pasta is done," she said. "Do you want wine?"

"Of course I want wine. What can I do?"

"Make the salad?"

"I'll make the salad. I'll open the wine. You're doing too much. I feel like you're taking care of me."

"I'm not taking care of you, I'm just making dinner."

"You're spoiling me."

"Let's eat. We don't have much time."

The subway to the theater district took longer than they expected. They were in danger of being late, of missing it.

When they saw the theater down the street, though, she checked her watch and darted into a restaurant with an espresso machine behind the bar. She ordered two shots, paid with cash, and returned to where he waited on the sidewalk.

"Drink this, we have to stay awake," she said, handing him one of the white paper cups.

"I slept. You didn't. You should have them both," he said.

"I don't want them both. Drink, drink."

They joined the crowd flooding into the theater and through the lobby and went up a side staircase to where they emerged at the balcony, stage right. An usher with thick glasses and a few locks of hair swept carefully over his bald pate stopped them. He looked at Geary's ticket, frowned, and shook his head as one might with a complete illiterate.

"You don't go up, you're not up here," he said. He pointed toward the thin strip of stage visible in front of the vast curtain. "Your tickets are for the orchestra level, down there. You're going to have to hurry, though, it's about to start."

They turned and made their way back, against the flow of people. When they crossed into the stairway hidden along the side of the theater, though, she sprinted down the stairs with athletic precision. He followed until they re-emerged and found another usher. She looked at their tickets and pointed further down the aisle. "Third row," she said.

They found the little brass numbers on the two end seats: 22 and 23. The man who sold them the tickets had told the truth—they were far stage right. He had not mentioned that due to the curvature of the rows, the last seats in the third row were against the stage. If they wanted, they could reach out and touch the boards. Kristen Scott Thomas would be playing Irina, an actress. Peter Sarsgaard, according to the playbill Geary had been handed, would play Irina's "younger lover, the feckless, somewhat amoral writer Trigorin."

Geary had read Chekhov short stories over the years, but he'd never read *The Seagull* and didn't even know what it was about. He'd made some attempts at theatergoing in Portland, but those visits had ended in disaster, in being witness to the violent disfiguring of Shakespeare or clueless failure at Beckett. The experiences had left him leaden and bereft and wanting to step quietly in front of a bus and thus be removed from the embarrassment of the human race. He did not have high hopes—theater struck him as starched and affected—but he was pleased they had good seats, that this would at least be something they could refer to as an experience.

The curtain opened. The stage was at eye level, a dark plane that stretched into the distance. There was no set, only a blank back wall and a dozen candles scattered across the boards, flames flickering.

He watched the opening scene—Nina's performance of Konstantin's disastrous play—with delight. It was as if Chekhov had known what Geary was thinking. Konstantin stopped Nina and stormed off. Irina offered a harsh assessment of the play and solicited Trigorin's agreement. Trigorin—Sarsgaard—shrugged. "Each of us writes as his fancy takes him and his talent allows," he said. Geary understood Trigorin was trying to sidestep evaluating Konstantin's attempt, yet the sentence was forceful in its economy.

He watched the succeeding character building of the first act with growing alarm. Kristen Scott Thomas stood directly before him, raising her nose haughtily, laughing the derisive, mocking laugh of an insecure woman. Sarsgaard—bearded, thoughtful, alternately distracted and considered in his responses—stayed on the other side of the stage, maintaining in his bearing and voice a benign distance. Geary recognized Thomas from the movies. Mackenzie Crook, who played Konstantin, had a featured role in *Pirates of the Caribbean*, a movie Geary's kids had watched dozens of times—Geary kept expecting Crook's eye to pop out, as it did in the movie. Sarsgaard was different. He seemed to have arrived at his position through alternate means. There was a strange energy bound up in Trigorin, or in Sarsgaard's performance of Trigorin, or in the intersection of the two.

In this, too, Chekhov seemed to be ahead of Geary. In the play it was Nina, the daughter of a nearby family, who became fascinated with Trigorin. When Konstantin laid at Nina's feet a seagull he had killed, Geary understood both positions. Of course Konstantin was in despair, of course Nina found him pathetic. When Nina told Trigorin she thought it must be wonderful to be a successful novelist and he responded with his speech about *ideés fixes*, Geary was stunned—again, the words seemed to him obvious and true. Yet this was the character who was supposedly *feckless, somewhat amoral*. Was Geary supposed to find Trigorin shallow? By the time Nina told Trigorin perhaps he was spoiled by success and he responded, "What success? I've never given any pleasure to myself. I don't like myself as a writer," Geary no longer had thoughts about the lines or the plot. Thought had been suspended. He was inside the play. Sarsgaard pulled a pencil from his pocket and wrote something in a notebook. When Nina asked what it was and he told her it was nothing, just an idea, Sarsgaard wrote in no particular hurry, as if the play itself could wait for him to finish. He put the book in his pocket and, with the hint of a smile, studied Nina as she stood before him. "An idea for a short story," he said. "A girl like you, living beside a lake since she was a child. She loved the lake the way a seagull might—she's as happy and free as a seagull. But one day, by chance, a man comes along and sees her. And quite idly, he destroys her. Like this seagull." Irina appeared in a window, happily shouting to Trigorin that they would not be leaving the estate as they had planned, but staying longer. Trigorin stepped through a door and disappeared. Nina turned to the audience, hands clasped, eyes cast beatifically upward. "A dream!" she exclaimed. The curtain fell.

There were gasps from the audience. When the lights came up, a woman down the row from Geary stared wide-eyed at the curtain, hands on her head. *Quite idly.* To Geary's ear, there had been something distinct about the way Sarsgaard had pronounced those two words.

He felt a hand on his arm.

"I'll be right back," she said.

He'd nodded without turning. He did not want her to see he was weeping.

10 | Louise lived in one of the city's oldest neighborhoods. It was an area of tree-lined streets, trimmed lawns, and, almost without exception, craftsman homes built in the early twentieth century. Her home was a ranch, though—someone had kept the lot empty for forty years and the house had been built in a different era. Louise was a writer. A small press had published her story collection. Those who had read it admired it, but the press didn't have much success with distribution, so this was a small number of readers. Her sons were twelve and fifteen. Her husband was a forester—he and two partners had their own company that helped private landowners manage their trees. Some days he went to the office, some days he went to the forest. He came home from the forest with scratches on his arms and sawdust in his hair, smelling of the oil and gasoline in his chainsaw. He was quiet. He preferred the days he was alone in the forest.

Louise was tall and thin, with high cheekbones and an infectious laugh. She woke at five in the morning and wrote until it was time to go to her job at the Cascadia Arts Council. She ran a program that placed local artists in the high schools, where they taught art to the students. She tried to do this well and then to stop thinking about it as soon as she left the office. Family, life, work—it was all too much, it threatened to overwhelm her entirely. Her older son had brought home C's and D's on a report card during his freshman year and she'd been so angry she'd started crying. You can't do this, she'd told him, I barely have time to breathe as it is, and now I have to keep track of whether you're doing your homework?

Her husband's inwardness was only something that occurred around other people. With the boys he was like a father bear, wrestling with them, taking them camping, throwing the football. Sometimes when he was angry at them his eyes went flat. Louise had grown up in Boston, in a home in which everyone yelled and cried and argued. Her husband's silent anger, the way his jaw tightened and he went completely still, this was novel. It was western anger, she decided. A different animal.

"People always talk about nature and nurture as if they're fifty-fifty," Louise said. "They're not. Nature is eighty percent of it, at minimum." She wore blue jeans and a white silk blouse. Her hair was cut short for the summer.

"Eighty?" Geary said. "How did you arrive at that number?"

"There's nothing I can do with the boys. They didn't become who they are because of anything I've done. They are who they are in spite of what I've done."

"But you've put them in certain schools where they've had a chance to find out who they are. You enrolled them in sports and activities so they could figure out what they like."

She took a sip of her wine. "Seventy-thirty," she said.

"And we still keep looking for things for them to try," her husband said.

Louise shrugged.

Her husband was standing at the barbecue, drinking a beer. "We also keep working on finding better ways of communicating with them. That's nurture, isn't it?" He flipped the chicken thighs sizzling on the grill.

"But has it changed the way we all talk to each other?"

"That was my question," he said. "I'm the one who asked that question, the other day."

"People always imply teenagers have problems because

of dysfunction in their family dynamics. The whole counseling profession is built on the idea. But no amount of counseling is going to alter hormones," Louise said.

"Let's not start talking about hormones."

The boys came out into the backyard together. The older one was over six feet tall now and walked with a slight stoop, as if uncomfortable with his height. The younger one was not much shorter but had the untroubled grin of a child.

"And here they are," Geary said.

The boys studied the adults gathered in their yard, looking for a familiar face. They were in shorts and t-shirts, their feet were bare.

"No one ever talks about friends," Louise said. "The friends I had as a teenager had more to do with how I turned out than my parents did. I had five brothers and sisters. My parents didn't have time for nurturing. There was food in the kitchen and after that we were on our own. We were raised by punk rock."

"Punk rock?"

"Zach's here," the younger boy said.

Louise looked toward the house. "Did you tell him we're in the yard?"

"He was…delayed," the boy whispered. "He's in the bathroom."

"Oh, well, the bathroom. I'm sure he'll find his way."

"Hello," a man said as he came around the side of the house.

"You found us," Louise said.

He crossed the grass to where they were gathered around the picnic table and the barbecue. There were nearly a dozen people there by then, enough that there were three or four conversations going.

Zach Sellwood was tall. His hair was ragged, like a musician, and he wore dark jeans and a tight gray t-shirt to complete the look. He'd opened three restaurants and each had won an award of some kind. Geary had been to one of them. Small birds—pheasants, maybe, or grouse—sat in cupolas beneath the stamped tin ceiling twenty feet overhead. He couldn't tell if they were taxidermy or fake, they were too far up. He couldn't remember what he'd ordered. He remembered she'd worn a black dress, the short sleeves lace.

"Louise, your sons just keep growing," Sellwood said. "I think Tim may be taller than me now. Is it true, Tim? Are you taller than me?" The older boy shrugged, walked over and stood next to Sellwood. "We have to stand back to back. Louise, you're living with a basketball team."

"It's the first time in my life I've been the shortest person in my house."

"Oh no, it's true," Sellwood complained. "Are you taller?"

"Maybe just a bit," Tim said.

"You must have all the girls after you. Don't get mixed up with girls. Louise, have you told him not to get mixed up with girls?"

"I think he has it under control. He doesn't take advice from me on that."

"He's taken," his younger brother said. "He has a girlfriend."

"Be careful. They mess you up," Sellwood said.

"She's very nice," Louise said.

"They start that way," Sellwood said.

He grabbed a beer from a cooler at the end of the table. His arms were long, the fingers long, too. He popped the top from the beer with an opener on his keychain.

"So you were traveling? Did you have an event?" Louise said.

"What do you mean?"

"In your email you said you weren't sure if you'd be back today."

"Oh, right. I was up in Seattle. I've been dating a woman that lives up there, but I don't have to go up there anymore. I'm tired of it."

"Of driving to Seattle?"

"No, just of dating women my age. The good ones are taken. I just drove all the way to Seattle to spend the weekend with this woman, and she got pissed off at me. She wanted to know where our relationship was going. We've been dating two months. We live in different cities. I told her I had no idea where the relationship was going, I thought that was why we were dating. That just made her angrier."

"I'm sure she was in love with you. That's hard," Louise said.

"After two months? We've spent four weekends together."

"Four weekends is enough time to fall for someone."

"If you fall for someone that fast, it's a red flag. She was smart, good looking, seemed normal. So why was she single? Now I know. If you met these women or were able to hear these arguments, Louise, you'd know what I'm talking about."

"I'm sure I already do."

"No, if you're not in the room, you don't know. I drive three hours to take someone out to dinner and she's throwing things at me."

"I've thrown things. Ask Jeffrey."

Her husband nodded. "More than once."

"I feel like I have to be so careful," Sellwood said. "I don't mean for my physical safety, I mean for my future. If you date women in their thirties who don't have kids, they're looking to have kids. They won't say it, though, which means the whole relationship revolves around a lie. I can't tell you how many times women have told me I don't need to use a condom. I'm sorry, boys, I know this is uncomfortable, but you've taken your sex-ed classes, right? When I say, *Wait, let me get something,* women actually get angry, like I'm insulting them. It's ridiculous. They're just trying to get my sperm."

"Come on," Louise said. "Women don't need a man to have a kid anymore."

"These aren't women of science. They want a man to beat the emotional shit out of and have a kid with. Those are the same thing for them. It's a package deal and they want the full package."

Louise liked Sellwood. He was unreconstructed. He didn't seem to care if people disliked him or if things he said made people unhappy. She worked in a community of artists who carefully complimented one another, keeping track at all times of who was in power, who one needed to flatter in order to get shows or grants or teaching appointments. Sellwood talked the way people had talked when she was growing up. People in Boston assumed base motives lay behind all behavior and judged each other accordingly. When she was in college, Louise volunteered at an abortion clinic. Later she'd worked for a non-profit that helped single mothers find housing. She considered herself a feminist, and Sellwood didn't bother her. She spent her early mornings with a cup of coffee and her conflicts.

She tried to write fiction that revealed emotional truths and then she drove downtown to an arts community that ran on flattery and paranoia. She was proud of what she did for work, but it could also be insufferable and depressing. Sellwood seemed free, he seemed healthy.

"What happened to your friends?" she asked her sons. "You told them they could stay for food, didn't you?"

"They had to go," Tim said.

"They had…a family thing," Michael said, as if having to leave a barbecue to go home was a slightly embarrassing thing to have happened to his friends, or perhaps an embarrassing thing to have to report about someone. The two boys stood near their father. They had lived in Michigan, then in California, and now in Oregon. Their father had moved from forest to forest, their mother was always working for organizations that tried to help poor people or artists. They remembered California, where they lived in a small town near the redwoods. In their memories the trees had fantastic powers—it was a mythical place, the Valhalla of their early years. Tim remembered a bit of Michigan before that, or at least claimed to. Michael had been a baby there and had no memories of it. He'd once asked if they had maybe gone fishing in Michigan—he had an image of something. Louise had laughed. Their father had taken the boys fishing every place they'd lived, so yes, they had gone fishing in Michigan. The boys had heard their parents argue in every house they'd lived in. Sometimes they woke up in the middle of the night and heard their parents' voices, tense tones quiet and then rising in disagreement. They sensed in their parents a partnership regularly and enthusiastically negotiated. They understood their job was to set the table, be polite, and do their homework. Be kind to kids less fortunate. If they did these things, everything else would work out. They grabbed sodas from the cooler, twisted the tops off, and watched their father tend the grill.

"Did I say too much?" Sellwood said. "I don't want to paint all women with the same brush. Boys, women are nice. They're smart and good. It's just the ones I go out with that are a problem."

"We know," Michael said.

11 | Arden owned a dog. Kira was a chocolate lab he'd bought shortly after his last girlfriend had moved out. The dog was three years old now and immaculately behaved. He knew *sit, stay, come, down, roll over,* and *wait.* For fun, Arden had also taught him to bark when Arden said "O'Reilly." Kira was less reliable in this, though, perhaps because they practiced it only when Arden had been drinking. On first learning the dog's name, people assumed Kira was female, but a glance revealed the truth. *Akira* was a syllable too long, though, and Arden decided he didn't care about people's confusion.

He lived in a one-bedroom apartment in Southeast Portland, just a block from a grocery store. The living room was arranged around the huge television. The couch was centered. Speakers sat on pedestals aside the screen and in corners at the back of the room. Though he was renting, Arden had installed blackout window shades at his own expense. His bicycle went in the bedroom, his jackets in a hall closet. The living room was clean, a theater awaiting showtime.

He had all of the Criterion Kurosawa titles available on Blu-ray. The films of Truffaut and Godard, of Jean-Pierre Melville, of Nicolas Roeg. He owned all of Tarantino's films and all of P.T. Anderson's films. He liked grand gestures, drama pitched at the edge of the believable, or beyond it and still somehow real.

"Watch this," he said. "Watch how many guys are running around here."

Silence. Mifune in close-up, chastising someone.

"It's in a second. Kurosawa even grabbed members of the crew, he just gave guys swords and told them to get out there and run around."

"Was this story based on anything that came before it?" Park asked. They were drinking tequila Arden had supplied. They'd had a couple rounds already.

"I don't know. But everything that came after it is based on it."

He was always searching for the best way to capture something, the right way to put it. He read all sorts of things, high and low: novels, biographies, tabloid newspapers, literary magazines, gossip websites. He had never agreed with a single teacher he'd had at any point in his education. Teachers didn't take their subjects seriously enough. They didn't take the deep dives.

A white cat stood on its hind legs, its paws on the screen door, peeking in. Kira raised his head at the shadowy form but didn't bother to get up.

"Your cat wants in," Geary said.

"That one comes by every evening. To see what I'm watching, I assume."

"Do you know its name?"

"I don't even know who it belongs to—if it belongs to anybody."

"It's a freelance cat?" Park said.

"I don't think he's for hire. Cats can be solitary. He's maybe a Scandinavian cat, spenting soam time ah-lone, on a sole-itary quest, to lurn deeper truths about loif."

"That turned into Bjork at a certain point."

"You're criticizing my Scandinavian cat accent? What are you, a Scandinavian cat linguist?"

"I'm just familiar with Bjork."

"I don't have to take notes from you."

He pursued his enthusiasms further than others, the trivial enthusiasms furthest of all. Other designers made friends laugh by creating a fake album cover for a fake band. Arden crafted a dozen covers for the fake band. Studying the covers suggested with astounding precision the years the band had been active, the predictable phases the members had gone through, the mysterious lineup changes.

There was a woman in his life. No one knew, it had just happened. She texted late in the evening and arrived shortly after. Black leggings and a black sweater, streaks of blonde in her dark hair, worn sandals she scooted aside with her foot. He made her a drink. Or he made himself a drink and one for her too, to be polite. With her he spoke differently. She was the one who made jokes. She led him into the bedroom. She took his clothes off first, then her own. She was confident, her hands worked swiftly. Three nights now.

"He edited at night, after they finished shooting for the day. He would have complete scenes to show people in the morning," he said.

"Seems like a nice way to wind down," Park said. "Editing a samurai epic."

"Who does that! No one does that!"

The late hour, the look in her eye, the feel of her body—she transforms him, he becomes another man entirely. She begins and something takes over. There is neither intention nor surprise in his movements. She starts as the aggressor but ends in the clutches of something, in agony. She arranges her own destruction and demands it of him. He's out of breath, at the limit of what he can do, but he pulls her closer, holds her tighter. There is a catch in her breath.

"How long did it take? From starting shooting to finishing the movie?"

"A year," he said. "Way longer than it was supposed to. The studio stopped it twice. Each time they shut it down he supposedly just went fishing. He knew they'd have to let him finish it."

Her eyes were closed. She was focused on a sensation that was elsewhere, only hers. It was not him—it was something he helped her conjure. His body made its own claims. He slowed. There was something contemptuous in it, in his changing the rhythm. Her hand was behind her head. He pressed, and then again, coming with each jolt. He slowed further and lowered his forehead to hers. They were sweating, exhausted, like people who had outrun something. He fell to her side, placed his hand on her stomach, lifted it and trailed it slowy down her breast. The wonder of her body, of what she had done to him. Her thighs were soft, relaxed. He slid his hand between them.

The samurais sprinted across the screen, they chased and clashed swords and tumbled in the dust and jumped to their feet again, wild-eyed. They were inexhaustible. He liked selecting the correct version of the movie, the length Kurosawa intended, the crisp Blu-ray drawn from the restored print, played on his high-quality television. Geary was divorced with two kids and Park was married with no kids and Arden had never married and couldn't imagine it. He trusted them, though. He could discuss this aesthetic triumph with them, he could make arcane jokes and they understood the references—if they didn't, they didn't mind. The light faded, the room fell dark. Park was quiet. Geary had nodded off. The movie was over three hours long. It was fine if they drifted in and out. Maybe even better that way.

She got up to go to the bathroom. The lights were still on in the living room and kitchen. He didn't know what time it was, how long they'd been asleep. He turned off the lights, turned off the muted television, too, and closed the front door. He didn't know if he should lock it—he didn't want to presume. With women he has been faithful, conventional, domestic. There have only been a few. He didn't know the conventions of this, the sophistications. He closed the door but left it unlocked.

"Sylvia said she thinks what Peter is doing isn't unethical, but it is immoral," she said. "Do you think something can be immoral without being unethical?"

"What thing that Peter is doing?"

"Sleeping with Marcy."

"You guys know about that?"

"Everyone knows about it."

He felt less judgmental in the small hours. He'd been thinking about birth control. She said she was on the pill, but how did he know? He hardly knew her. Larsen seemed distant, abstract, a situation more than a person.

"Is what we're doing immoral?" he asked.

"Are you married?"

"No."

"Then no."

"So your morality isn't biblical."

"Is anyone's?"

In the morning she rose early. The sound of the shower lasted only a minute and she returned dressed. He offered to make coffee, but she told him it wasn't necessary, that he should sleep. She kissed him on the forehead and was out the door before he could catch up. She was in a grad program in design at the University of Oregon, was spending the summer as an intern at Larsen's firm. From what Arden could tell, she had attempted to understand, critique, and dismiss Larsen's entire operation within her first three weeks. Her mastery of a knowing, sardonic tone, her skeptically raised eyebrow, and the ferocity of her ambition impressed and offended him. He'd worked for Larsen eighteen months before dismissing the endeavor.

He has been a certain kind of man for three years now. He does his work well, according to his own hours and his own terms. He watches movies. He reads political news. He knows which films of the seventies are being restored in advance of a new video release, and knows which Oregon senator has supported a bill in contradiction of a campaign position. He knows how many drone strikes Obama has signed off on and can explain how this is in complete contradiction of the Obama he voted for.

Reina had come along to a lunch meeting Arden had with Larsen two weeks ago. When he'd asked how she liked Portland so far, she said she'd never seen so many white people in one place. They sat outside and she kept her sunglasses on. When Larsen went to the bathroom she said she didn't know anyone but the other two interns, whom she'd just met. Would it be okay if she got Arden's number? She didn't ask if he was seeing anyone. Maybe she assumed he would tell her if he was, or maybe it was somehow obvious.

The movie ended. Park and Geary squinted when Arden turned the lights on.

"I'm not sure what more can be done with samurais," Geary said.

"There's *Yojimbo*," Arden said. "There's *Sanjuro*."

"But do those have seven samurai in them, or are there fewer?" Park said.

"You're right, he did it wrong. There should have been sequels named *Eight Samurai, Nine Samurai*."

"*Samurai's Eleven*, with Sinatra, in Las Vegas."

Kira circled them, tags jingling. Arden grabbed the leash and went out the door with Geary and Park. They headed their separate ways. Kira turned in the direction of the longer walk—the one that ended at the dog park—but Arden pulled him the other way. Kira followed obediently, head lowered in disappointment.

"Tomorrow, Kira. Tomorrow."

They were home ten minutes later. Arden straightened the living room and washed the glasses. He could read for a while before going to bed. He could watch Jon Stewart. He was tired, it had been a full day. He was fine.

She texted at eleven-thirty. *Sure*, he texted back.

12 | "Do you have a sense of what your highest priority is?" Geary asked. "Is there something specific you're looking for first?"

He was a face on a screen, a low-resolution image that froze, shattered into a mosaic of tiles, and then lurched into blurred movement. His voice continued, though, hollow and echoing.

Bouros and Norman were in a different city. They sat next to each other at a round table with a strategically placed laptop. Behind the laptop was a glass wall through which they could see the main room. Young people in slacks and dress shirts peered into screens, nodded to music on headphones, and laughed with each other. Bouros had a second laptop open and studied its screen. Norman looked at a legal pad on which he'd written notes in his tiny, precise print.

"The column-width issue will affect every page, so maybe that first?" Bouros said.

"Then the icons," Norman said.

Bouros couldn't think of any reason the icons should be a high priority. He suspected Norman just wanted to see everything together, done.

"And then we'll pretty much be seeing the new look, right?" Norman said.

"It looks great right now, though, too," Bouros said. "It's way better than dumb wiki sites. This is in a different league."

"Design is everything," Norman said.

Geary's face froze again, his gaze to the side in a look of concern or confusion. "So then after I do those things you want me to get back to you, so you can take another look?" the frozen image asked.

Bouros looked at Norman. Norman shrugged.

"Sure. Sounds fine," Bouros said.

The image moved again. Geary did not appear to be looking at Bouros and Norman so much as peering from beneath the surface of some strange liquid or glass. "Are there other deadlines I need to be hitting? I know we have the launch, but in advance of that? Are there dates for locking in the layout, or stopping work on the icons, or settling on the filtering?"

"Good questions," Bouros said. He was disappointed in himself—he should already have considered these things. He worried he and Norman were lazy, slipping. Too much money, too many projects, too little attention.

"I wouldn't worry about that," Norman said. "We'll take care of that."

The image froze, and this time the audio disappeared too. Then both returned.

"—you guys are in town?"

"Don, you broke up there. What did you say?"

"Sorry. I asked if we'll be doing this remotely all the way through or if you guys will be back in town at some point."

"We'll be back," Bouros said.

"We'll definitely be back," Norman said.

"So the columns and icons first, then the filtering, then the tagging issues and the whole data analysis system. And then of course there's still looking into the copyright stuff."

"And the editing," Norman said.

"Okay."

Geary looked down, appeared to be writing something. It was hard for Bouros to believe this was the person who had written the humor piece that had made him laugh.

Over the last year Geary had been so earnest. He hadn't made a single joke Bouros could recall.

"One last question, maybe slightly less procedural—or maybe it's still procedural," Geary said. "Is there going to be any publicity? I haven't told anyone about it, of course, but at some point we'll want to publicize it, right? To bring people to the site?"

"That will all be taken care of. We have a way we do that, reliable outlets. We'll put that in motion when it's time," Norman said.

"Don, it looks good," Bouros said.

"Thank you."

"We'll talk soon," Norman said.

"Okay, I'll—"

With a tap of his finger, Norman ended the connection. He flipped a page on his legal pad and read with a furrowed brow, as if confused by his own notes.

"That was nice," Bouros said.

"What, that I cut him off? The endings of those things are always awkward. I'm thinking about San Rafael."

"You're thinking about San Rafael?"

"I'm not sure they're really doing it."

The way he so entirely believes that he is the center, that everything revolves around him, Bouros thought. It wasn't just the way he cut Geary off, but that the gesture betrayed something. It was sloppy. "San Rafael is all about whether they can write the code or not. And we don't write code, so we can't know."

"I'm not even sure San Rafael is a thing," Norman said. "Is it even a thing?"

"Is it even a thing?"

"Yeah. Is it a thing?"

Bouros was tired. Not physically. It was the repetitions. "I don't know," he said. "Is anything a thing?"

Norman laughed, flipped another page. "I think too many things are things."

The man was a case study, but in what, Bouros wasn't sure. "And we are alleviating that how?" he said.

Norman looked at him and smiled. "Not at all," he said. "It's to our advantage."

Two

1 | He was mostly alone. Old dreams trailed him, reduced now to habits, ways of being. No one observed how many times he listened to the same albums, whether his taste in music was good or bad. No one knew he was reading John Berger novels and rewatching Fellini films. No one saw how many evenings he ended drinking a glass of wine while watching Letterman. His studies—borrowing the third season of *Taxi* from the library and watching every episode, reading theories about Area 51 and aliens for two hours on the internet late one night—were eccentric, unsustained. He was not a person who kept a journal. His thoughts went unrecorded and his actions were not noted. He left no mark.

He received an email from his landlord:

> Hi Don,
> I hope all is well with you and the kids.
> I want to share my thoughts about an upcoming
> increase in rent that I will propose for the house.

As I think you know, it is not my customary practice to ask stable long-term tenants to shoulder significant rent adjustments. On occasion, as only happens with long-term tenants in an environment of escalating rents, the unit's rent falls considerably below 90% of the actual market rent. In this circumstance, my sense of fairness is that there needs to be some kind of rent adjustment to bring the rent to that lower limit of discount. In the circumstance of the unit today, my best estimate is that the fair market rental value of the unit is $1,750. On this basis, the target lower limit is $1,575 which is an increase of $100, far larger than customary. I am proposing that this increase go into effect with your June 1 rent which is your 3rd year anniversary. Your original rent was $1450. Obviously I hope that you will find this fair and tolerable since I am certainly not trying to spur you to relocate. Please let me know your thoughts.
Onward,
Jerry Kessler

The only thoughts Geary had were that being able to increase your income by sending an email seemed enviably convenient. Kessler was a retired engineer who lived on Long Island. He was tall, kept his gray hair shaved almost to the scalp, and wore rimless glasses that lent him a patrician air. He visited Portland twice a year to see his daughter, who lived in the suburbs, but he was otherwise out of touch except for occasional email missives.

Geary did not respond.

As a child he had often been told what things would

be like in the real world. Once he had grown up, though, he noticed adults in the now supposedly real world often thought about, relived, rehashed, or repeated many of the relationships or experiences they'd had when they were children. So which was real? Adult life, or the child-life that adults' psyches were built upon and constantly referred to?

Other people remembered school dances, boyfriends and girlfriends, popular music and movies from their childhoods—and Geary remembered those, too—but he had been more fascinated by sports and games: the used, yellow-felt pool table his parents installed in the basement, the contours of whose uneven surface Geary soon came to know by heart; the plastic lawn tennis racket he used to hit a yellow foam ball against the garage door; the orange rubber ball he pitched against the front steps, imagining the caroms to be the hits of phantom batters, playing nine-inning games in his head; the dice baseball game his father devised one evening to entertain him and which he then played for years, tracking entire seasons of an eight-team league roll by roll, inning by inning; the rounds of golf he played with wiffle golf balls and an adjustable iron his father had whose head could be ratcheted to serve as everything from a four- to nine-iron as Geary picked out distant tufts of weeds to serve as improvised pins; most of the little league baseball games he'd ever played, but especially the night games under the lights; and also—in greater detail than any of the other sports—the games of basketball he had played, whether on the little aluminum basketball rim his father hung on the basement wall, on a Nerf hoop in a friend's bedroom, or on a full-size hoop in a driveway, a parking lot, a church gym, a playground, a high school gym, a college rec center, or any one of the thousands of games of basketball he had played alone in the driveway of his childhood home. All of these games had been just as real to Geary as anything else that had happened. Some part of his mind, or some somatic self constructed in the place mind and body meet, was unaware he had been alone. This self did not experience life as dependent upon the presence of others. It did not wonder if the games Geary had played were real—it knew they were real. Because it had played them.

He turned thirty-eight. It was a Tuesday. He did not like to celebrate birthdays, but the kids wanted to do something, so he took them out for hamburgers and shakes. Nathan talked about D-Day: how many beaches the men had landed on, what kind of guns they had used, what had gone right and wrong—it had mostly gone wrong, he said, but people didn't know that. Emily listed the boys in her kindergarten class and the ways they misbehaved. The boys had different names but the types of misbehavior repeated. After the kids were in bed, his phone buzzed. *Thinking of you & wishing you a wonderful birthday*, the message read. He did not understand. *Thank you*, he wrote back.

He did not understand.

2 | Sunday evening. A time for solitude, reflection, and rest. But he stood in the polished white aisle of a sporting goods section staring at a pallet of large white boxes. His jeans were torn at the knees. His green t-shirt was faded. He was thirty-eight, single, a father. Somehow nothing more.

The local news had warned a heat wave was on the way—it would be ninety on Monday, above ninety the rest of the week. Each of the last two summers, Geary has bought an inflatable pool and set it up in the backyard. He forces an electric air mattress pump over the valves on the pool's three stacked rings, and the inflated pool rises from the grass. Four people can stand comfortably in it. The water comes to the kids' waists.

The pools do not survive. Each becomes dirty and mildewed and is deflated one late summer afternoon and dragged into the back corner of the yard to rot beneath fallen leaves. Two years ago the pool had been white with blue stripes and had cost Geary thirty dollars. Last year it had been white with green stripes and had cost the same. Over the weekend, while on their way to a barbecue, home from the library, or between other errands, Geary had held the kids' hands as they made their way through congested parking lots into busy stores. He knew the pool would be white, with this year's color of stripe, and it would cost thirty dollars. He would inflate it with the mattress pump and summer would begin. The kids believed the purchase of the summer pool was an immortal tradition. They had asked Geary weeks ago when he would be getting this year's pool.

The stores did not have it. Geary, Nathan, and Emily left

one store, went to another, left that one and tried another. The stores weren't sold out. The thirty-dollar pool just wasn't available. There were plastic baby pools for twenty dollars or huge inflatable pools for sixty dollars. The choice was between a joke and an impossibility. His kids were too big for the baby pool, his yard too small for the big pool.

He had to do something. This feeling—the feeling that action, from him, was urgently necessary—had quietly blanketed every aspect of his life. He did not know what it was he needed to do, he knew only that it was for him to do it.

He'd searched the internet. There were endless pages of swimming pools and water guns and sprinklers, but the thirty-dollar pool did not appear. It had been an example of a manufacturer nailing a market too exactly, he decided. People who might have bought the bigger, sixty-dollar pool saw the thirty-dollar pool and decided it was nearly as good, for half the price. People considering the little plastic pool saw the thirty-dollar pool and realized it was more fun, for just a few dollars more. The thirty-dollar pool was so perfect that it had annihilated its own manufacturer's other market positions. The company had wised up, Geary decided. They hadn't manufactured the thirty-dollar pool at all that year. Last year's unsold twenty- and sixty-dollar pools had spent the winter in warehouses and were then shipped right back to the stores. No manufacturing costs this year. No thirty-dollar pools. People would have to choose. This was his theory.

He had already been to this store once over the weekend, had stood in this very aisle, this exact spot. On his way this time he'd convinced himself that because of his indecision and stubbornness and the repeated warnings about the coming heat wave, the pools would be sold out. He would be punished, and his children would be punished by proxy, left without a pool during the heat. He couldn't have his children growing up telling stories of how their father was stubborn, the kind of man who refused to buy a pool if the stores didn't offer exactly the same model year after year.

The twenty-dollar pools were gone. The country was in a recession. People were losing their jobs and houses and they had chosen the twenty-dollar pool this year—it was enough, or would have to be. Only the sixty-dollar pools remained. They were stacked three high on the pallet, fields of latex tightly folded into white cardboard boxes. An image on a wrinkled sheet of paper glued to the side of each box showed children splashing happily.

Nathan and Emily wore hand-me-down clothes. Geary had no money for college savings accounts and he rented instead of owning. He believed they were trapped. He had trapped them—because he could not, for whatever reason, catch on somewhere. Because he insisted on continuing to try, they sank further. He did not have the money to pay next month's rent and was not sure how to get it. He had invoices out, but agencies paid freelancers at their leisure, almost casually. He had already considered his car. Selling it would be self-defeating, though. How would he pick the kids up, how would he take them places? He should not be purchasing a pool at all. And if he must, it should be the twenty-dollar pool. The pallet of sixty-dollar pools stood before him, three boxes high, four wide, four deep: forty-eight pools responsible parents had rejected.

His phone buzzed. The screen read *Elizabeth Barrow*. Elizabeth was a friend from graduate school—she knew him from when he'd wanted to be a writer and had called himself one. She was the communications director for the Cascadia Arts Council now—Sheckley's boss. She'd given Geary some work a few years ago redesigning CAC's newsletter. It was just a one-time job, but it had been kind of her to offer it to him. He hadn't spoken to her in probably a year. When he was working, or in a store, or sometimes even just absorbed in a book, he often ignored calls that weren't from family. Her name continued to glow on the screen, though. The phone buzzed. He answered.

"Don. How are you?" she said.

"I'm looking at swimming pools."

"You're building a swimming pool?"

"No. Looking at one. The blow-up kind."

"God, my kids are on me to do that, too. I'm sorry I'm calling on a Sunday, but I have a time sensitive issue, something I need to know by tomorrow. It's a work thing—a job."

"Okay."

"First, though, how are you, really? It's been too long."

He could not remember having spoken to Elizabeth on the phone before. He wasn't sure how he was, but said he was fine. She asked about his kids and he asked about hers. He'd been raised when phone conversations were considered private. He'd also been taught it was rude to ignore others in public, so he instinctively moved into an empty aisle: automotive supplies. He contemplated black bottles of Armor All while they talked.

"About the job," she said. "We rebranded last year, as you know. New logo, name, website, everything. Occasionally we get outside people to evaluate our projects, and then our board looks over the evaluations. It's part of our annual review. And I need someone to evaluate the rebrand."

"David Hulme did the rebrand for you, didn't he?"

"Yes, but the review is about more than just him. You would look everything over and write something about the strengths and weaknesses of the whole process. You'd have to address our position in the field, the design and functionality of the website, some cost analysis of the project, that kind of thing."

Cost analysis? He'd plagiarized his own rates from a magazine he'd found in the trash. "I don't think I'm in a position to evaluate the projects of other designers," he said. "I don't run an actual agency, Elizabeth. I don't have employees or an office. I have a computer, and that's it. I work on my computer."

"I think that's what everyone does, Don. David Hulme doesn't have employees. How have you been making your living this year? The primary way."

"Design stuff."

"I asked some people about you—clients of yours. You've worked with other non-profits."

"A few times."

"They said you're working on some long-term project— you listed it in your references. It took a little bit of work, but I figured out you're doing something for those guys who call themselves Apogee, right?"

"You're a very skilled detective."

"Not that skilled—I don't know what the project is. But I know they're venture capital guys, and I know some other things they've done, and they're not small things. If you're working for these guys and it's a long-term project, then I think you're a professional. You should just admit you're a professional."

"It's just one project. I don't have some long career of experience to draw on in order to evaluate other people."

"When is the Apogee project rolling out?"

"What do you mean?"

"When will we be allowed to see this supposedly non-professional thing you've been working on?"

"I didn't say it was non-professional."

"When does it roll out? You're being weird."

"In the fall. October." As soon as he said it he wondered if he'd violated the non-disclosure agreement.

"And what will you be doing for work then? When that project is done?"

Elizabeth had gone to graduate school with him. The cadence of her voice was the cadence of an entirely other community. She was the managing editor of a magazine, she worked with writers. Her cadence was like the cadence of family—the thing he wanted to return to, the thing he could never to return to. He couldn't chase the past. It no longer existed.

"I don't know what I'm going to do when the project is done," he said. "I just think about the week in front of me."

"I don't want to claim I'm an important person," Elizabeth said. "I'm not these Apogee guys, I'm aware of that. But CAC pays, and I'm offering you work for hire. If you accept, our staff and board will see your work. You'll be the designer we chose to evaluate our rebranding. Won't that help you get more clients? Would you at least meet me for lunch and let me show you what I'm talking about?"

"Of course I'll have lunch with you, Elizabeth."

"You always say you're not up to anything, but then other people tell me you did a project for them, or they know you're working for someone else. You're very secretive."

"I'm not secretive at all. Everything I've told you is the truth."

"No. You leave things out. There's always something else going on. I'll email you to figure out a time for lunch. It's really an easy job, Don. Think of it as an opportunity for professional advancement."

After he thanked her and hung up, he wondered why he was looking at bottles of Armor All. He couldn't remember. Then he snapped back to focus—swimming pools. He returned to the cardboard boxes.

He had a personal credit card and a business credit card. The combined debt was both a real amount and a kind of nonsense number and he looked for the strength not to care. He had children and they required things. Their childhood would not last forever. He and Nathan and Emily were flickering lights in the emptiness of space and time. Should his children not know happiness? Should they not know moments in which he had provided? In which they had entered his house and felt surprise and delight and knew him as a father who came through, who was good?

He began to wrestle one of the boxes from the stack. It was heavier than he'd anticipated.

3 | Hal Bermea was in his fifties, bald, with thick glasses, but boyish in his enthusiasm as he scrolled through a page on the ESPN website. It featured an article in which an aging player considered his legacy. "What about this?" he said. "You see the way it rolls down like a curtain?"

"You want that for your site? Do you have content like that?" Sheckley said.

Bermea scratched his chin and studied the screen, which

he'd turned so everyone could see it. The scent of his mint gum filled the room. He owned Broadway Plumbing, a business whose website had been built in 2004. Bermea liked to update the site himself. He had, over the years, begun tinkering with the code, but he'd tinkered himself into a corner. Certain pages didn't load. Others had photos and text in incorrect places. Chunks of code appeared on screen.

"What about the company history?" Bermea said. "That would be cool this way. Really dynamic."

Sheckley looked at Geary. He couldn't tell how Geary felt about this. He suspected it wasn't good.

"That kind of thing can be done, but it's an entirely different kind of page. It's many more hours of work," Geary said.

"How many hours, do you think? I just want something super, super dynamic," Bermea said.

Sheckley explained that the site Bermea currently had was a single design consistent across all individual pages, which gave the site a unified feel. What Bermea was suggesting was a completely different design—it would be like designing a whole other site. Bermea clicked some more, his eyes on the screen.

"It's just so dynamic," he said.

The door opened and a man in a Broadway Plumbing shirt poked his head into the office. "You said you wanted to know when that Adirondack shipment showed up?"

"Oh, yes. Thank you," Bermea said.

The man disappeared. Bermea turned his computer monitor back to where only he could see it. Frowning, he clicked his mouse and studied the results. Sheckley had no idea what Bermea was looking at so intently.

"Gentlemen, I'm sorry," Bermea said. "This will just take a minute." He clicked once more and, apparently satisfied, stood, smiled, and walked out of the office. After the door closed, Sheckley and Geary were alone.

"What's the budget on this job?" Geary asked.

"I can't get him to say. I was hoping we could figure it out today."

"He wants the ESPN website, but full of plumbing products and stories about his life. Who's going to write that?"

"Maybe he'll ask us to."

Leaning stacks of manila folders and plastic binders filled Bermea's desk and the top of his filing cabinets. Pipe joints lay in the corner. The room was dusty, the vinyl shades on the windows discolored.

"How did you meet him, again?"

"He's a donor," Sheckley said. "He's on the board, too."

"This guy is on the board of the Cascadia Arts Council?"

"You put business leaders or connected people on a non-profit board. They help you get money."

The warning beeps of heavy equipment in reverse were audible from somewhere nearby. Bermea's computer made an odd sputtering noise—a strangled voice—and then returned to silence.

"Do you want to run?" Sheckley said.

"No. I need the job. But why are *you* doing it? I thought your position at CAC was full-time."

"I'm trying to hand off all my old clients personally."

"Did you write the stuff that's on his website now?"

"No, I just wrote marketing materials and their email newsletter."

"Who wrote all the copy on the site?"

Sheckley didn't say anything.

"He wrote it himself," Geary said.

"You can still walk."

"No. But do you think there's any way we can ask for half of the payment up front? I'm kind of cash poor right now."

"He's never done that with me. It's all invoices, sixty days. That doesn't mean we can't ask."

"It's not a big enough job to get into that if that's not how he operates."

"It's big if we're remaking the ESPN site."

"We're not remaking the ESPN site."

"It would make him really happy. It would be dynamic."

The door opened and Bermea strode past them, back to his desk. "Sorry. They always ship the wrong stuff, so I have to check. Where were we? Wait, right, it was ESPN. Look, there's another site I want to show you. Do you guys play video games?"

"Don?" Sheckley said.

"Not lately."

Bermea rubbed his hands together and leaned over his keyboard. "Okay, get ready to have your minds blown. PlayStation." He clicked a few times, studied the result, and then looked down, hunting and pecking. After each letter, he glanced at the screen to confirm he'd hit the right key.

4 | "How are you getting this effect?"

It was two thirty in the afternoon. The employees worked at their stations—long stretches of quiet clicks, an occasional clatter of typing, and then another stretch of quiet. Larsen and Geary sat at the long white table at the side of the Polymath office. A dozen large color printouts lay before them on the table, each a spread from the project.

What was Larsen asking? Geary did not want to describe his process. There might be something wrong with it, something foolish he'd done. But he also wanted to talk. Larsen was someone from whom he could learn.

"I took some photos of curtains."

A woman left her workstation and walked barefoot out the back door to the parking lot. She disappeared into the light, her wireless headphones still on her head.

"And then you made something based off the photos?" Larsen said.

"No. That is one of the photos."

"What about the screenprint effect here?"

"I did a screenprint."

"You made a full, physical print?"

"Yes. And then I took a photo of it."

There were no clocks visible, but Geary didn't want to look at his phone. The kids' school day ended at three. They would be in after-school care until four thirty. He hoped the meeting would last a bit. He wanted Larsen to like his work, to be impressed, to want to discuss it. Yet a part of him was always keeping track of time. If the meeting was short, he might be able to get home in time to work on Gielgud for thirty or forty minutes before he had to get the kids.

"How long did that take?" Larsen said.

"Don't worry, I'm not billing for the screenprint time. I've been doing screenprints just for fun."

"I don't care about the billing, I'm just wondering how long."

"I don't know. A few hours, maybe."

Larsen moved the spread aside and grabbed a different one. "They're going to ask for this stuff to be removed. It's too natural," he said. "They like digital curves on a digital grid. I think you said Vidal Sassoon the last time you were here."

"Sorry. I thought—"

"Don't be sorry. I'm trying to tell you they'll want this changed because they have surface aesthetics. They'll sense there's something subtle going on and they won't like that. It makes them nervous. They are the least subtle people in the world. They want a quick hit from design and then the thing is done—the book's closed or the shoes are purchased. The copy is corporate speak and ad slang and the design has to match that. What you're doing is trying to elevate the text, but you can't elevate corporate buzzwords."

This was the day Andrea had told him she wanted to have Emily tested. They'd tried the powder laxative, to no effect. Emily was still in pain. Geary had read an article in the *Times* about the mystery of girls and stomachaches and had suggested sticking with a wait-and-see strategy, but Andrea wasn't interested in ambiguity. The doctor who'd prescribed the laxative had told her they could run a scope down Emily's stomach and take a look. This sounded invasive to Geary. Andrea's professional life was wandering into their personal lives—she was diagnosing their daughter. It was also true, however, that Emily continued to cry and lie curled on the couch, and Geary felt helpless.

Rubbing her back made no difference. She refused to take Tums—they didn't do anything, she said. He didn't know what to do.

"When was the last time you were in San Francisco?" Larsen asked.

It took Geary a moment to understand the question. "Maybe a year, year and a half. Why?"

"Ever heard of an agency called Ad Astra?"

"No."

"They do this. The CD used to live here. She came out to work for Wieden like all of us do, and then she started her own thing—like all of us do. But then she moved to San Francisco. What you're doing here, all this sourcing of the images, photos of actual curtains and actual prints? That's what they do. She's the kind of person who at this point probably wouldn't even take Nike's money. She's arrogant, she won't do certain things. I always found her to be kind of an asshole, personally, but her work is pretty cool. *Their* work, I guess. I don't know how many people she has now. I feel like the artisan stuff is a waste of time. It's beautiful and I like looking at it, but nobody does this. I mean, except for them. Maybe a couple places on the East Coast."

"Are there campaigns of theirs I know? Would I know it if I saw it?"

"They do some big museums, I think. And probably companies that make...yachts or something. Ad Astra would actually pay you for the hours you spent doing the screenprints is what I mean. They probably have a screen-printing studio in their building." He gathered the spreads and clipped them back together. "Ever think of moving to San Francisco?"

"No."

"Well, if you ever do, let me know."

5 | "Is your poster up yet?"

The back door was open so Geary could see and hear Emily in the yard. She dashed from the pool to the grass and back again, immersed in the urgency of an imagined drama. Nathan had told Geary the evening wasn't warm enough for him to go in the pool and had disappeared into his room. Now he was standing at Geary's elbow.

"I think they're going to put it up at the beginning of next month," Geary said. "Why?" He'd been drinking a beer and reading a magazine. He placed the magazine spread-down on his desk. George Clooney gazed up from the cover. The back cover featured a man with a brooding gaze standing on a yacht in a suit and tie, his hair slicked back, a checkerboard-patterned bag hanging from his shoulder.

Nathan held a folded piece of paper in his hand. Geary could see his block-letter handwriting on it.

"What do you have there?" Geary asked.

"An order form," Nathan said. "For people to order books."

"What books are you selling?"

"Just the books I've written."

"Let me see."

Nathan liked to fold a few pieces of paper in half, saddle-stitch them with a stapler, and make little books. They contained variations of the stories he'd seen in movies, or placed the movie's characters in new situations. He handed his list to Geary. It had three titles: *IronMan $5, Star Wars $7, Skatbording $10.*

"You wrote a book about skateboarding?"

"Not yet. I'm working on it."

"You should probably finish it before you advertise it for sale."

"I will." He touched his chin once to his right shoulder and once to his left. "How long is it until your poster is out?"

"Next month. About four weeks from now."

"Why is it taking so long?"

"Right now the stores have posters up for the concerts that are happening this month. Everyone has to wait their turn. It doesn't have the monster on it anymore, though."

"What's on it?"

"A picture of a really big wheel."

"Why does it have a picture of a wheel?"

"They didn't think the monster was a good idea."

"I thought it was good."

"I know, but other bands have had monsters on their posters, so these guys wanted to do something different. What do you think would be good on a concert poster?"

The boy rubbed his nose. The sun had brought out the freckles on his cheeks. "I don't know. I haven't heard their songs."

"Neither have a lot of the people who will see the poster. You might still know a good idea for a picture."

"I liked the monster."

"I know."

"I told my friends there was going to be a monster on it."

"It's okay. You can tell them I had to change it to a different cool thing."

"What's the band's name?"

"Pages."

"Are their songs about books?"

"No."

"Do people in the band read books?"

"I assume so."

"Is that why their name is Pages?"

"I don't remember."

"You don't remember why they chose their name?"

"I've talked to them about a lot of things, Nathan. I don't remember everything they've said."

Nathan seemed unsatisfied. It wasn't clear if the dissatisfaction was with the band name or with the idea that his father might not remember things people said.

"What's your favorite book?" Emily asked him at bedtime. She and Nathan were climbing onto her bed after she'd selected a story for Geary to read. It was about a town of people drawn in loopy scribbles and what happens when a stranger drawn in straight lines comes to town.

"I don't know," he said. "I like different books for different reasons. What's your favorite book?"

"Are my cards a book?"

She had a stack of quiz cards with questions about letters or words or animals or pictures. She liked to do two or three cards before Geary turned out the light.

"I don't think the cards are a book. They're cards."

"Then my favorite book is..." She narrowed her eyes while considering the ceiling and then the wall, drawing out the drama. "*The Lost Thing*."

"*The Lost Thing*?" Nathan said.

"We haven't read that for a while," Geary said.

"Because I already know it. But I like it. It's my favorite."

The Lost Thing was about a teapot-shaped object a boy encountered in a fantasy city. No one else seemed to notice the thing, which was odd, since it was as big as a shed. The boy tried to figure out where the thing belonged, but had a hard time.

"That's a good one," Geary said. "What's your favorite book, Nate the Great? Is it *Nate the Great*?"

"No. Don't call me Nate the Great."

"Sorry. Nathan the Grathan."

"Dad."

"Sorry. What's your favorite book?"

"The skateboarding tricks book I got at the library."

"Today?"

"Yes."

"You got four books about skateboarding tricks. Which one are you talking about?"

"It's called *Fourteen Skateboarding Tricks*. It shows you how to do tic-tac, ollies, kick-flips, some other stuff I can't remember."

"And it's your favorite book? After only seven hours of having it?"

"Yes." He was quite serious about it.

"That skateboarding is a hot topic with you."

"What does that mean?"

"It means it's very popular with you right now. You're very interested in skateboarding."

"It's my favorite sport."

"I know. I know that, Nathan Geary."

"So the skateboarding book is my favorite book."

"Makes sense. I know what you're saying."

Nathan's pajamas were red and black. The shirt featured repeated images of movie cameras, film reels, and the word *Hollywood* in blinking-lights type. "You didn't tell us what *your* favorite book is," Nathan said.

"I thought I said I like different books for different reasons."

"But what's your favorite?" Emily said. Her pajamas were pink and white. The top featured a drawing of a typewriter. The drawing was gray except for the *L*, *O*, *V*, and *E* keys, which were pink.

"I don't think I have a favorite," Geary said.

"Tell us what your favorite book is!" she cried.

"Emily!" Nathan said.

"Calm down!" Geary said. This pattern occurred often: Emily became frustrated and yelled, Nathan yelled at her to stop yelling, Geary yelled at them both, and then they all glared at each other, wide-eyed and breathing hard.

"You don't need to yell," Geary said. "My favorite book is probably *The Lost Thing*."

"That's *my* favorite book!" Emily said.

"Mine, too!" Geary said. "I like *The Lost Thing* a lot. But fine, if I have to choose something else...*Curious George Goes to the Hospital*."

"But that's for kids," Nathan complained.

"So? I can like it, too. I think it's a perfect book. In the beginning, George swallows a piece of the puzzle. For the whole story it's down in his stomach and no one can finish the puzzle. And then what does he get back on the last page of the book?"

"The puzzle piece," Nathan said.

"Yes. Don't you think that's good?"

"I guess so."

"I like that book," Emily said.

"See? Emily likes it, too."

"I thought you were going to tell us what grown-up book you like best," Nathan said.

"Grown-up books aren't as good as kid books."

"That's not true. *True Grit* is good."

"I forgot you read *True Grit*. You're right, *True Grit* is good. But it doesn't have a missing puzzle piece in it."

"Why are you so interested in puzzles?" Nathan said.

Later in the evening he was watching Letterman when he heard the sound of splashing in the backyard. Had some drunk person walking past the house spied the pool and decided to jump in? Was a homeless person worn down by the heat taking advantage? Or was the sound coming from some other yard?

He listened. Silence. Then: more splashing.

He went downstairs and stepped out the basement door. The pool was silent, its walls faint orange in the glow of the light by the back door. He moved toward it and looked into the water. Glints of half-seen ripples twisted slowly across the surface. There was no one in the water.

Then a face poked above the edge of the pool and he shouted. No more than five feet away, black eyes studied him without a trace of fear. Claws gripped the rounded latex side of the pool, holding the creature up. It was a raccoon.

"Get out of here!" Geaery yelled, clapping his hands.

The raccoon lowered itself from the edge of the pool and ambled a few steps off. Over the other edge of the pool another face appeared.

"Hey! Get!" He clapped his hands again, as loud as he could. They just looked at him.

He jogged back into the basement and found some pennies on his desk. Returning to the yard, he set one of the coins in the crook of his finger and, using the same motion he'd used to skip stones across a pond when he was young, winged the penny at the nearest raccoon. He missed, but the animal sensed something had flown past, and began moving away.

"Go!" Geary yelled.

He threw another coin, this one at the other raccoon. He heard no result and so didn't know if he'd hit the raccoon or missed entirely, but that one also began to move unhurriedly toward the cedar fence at the back of the yard. Geary yelled more and slung more pennies and the raccoons looked back at him a last time before they slipped through the gap under the fence. He noticed two more faces peering at him from the gap beneath the boards— the rest of the family. He threw the remaining pennies at the fence and heard the sharp reports of the coins against the planks. The faces disappeared.

So raccoons were washing their paws in the pool he'd bought for his kids. They were probably swimming in it, too.

When he woke in the morning and went out to the yard, he found the top ring of the pool soft and sagging. He ran his fingers over it until he found the line of small holes in the latex—claw marks. After he covered the holes with gray duct tape, he reinflated the ring. It seemed to hold.

6 | A couple dozen people sat in the rows of folding chairs set up in the middle of the gallery. Half of the attendees had white hair, they wore glasses and slip-on shoes and whispered to each other, a word now and then followed by silence, and then another comment, a nod. Everyone held a flimsy paper program. A few of the men had folded the programs in half, though there was no apparent reason to do this.

Geary took a seat in the back row. There was a wooden podium to the right front of the room and behind it nine large video monitors locked together in a three-by-three grid to form a single large screen. He could not see what scaffolding or support system held the monitors together, but there were no gaps—they were a single, perfect entity, a screen of screens that did not yet hold an image but stood noble and luminous, a field of white light.

Younger people—men and women his own age wearing jeans and sneakers—occupied the row immediately before him. The men wore baseball hats and chatted and laughed with one another, trading information. Geary hoped to be ignored, to sit silently in the back row. To be in the middle of the scrum, talking, laughing, pumping hands— it looked like torture.

Back beyond everything, beyond the podium and screens, in the far corner of the gallery, a woman stood watching. Geary was in the last seat in the last row, but the woman seemed to be looking directly at him. The chairs were filled, the screen was large and there was much commotion, but Geary saw her head tilt ever so slightly, as if she had noted something interesting. She was short, slight, older, dressed in dark slacks and a dark blouse. Her hair was gray, pulled tightly back. She occupied the back corner the way a security guard would—motionless, expressionless. She did not wear the uniform of a security guard, though, nor did she possess the professionally bored mien.

A door near the woman opened and two men stepped into the gallery. The first was tall, lean, with a slight stoop or perhaps just a slight forward lean. The second was shorter, heavyset, with thinning gray hair and a gray goatee. The taller man leaned down to speak to the woman. It was difficult to read the nature of their exchange, but the woman nodded—the tall man seemed to be asking questions. From Geary's distance the man appeared to wince, in pain or perhaps merely uncertain about something. The woman nodded in the direction of the podium, as if encouraging him.

The screen changed—someone had activated whatever technology enlivened the blank white canvas. A computer desktop appeared, a cursor flitted across the field and stopped over an icon, and the desktop was replaced by a single image. In the foreground, a male figure in an earth-colored tunic over a red shirt trailed a horse pulling a plow. A wooden blade on the plow sliced neat ribbons of earth. Beyond, a smaller figure looked to the sky. This figure was on some kind of outcrop or cliff over a green sea dotted by rocks and boats. The horizon and sky were a white and cream and gray-blue murk above indistinct mountains rendered in the same tones. It was a painting familiar to Geary, though he could not recall the painter.

The two men had approached the screen from the rear of the gallery and moved past it now to the podium. The shorter man stepped behind the podium first. He introduced himself as the museum's director, welcomed everyone to the event, and began to speak about the power of images, how there had been a time in history when humans made long treks, pilgrimages, really, just for the opportunity to see certain images: a painting of the Virgin Mary, stained glass panels, haunting faces that gazed from canvases. "As noted by John Berger, however, images have, for some time now, traveled to us. The advertising industry is the primary maker of images now, and though we may think of them as different in kind, many of their goals are shockingly the same—to inspire wonder, to communicate values, and, ultimately, to connect people to a way of living, to establish a culture."

Geary tried to understand the man's motivations. He was elevating the practice of advertising to the position of art, mentioning religious and spiritual traditions—the care of the soul—alongside television commercials and magazine advertisements.

"I'm excited, then, to introduce today's guest speaker, a man who is an expert in identity and brand management. He has served as Executive Creative Director at Cumulus, as Group Creative Director at The Alexander Agency, and as Creative Director at Cumulus Amsterdam. He was a founding faculty member of the Penn State University Marketing Program and an adjunct professor in the University of Oregon School of Journalism and Communication. He is also the founder and director of SpeakMillenium, an experimental education experience that helps students explore the intersections of narrative, communication, and identity. His new book, *Purpose is a Story: A Manifesto*, published by Simon & Schuster last year, is, according to the publisher, 'a rigorous and radical attempt to reframe how we think about brands, story, identity, and the lives of consumers.' Chad Taylor, in *Adweek*, called it 'a spirited polemic on behalf of purpose-driven marketing. The debate over whether narrative- or impact-driven campaigns are best suited to the contemporary consumer environment'—this is still the reviewer in *Adweek*—'has become intense in recent years, and Hulme cranks it up a notch. The book is smart, stimulating, and aphoristic. It is a provocative and entertaining manifesto.' Our speaker has been a brand and identity consultant to numerous Fortune 500 companies and national non-profits, and currently researches and speaks about story, collaboration, thought leadership, and the role of purpose and story in our changing culture. With this list of achievements and experience, I know he will offer particular insights into how we respond to art and images, and how the relationships we form with images offer us a shared sense of identity. Ladies and gentlemen, David Hulme."

Someone in the audience turned and looked back. Geary recognized Lana Luft-Castillo, the executive director of the Cascadia Arts Council. She was gauging the size of the crowd, it seemed, or perhaps looking for someone. The tall man—Hulme—stepped to the podium, thanked the museum director, and began to speak. His voice was higher than Geary had expected from a man his size, and his sentences were peppered with hesitations.

"In 2008, I took a sabbatical from my job. I wasn't burned out, I wasn't questioning what I was doing. I had a sense there was something going on that I couldn't see, though. I could sense something, a dynamic, or an energy—it was bound up with what I was doing, but I didn't understand it. So I took some time away from the agency I worked for. I continued to work, but only with students in my SpeakMillennium program, and also with a small group of new clients on a freelance basis. I worked with clients who were okay with the fact that I didn't want to be a traditional brand manager for them, that I no longer wanted to do traditional identity creation."

Were the hesitations an affectation? A rhetorical trick that suggested an improvised speech from the heart, despite the fact that the screens seemed set to unfurl a prepared presentation? Or was this the way he spoke, was the uncertainty real? Impossible to tell. Hulme's lack of charisma was striking. He reminded Geary of no one Geary knew. He was like a boy who had been pushed in front of the microphone and was only warming to it slowly.

"But what did that mean, that I didn't want to be a traditional brand manager? I wasn't sure."

He stepped from behind the podium and began to pace slowly, back and forth, in front of the audience.

"I didn't even want to be called an identity manager, or a brand manager, or anything like that. I asked them to think of me as a narrative consultant, to understand that stories are how people make sense of themselves, of their place in the world, of their purpose in life. What I wanted to do, what I wanted to understand, what I wanted to practice, was the idea that when we create a brand, what we're really doing is creating a new narrative that is in addition to our already existing self-narrative. We're creating something larger than ourselves as individuals."

He was not looking at the audience, he was looking at his shoes. Geary noticed a small camera on a tripod off to one side of the audience, and another, set lower, on the opposite side, near the front. Hulme's affect was perhaps not for the immediate audience, Geary realized, but for the cameras, for posterity. For the internet.

He talked about deciding not to return to the agency, chosing instead to continue developing a client list of his own, operating on the principle that the most effective brands develop narratives that place purpose before profit. He rubbed his chin. He nodded while gazing into the distance. He was forty-six years old, was born and grew up in Los Angeles. His BA was from Brown, his MA from the Rhode Island School of Design. Geary knew these things because he had read Hulme's Wikipedia page.

Hulme said when he was young he wanted a life driven by meaning and by purpose. "The career as the measure of the human," he said. He talked about being a child, the assumption at all times, everywhere in American culture, that family life was not a pleasure in and of itself, but preparatory. What it was preparatory for were the careers of the children. He held his fist in his palm as he spoke about imagining a career in which he was entirely committed, in which each day would offer the opportunity to express something of himself. The fingers of his open hand kneaded the back of his fist. Geary realized the woman in dark clothing had disappeared from the distant corner of the gallery. She must have slipped out the same door Hulme had come through. Geary had heard nothing, had no idea when she had left, what function she had served and had apparently completed. Hulme paused—an extended pause, the silence significant.

"On one side was soul-deadening cynicism. On the other, naïve optimism. And I could not resolve them."

Another pregnant pause. Hulme was beginning to indulge the theatrical aspects of the presentation, Geary thought. He was slipping deeper into character. Cynicism versus optimism, dark versus light, life versus death, and Hulme perched precariously above, brooding over the conflict.

"Purpose. The beauty of being purpose-driven. Not money-driven, not pleasure-driven. Purpose-driven. What I wanted to create were purpose-driven brands. The beauty of brands underwritten by purpose is that they can find a place in which they are productively situated between the extremes of that soul-deadening cynicism and that unreflective optimism. A brand situated between those poles can find a tension, a *creative* tension, in which every aspect of the business can appear—can become—purpose-driven. The brand suddenly looks, and is, more interesting. It begins to build a narrative of itself, of how it operates in the world. Of what kind of relationship it wants to establish with others."

Geary had read Hulme's blog and facebook posts. Hulme was a husband and a father. Geary imagined a home from the pages of *Dwell* magazine, a clean white study in which the family gathered to read and think.

"The center of effective brand building, for me, is the struggle to transform feelings, insights, or values into an overarching symbol. And then to make that symbol stand for everything."

He had two boys, Geary decided, with nice haircuts, good clothes, the ability to sit quietly. A smiling wife paging through a book, relaxed and at leisure. The image was unlikely, but it was the only image Geary could come up with.

"The painting behind me: *Landscape with the Fall of Icarus*, by Pieter Brueghel the Elder."

He decided to escape the images of Hulme's home by deciding what sport Hulme would play—to try to imagine him in movement. He was tall but did not seem swift. There was something mechanical in his pacing. Brown, RISD, these were upper-class places. He played competent tennis, Geary decided. He had a fundamentally sound golf stroke. Individual sports, non-contact sports.

"A single image, but with a number of things going on in it. Tension. The tension between the painting as a whole and the multiple human beings in it, each with their own position. Icarus falls into the sea. The others don't see it, they're looking the wrong way. Is the subject matter cynical? Is this painter a cynic? The fantastic care that has gone into the craft. The use of perspective, of color. Is this painter an optimist? Someone who believes, in some naïve way, in the importance of painting? The image spurs many thoughts in us—it spurs thoughts in me, at least. There are so many individual moments to investigate here. And yet at the same time, the painting confronts us immediately, at once. It's one thing, a single entity. *Landscape with the Fall of Icarus*, by Pieter Brueghel the Elder."

He decided he would try agreeing with everything Hulme said. To keep himself flexible, to open his mind. Hulme was a successful person, had achieved highly and worked with scores of clients, and the art museum had invited him to share his thoughts. Geary would agree. There was no harm in sitting in the back row and practicing agreement, being agreeable.

"I want to show you a plan. It's simple—deliberately so."

The painting disappeared from the screen and was replaced by four concentric ovals, each containing a label. The diagram was not refined—it could have been made in a word processing program in two minutes. The ovals' arcs were chunky, digitized. The innermost oval held the word INTENTION. The oval surrounding it was labeled WORTH. The next was NARRATIVE, and the largest was HUMANITY. The labels were in Times New-Roman. The ovals were weighted to the left, like a solar system in which the planets' orbits track closely on one side of the sun and spread wide on the other. No, Geary thought, it's not a solar system. It's an avocado.

"People, groups, organizations, businesses—they all find meaning, find a sense of worth in life, by living with intention. When an individual or a group lives with intention, other human beings, whether a mass audience or just an individual, they see this as a narrative."

So the goal was to have a goal. Managing to rouse oneself from passivity was the spiritual breakthrough? Geary wanted to suspend analysis, to just listen. He tried to imagine Hulme outside of the event, somewhere he would be other, perhaps more himself. He could be surprisingly good at croquet. He could have extensive experience with tai chi.

"We consider ourselves a bespoke identity agency." The transition to the plural first-person went unexplained, the move from private sojourn to team destiny apparently too natural a step to mention. He described, with thoughtful hesitations and effortful hand movements, how their goal was to share narratives so luscious they were almost delicacies. This was why they worked only with intention-driven people and companies. Art and craft were important, but the most powerful narratives were built on the engine of intention. Those were the narratives people were hungry for, now more than ever.

7 | They left the house at five thirty. The kids grabbed their backpacks and lunchboxes and jackets and piled into Geary's gray Corolla and he drove down to the Morrison Bridge and onto the freeway and picked up speed. It was fifteen minutes to the north side of town. Geary chose

the music and turned up the volume. He negotiated the freeway and experienced it according to the terms of the negotiation: signs and limits, directives and warnings. The kids chewed gum and slipped into reverie, the windows half-reflecting their upturned faces. Their thoughts were unguessable. Perhaps they had pure impressions—of cars and warehouses, the basketball arena that rose like a concrete drum, the slate river and green hills. The train yard. A man pushing a shopping cart, a dog running loose. The sky with its clouds and contrails.

When he parked, the kids tumbled from the car and walked across the common lawn surrounded by half a dozen houses, all of which were five years old. The massive apartment buildings that once stood there—"the projects"—had been razed and replaced with a park, a community garden, and a strategic mix of houses, townhomes, and apartments. An elementary school, a small grocery store, and a boutique police station on the corner each looked the same: crisp brick and clean glass.

Emily knocked solemnly on the door and was answered by barking.

"Buddy!" she yelled.

"Oh, Buddy!" Nathan sang.

Andrea opened the door and held the dog back with her leg. He barked while turning in a circle, backside wiggling as the kids stepped past Andrea into the house.

"Don't drop your backpacks here. Backpacks belong in your rooms," she said.

"Buddy, Buddy!" the kids sang, adoring him with their hands and voices. This was his second family. The first had left him in the backyard of a foreclosed home. That, at least, was what the people running the animal shelter had told Andrea and Tom when they'd met Buddy cowering alone in his cage. He peed on the concrete the moment they petted him. His muzzle and haunches were white, but his true age and breed were a mystery. To Nathan and Emily he was just *Buddy*, wholly sufficient. They had saved him.

"We're barbecuing," Andrea told Geary. "Do you want to eat something?"

The kids looked at each other, aghast. Except for birthday parties, Geary did not step further into the house than the entryway.

He shrugged. "Sure."

Unprecedented. The kids sprang into action. They demanded he look at their rooms, scrambled ahead of him up the stairs chattering excitedly about the wonders that awaited. Andrea had repainted Nathan's room in colors he had chosen: three walls aquamarine, one orange. They were Denver Broncos colors, Nathan said. The shades were closer to the Miami Dolphins, but Geary nodded and said it looked good. Nathan showed him a desk Andrea had bought him, shelves she and Tom had put above it, and then the *coup de grace*: opening his closet doors, he revealed a dresser on top of which a television with a built-in VHS player sat. VHS tapes Nathan had liberated from a box in Geary's basement lay scattered across the closet floor. Nathan hadn't asked permission to take the tapes—he must have smuggled them out in his backpack, Geary decided. He noted the Disney *Robin Hood*, Tim Burton's *Batman*, and the two-tape box with the unmistakable picture of the Alps.

"Do you watch *The Sound of Music*?" Geary asked.

"Yes," Nathan said.

"You like that? How often do you watch it?"

"I like it."

Emily pulled Geary to her room. It was pink, with a pink play kitchen, and on top of her dresser a pink Disney princess television set with a built-in DVD player. She had a little remote control for the television and proudly demonstrated how it worked. The kids' rooms were large, with clean windows and television sets they could operate. At home, Geary still kept his remotes on a high shelf. It wasn't unusual for the kids to discover they couldn't make the stereo or television do what they wanted. Their rooms were small. No television sets. Small windows. Emily began to demonstrate how to put plastic pieces of toast into a pink play toaster. Geary said their rooms looked great, but he should go downstairs and talk to their mother and Tom.

"Can we watch some Disney in Aiden's room?" Nathan asked. Aiden was Tom's ten-year-old son, whose room was across the hall.

"You just showed me you have televisions in your own rooms," Geary said.

"But he has cable," Emily said.

"It's satellite," Nathan said.

"Same thing!"

"Mom lets us watch Disney in there when he's not here."

Curtains covered the glass of the French doors that opened into Aiden's room. The space was intended to serve as an office or television room. The doors were closed, the room dark.

"You'll have to ask Mom," Geary said.

The kids thundered down the stairs. By the time he reached the end of the hall and started down, they were running back up, Andrea trailing.

"I didn't know what to say," he said.

She shrugged. "It's an ongoing issue."

In the kitchen, Tom set barbecue tongs across an empty plate. "I was at the track this afternoon," he said. "Our house is louder. Do you want a beer?"

There was something of *Rockford*-era James Garner about him. He was a man neither critical nor impressed, just getting through and assuming others were doing the same.

"How'd you do at the track?"

"I did not do...as well as I should have."

"Do you study ahead of time?"

"A bit. At little tracks like the one here in town there are always horses just there to fill out the field. You can kind of figure out which ones those are. There are a couple sites on the internet that are good on it."

"And then you've increased your odds."

"Supposedly. Of course once in a while a field horse wins."

"The field horses don't know they're field horses," Geary said.

"They're so dumb they actually try. It ruins the system."

"Are you still complaining about the bike path?" Andrea said, returning to the kitchen. "There were too many people on the bike path today for Tom."

"I was complaining about horses. Maybe there were some horses on the bike path today, though. A couple of those ladies."

"Tom."

"I may have seen them again later, at the track. I probably bet on them."

"Stop."

He stepped into the backyard to attend to the barbecue.

Geary sat on a stool at the counter between the kitchen and family room. The television was tuned to a music station: *Hits of the Fifties*, the screen read. He couldn't guess who had chosen hits of the fifties.

Andrea stood on the other side of the counter, shaping ground pork into patties. "So what's new with you?" she asked.

He laughed. "What's new with me?"

"Is that a weird question?"

Even when they'd been together and planning a life, she'd sensed his contract was not with her. It was with some other thing. It was impossible to ask about, though, because how could she ask about a thing she couldn't name? Its whole power was that it was nameless. When he said they'd fought enough and he wanted to end their marriage, she had in confusion and anger asked if he was gay. He'd just laughed his same laugh, as if her question were final proof of something, which had of course further hurt and angered her.

"Are you working on a new project? New clients?"

"No, still working on the old one. It's supposed to go live in the fall."

"Are you looking forward to being done with it?"

He was hoping never to be done with it. He was hoping it might be the thing, the project that launched him. This was not something he would say, though. "I'm looking forward to it going live. I'm trapped in an end-of-the-project period of constant tweaking and testing. And I'm having a hard time communicating with the clients."

"You're not sure what they want? Or they're not sure what they want?"

"Something like that."

He tried to describe the situation as simply as possible without getting into specifics. Tom returned to the kitchen midway through the explanation. "It sounds like you're building Wikipedia," Tom said.

"And every time I mention Wikipedia to them, they say that's exactly what they don't want. But then when they describe what they want, that's pretty much what they want."

"When you're a famous designer, you'll be able to drop that stuff," Tom said. "I'm sure Steve Jobs doesn't do that stuff."

"I'm not sure Steve Jobs actually does anything."

"Sure he does. He stands on a stage with a big screen behind him."

"Well—they may be the Steve Jobs in the relationship."

"Do you get a percentage of the profits?"

It was a common sense question Geary tried not to think about. "No. I'm just a hired gun."

"Hired guns can always get hired by someone else."

Andrea's house still seemed new to Geary, still carried the sense of fresh paint and crisp trim—especially in comparison to the house he rented, with its crooked doors and wobbling fixtures. He had a futon for a couch. His desk took up too much space in the front room, and he left stacks of books everywhere. Andrea's chocolate brown sofa had matching pillows. Her mantel featured framed photos of the kids.

They traded thoughts on Nathan's tic. Geary saw him jut his chin toward his shoulder a few times a day, but it used to be a few times a minute. Andrea agreed it seemed better. She asked about Emily's stomachaches.

"When she says she has a stomachache in the morning, I've started saying, 'I know, honey, you say that every morning. But what we need to do...' and then I just move forward with getting ready," Geary said. "It seems like she always says it when she doesn't want to do something, like getting ready for school or bed."

Andrea was arranging the meat into neat stacks on a plate. "I'm thinking about taking her in to get some blood drawn. I just want to rule out anything serious."

He nodded. He deferred to her when it came to the children's medical lives. He found it unlikely anything was wrong with Emily. She ran and laughed and played like any kid. It was also true she kept curling up in pain.

When the burgers were done, everyone moved to the dining room. Geary stood to the side until Emily took the chair at the head of the table. He decided it would be logical to sit next to his daughter. Tom sat next to him, and Nathan and Andrea sat on the other side. Nathan was describing something funny that had happened in the show he and Emily had been watching, a complicated situation that had to do with mistaken identity. Emily supplied additional details. When Nathan finished explaining, the two of them laughed.

The framed photo of elk in mist that hung on the wall behind Andrea was a Christmas gift she had given Geary when they were dating. Through the arched doorway into the family room he could see a Maxfield Parrish print he'd bought for her when they moved into their first house. The Italian espresso machine she'd spent weeks researching on the internet before finally purchasing sat on the kitchen counter. When she went to bed at nine thirty each night, exhausted by work and dinner and diapers and baths, he used to use the machine to make the coffee he drank while building websites, looking at design books, and reading novels. That was when he had stopped writing, stopped the exact thing he had claimed he would be doing for the rest of his life.

"What are you looking at?" Andrea asked.

"Nothing," he said. "I was just wondering when school starts again."

"Tomorrow," Tom said. "Right, guys?"

"No!" the kids yelled.

Andrea stated the correct date. Geary repeated it silently to himself. Because he wasn't writing it down, though, he knew he would almost certainly forget it.

8 | The sky was white. The trees were full and green, everything was growing. He wore gray wool slacks and a crisp white shirt and drove instead of riding his bike. He wanted to arrive clean and cool, professional.

Norman had called the day before. "We're in town this week," he'd said. "Could you come into the office tomorrow? Maybe in the afternoon?"

Geary had told him he was free until three thirty.

"Let's do two thirty, then," Norman had said.

Geary found a parking space ten minutes early and stopped to buy a cup of coffee and a cookie. He took a chair and instead of opening his laptop and checking email, he looked through the weekly newspaper. He'd worked hard, he decided—he deserved the small luxury of the newspaper. He finished the cookie and walked to the brick building that had once been a brewery and was now filled with title companies, real estate agencies, small tech firms, and mysterious suites marked only with numbers. Bouros and Norman occupied one of these.

"Hello, Mr. Geary." The welcome from Ramel, Bouros and Norman's clean-cut collegiate assistant, surprised Geary. He'd only been in the office twice before, both times to sign contracts, and Ramel had been behind the reception desk each time, in the same alert posture. He wore a crisp shirt and tie, his hair was carefully styled—he was obviously ambitious. Geary assumed assistants in the finance or venture capital world moved on, climbing whatever ladders structured their field. Ramel was still at his post, though. Maybe he wasn't done making contacts, or maybe there was more to learn. Maybe he was paid well.

"You can go right in. They're waiting for you," he said.

As it had been on Geary's previous visits, Bouros and Norman's office was alarmingly clean. Two old Steelcase desks occupied the side of the room with windows that looked out over the street. The other side held a round meeting table, cabinets and a counter with a sink, and at the back, a ping-pong table. Previous tenants had probably divided the room into a dozen cubicles. There would have been a copy machine, a fax machine, telephones on the desks, notes and announcements tacked to the walls. Bouros and Norman had none of this.

"Don Geary! Good to see you," Norman called from his desk.

Bouros said nothing as he stood and shook Geary's hand, but he looked Geary in the eye and seemed genuinely happy to see him. Geary realized he actually liked

Bouros. He had a similar bearing and sense of courtesy. They were somehow on the same team.

"Code," Norman said after they had all settled at the table. He shook his head. "Code has always been a vast, foreign country to me. I don't know what's possible and what's not."

"I tried out that javascript that would allow users to enter corrections," Geary said. "We talked about it last time, I don't know if you remember. It works, but it's a little clunky."

"I'm sure there's something better. There's always something better," Norman said.

Geary told them the code worked differently on different devices—it was hard to predict. The trick was that it had to work equally well on all platforms and in all browsers. He could probably spend the next few days custom coding something. It would take time, but it would—

"No," Norman said. "Don't do that."

"It won't affect us being ready to launch. I also had some ideas on promotion. Just a list of publishing world media you could—"

"Don't worry about that," Norman said. "That's not something we're going to do."

Norman was obtuse. Did he think people would just discover the site on their own, with no publicity? Geary looked to Bouros, but Bouros was watching Norman open a folder he'd brought to the table. Norman removed an envelope and put it in front of Geary. "We tried to transfer this to you electronically, but the bank said the account was closed. Where are you banking now?"

"Oh, I meant to tell you. That just changed," Geary said. "Sorry about the physical check. I know it's annoying."

Geary looked at it. "Why are you giving me a check? Is this a bonus?"

Bouros sat straight, hands on the table, fingers interlaced. Norman sighed. "Don. It's not going to happen."

Geary couldn't read Norman. He never understood the man's tone. "What do you mean?"

"We're trying to tell you—we're not going to go forward with Gielgud," Norman said. "You understood this was a possibility, right? We incubate multiple projects. We don't implement all of them. We're always working within a range of possibilities."

"Right," Geary said, nodding. "A range of possibilities."

"There's an evaluative process."

"Sure, I knew we were evaluating this. It's just been in development." He felt he was speaking the wrong language, that his grammar was somehow off.

"I'm sorry, Don," Bouros said.

"So what is this? Is this is a final paycheck?"

"It pays you to the end date of our contracted term," Norman said. "It's twenty-seven days instead of a month, though, so it might be a smidge less than your usual checks."

"Right—I didn't remember what the date was. I didn't realize that was coming up."

"There's no easy way to handle this moment," Norman said. "You should be really proud of the work you've done. We just don't think this is something that would be profitable."

"The site is better than I ever would have imagined," Bouros said. "I love everything about it. This decision doesn't have to do with your work, it just has to do with the focus of the venture."

"We have to believe a certain number of people will become users, and I just don't think the audience is there," Norman said. "I thought maybe it was. I know people are interested in books, I just don't think they care who designed the cover, or who the editor was, or when the first edition was published. We thought there could be an ultimate site of book data, but we were wrong. Or I believe we were wrong."

"Did you do market research?" Geary said. "Is this a recent conclusion?"

"I don't believe in market research," Norman said. "Market research tells you what people think now about the past, which is not that illuminating. People can't be trusted in surveys, anyway. This is just my call. You might disagree, but I just don't think the numbers are there."

"This happens a lot, Don," Bouros said. "It's the downside of what we do."

Geary wondered what the upside was. The upside maybe did not involve him. "So is there a wrap up?" he said. "Should I just stop?"

"Your work is your work," Norman said. "Our contract stipulates that you can't start a similar project anytime in the next two years, so you can't take Gielgud live on your own—you do have to put it away. But the general design, and the things you've figured out in the coding, that's your knowledge. I'm sure you'll use that knowledge in various ways in your own future projects."

"You can't take this live, but your code is your code," Bouros said.

"Exactly," Norman said. "Your code is your code."

9 | He understands habit, he understands repetition. Move toward goals resolutely, without distraction. You are what you do every day.

He assumes the mien of a quarterback returning to the sideline. The drive has stalled and the punt team is headed onto the field, but the quarterback is calm. He will talk to coaches and teammates, study photos of the defense, and prepare for the next drive. Success is persistence.

He walked to his car. Moss darkened the metal plate that read *Corolla.* The roof, trunk, and hood were spotted, the windshields streaked. He didn't have a garage—leaves fell on the car, dust and pollen settled on it, and the night air bonded everything to the surface. Garages had been standard where he grew up, every kid he'd known had lived in a house with a garage. In the Geary garage, a Chevy Astro minivan occupied one side, a Honda Prelude the other. He retained clear memories of the days on which his parents had bought each vehicle. The Astro had replaced a blue Ford station wagon. He and his sister sat in plastic chairs in the waiting area as a cold December afternoon darkened into early evening. "Chevy! Chevy! Astro! Astro!" went the chorus in the vaguely "Age of Aquarius" television jingle as the minivan cruised smoothly along the rings of Saturn. His memory of the day remained vivid because the television in the dealership's waiting area had been tuned to a Broncos game. The Washington Redskins led the Broncos by six in the fourth quarter, but the Broncos were driving. His parents were negotiating with a salesman in some office down a hallway and he hoped the process would take long enough that he could see the end of the game. His parents could tune it in on the car radio on the way home, but what he had before him in the waiting room was the real thing: the Broncos in orange at Mile High Stadium, Pat Sumerall and John Madden calling the action, and John Elway dropping back to pass, attempting to bring the Broncos back from the abyss.

Geary's sister sat next to him, reading *Island of the Blue Dolphins*. It was just the two of them there by the white plastic coffee table covered with sections of the *Denver Post* and *Rocky Mountain News* and old issues of *Time*, *Newsweek*, *Sports Illustrated*, and *People*. Geary didn't know what *Island of the Blue Dolphins* was about. He understood it was for girls, and though he'd read most of his sister's *Babysitter's Club* books, *Island of the Blue Dolphins* hadn't much tempted him. Nothing in *Island of the Blue Dolphins* could be as important as John Elway dropping back to pass on third down, at least. Through the windows to the west the peaks of the Rocky Mountains became massive black silhouettes against the plum-colored dusk, but Geary didn't see them. He gripped the arms of the chair as he watched Elway spin away from pressure and scramble, looking downfield. He stopped, planted, and threw. The camera panned left and an orange blur appeared: number eighty-one, Steve Watson. Watson caught the ball at the goal line and fell into the end zone. Geary leaned forward, squeezing the arms of the chair. "Touchdown," he whispered. "Touchdown." He could not shout, he was in public. He looked at his sister. Her bangs hung from her forehead as she peered down at her book. He looked back to the television, here the image shook as Watson spiked the ball. The volume was low, but he still heard the roar of the seventy-five thousand fans in Mile High Stadium. He was seventy miles north, but thought he could feel it.

The images continued to shake: Elway with his fist raised, teammates surrounding Watson, coach Dan Reeves removing his headset. Geary sipped his soda. The Broncos' defense endured the last minute. The field was ruined, the players ran and hit and tackled on dirt. Time ran out, the announcers said goodbye, and a ticking stopwatch filled the screen. Morley Safer said he was Morley Safer and this was *60 Minutes*. Geary's mother and father appeared. "The Broncos won!" Geary exclaimed before they could even ask.

He wasn't at the dealership the day his father picked up the Honda Prelude. While he waited at home, his mother referred to the car as his father's "toy." This sardonic, marriage-insider talk surprised and impressed Geary. His mother had never spoken about his father that way—at least not in Geary's presence. When his father arrived with the Prelude, everyone piled in. The car was small and silver and felt dramatically low to the road, but Geary was most impressed by the dashboard: it glowed fluorescent green. He had seen fluorescent green dashboards in science fiction movies, but never in a real vehicle. As they backed out of the drive and headed down the street, he was further impressed to see his father changing gears. He had never been in a car with a manual transmission before, and he had the sense that, for the first time, he was seeing a person actually drive a car. Even though this was just the car in which his father would be commuting thirty minutes to and from his job at Hewlett-Packard, Geary felt everyone in the family was proud to own this car. His mother and father didn't use nicknames for each other or buy monogrammed towels or otherwise label the house or each other, but the Prelude turned out to be the exception. His mother bought a license plate frame for it: "My Toy" it read across the top, and across the bottom: "The Phantom." The name, the result of little more than the car being sporty and silver, became the vehicle's standard designation. If his father were going to head into town to run an errand, his mother would say, "Which car are you going to take? The Phantom?" and his father would say, "Sure, The Phantom." It ceased to be a joke, just became the name of the car.

The afternoon had grown warmer, the sun's spangled reflection on the river too bright to look at as Geary drove over the Burnside Bridge. Traffic was light, but there were scores of cyclists. The envelope Norman had given Geary was in his black briefcase. He wondered if he should deposit it immediately, if only for the clarity of a formal ending. Emily's pink and gray booster seat, spotted and stained by food crumbs and sloshed drinks, sat in the back seat. Empty cardboard gum packages filled the door handles, food wrappers littered the floor. What was the car worth? He could not sell the car. He needed the car.

He took small, neighborhood streets to get to his house. When he passed the kids' school, the asphalt playground was filled with summer day-camp kids playing kickball. He scanned them quickly, looking for Nathan or Emily— he felt a kind of magic anytime he saw one of his children. And he got his wish: Nathan stood between second and third base, laughing with a boy standing next to him. It felt like a small victory.

When he signed Nathan and Emily out of camp later that afternoon and the three of them walked home, he told Nathan he'd seen him playing kickball.

"What was I doing?" Nathan said.

"It looked like you were playing third base."

"No. Maybe I was standing by it."

"That's where you stand to play that position. You don't stand on the base. The runners stand on the base."

"Oh, yeah. I was out there."

"Was it fun?"

"No, kickball is boring."

"Did you see me?" Emily asked. "I was on the bars."

"I didn't notice who was on the bars, they're too far from the street. I was driving, so I only had a second to look."

"I can do a flip off the bars now."

"That sounds dangerous."

"It's not dangerous. I can do it every time."

"Just make sure you're careful."

"It's not dangerous!"

"I'm sorry to outrage you with my concern for your physical health."

"What does that mean?" she said.

"It means he knows he's being annoying," Nathan said. "He's just being a dad. Is that what it means?"

"That's pretty much what it means," Geary said.

10 | He walked past the rooms along one side of the crowded gastroenterology ward without looking in the windows or open doors, less out of respect for patient privacy than out of a desire to avoid the helpless feeling that came with seeing a child in pain. The washed whites and pale yellows of the walls and beds and monitors, flat and dimensionless beneath the overhead fluorescents, struck Geary as ominous. Andrea, Tom, and Emily sat by one of the cots that lined the back wall. Curtains divided the cots, leaving just enough space for the bed and two chairs, and Tom stepped aside so Geary could give Emily a hug. He kissed the top of her head and asked how she was doing.

"Good," she said. She looked at Andrea, Tom, and Geary and laughed. "Why is everyone looking at me?"

"Because you have on a weird gown," Tom said. "Everyone can see your underwear."

She checked her backside. "No, they can't!" she said.

The anesthesiologist arrived and shook hands with the adults before grabbing a chair and sitting before Emily. He had a closely trimmed gray mustache and beard and soft pink hands he gestured with as he began to explain, in his talking-to-a-child voice, what Emily would experience. She would lie down and he would put a funny mask on her. It would fit over her nose and mouth, and she would breathe through the funny mask. He could give the funny mask a flavor if she wanted—he could make the funny mask smell like strawberry or like grape. Would she like that? Would she like the funny mask to smell like strawberry or like grape? After she breathed through the mask for a bit she would start to feel sleepy, and she might have funny thoughts, or feel like she was floating, or forget where she was, or get really interested in the ceiling, or even just not think anything at all. The anesthesiologist's descriptions continued past the point of necessity, until the number of possibilities sounded alarming rather than reassuring. When he finished what was clearly a well-honed speech, he told Emily he would see her when she was wheeled into the room where they would look in her stomach. He stood, nodded to the adults, and departed. Andrea looked at Geary and shook her head—a bad review for the anesthesiologist.

"How will they make the air smell like strawberries?" Emily asked.

"It's just something they put on the mask, like a lotion," Andrea said.

Geary, Andrea, and Tom each hugged Emily, and a nurse stepped forward, unlocked the cot's wheels with the toe of her clogs, and wheeled Emily away. She lay flat on her back, holding a stuffed animal against her chest: a koala bear she liked to sleep with.

"So is this it?" Geary asked. "Is this test definitive?"

"They'll look to see whether her cilia are damaged. They look at the cilia and the bloodwork and that's how they diagnose it," Andrea said.

Geary nodded. Tom headed to the waiting area to make a phone call. Andrea stepped over to the nurses station and chatted with the women working there. For her, the coiled cords, sighing equipment, and tired children were familiar terrain. There were five bays for cots along the back wall of the ward. Four were unoccupied. The cots were freshly made with white sheets, the chairs perfectly placed. Geary sat alone in the fifth bay in his jeans, brown t-shirt, and worn blue tennis shoes, and studied the spot where Emily's cot had been. He prided himself on enjoying any cuisine, having no food issues. If Emily's stomach and intestines looked a certain way, though, and if her blood had the wrong amount of the wrong thing—Andrea and the doctors spoke in numbers and vocabulary Geary didn't bother to look up—she would become part of a food trend. He would enter the world of gluten-free food and conversations about gluten-free cooking and jokes about gluten-free eating. He would have to read or hear about digestion, people's beliefs about the magical properties of certain ingredients, the need to eliminate others. There were already too many topics and events and things to think about every day. More than ever, he needed to focus, to figure out a way forward. Instead, he was going to drown in trivia. He needed the world to stop so he could think, so he could figure things out.

When the nurse wheeled her back, Emily lay flat on the cot and held a popsicle in her mouth. She waited for the nurse to lock the wheels of the cot, and then sat up and smiled. "Hello!" she said.

11 | Sheckley and Brooke's friends that summer were Ana and her new boyfriend, Lee. Ana was Brooke's former roommate. She was in a grad program in botany now and sometimes spent days in the field, scouring Oregon's forests for a specific ficus or moss. She was tall and kept her hair long, almost to her waist. She'd been born in Russia and moved to Oregon when she was eight, learning English in the school hallways and playgrounds and through television. She still had the hint of a Russian accent—certain weather accentuated it, or sometimes her mood.

Lee worked for a wine distributor. His parents were

Cambodian but he'd been born and raised in San Francisco. Tattoos on his arms extended from beneath the sleeves of the immaculate polo shirts he wore with pressed chinos and designer sneakers. He radiated a relaxed energy, as if he already knew everything would be fine.

Lee had invited Sheckley to a wine tasting in a warehouse in the industrial eastside. Sheckley had always ignored wine culture—he'd never had the money to afford anything but cheap wine, and the florid language of wine descriptions struck him as comically false. As soon as he stepped into the warehouse, though, with its stacked oak barrels and strings of lights and tables filled with sparkling clean glasses, he felt at home. The simplicity of the concrete floor and wooden warehouse rafters appealed to him. When Lee handed him a glass of wine and started talking about where the grapes had been grown, why the vintner had decided to rent this warehouse in Portland even though his winery was in Dundee, how the whole enterprise was a story of work and creation and risk, Sheckley felt he understood. The motivations were the same as those of art or literature. One enjoyed the wine as a tribute to the surprise of its existence.

He watched the NBA playoffs with Lee. Lee had his own place, a large one-bedroom apartment with separate kitchen and dining areas. He had a television mounted on the wall, a new couch and a couple nice chairs, and a set of shelves with a dozen books. He'd sold all of his other books and compact discs and DVDs, he said— he'd gone digital, no clutter. Sheckley and four or five of Lee's friends opened beers and pulled dining chairs into the living room and watched the Trail Blazers. Sheckley and Brooke didn't have a television, and he'd never been much of a basketball fan. When he started watching the

Blazers, though, something in him responded. He leapt from his chair, yelled at the screen. In one of the games, the Blazers came back from twenty-three points down to win. One player, Brandon Roy, had taken over. Sheckley was aghast. There were five players on defense, but they couldn't stop Brandon Roy. Sheckley rode home alight with the victory—Roy had demonstrated the impossible could be defeated. When the Blazers lost a game and were eliminated only a few days later, it seemed a mistake. How could that incredible victory be part of the process of losing? He understood the teams were playing the best of seven games, but emotionally, it was confusing. With the Blazers eliminated, Lee transferred his rooting interest to another team for the next round. There seemed something sophisticated, almost professional, about this shift of allegiance. Lee continued to invite Sheckley to watch games, but Sheckley declined. He couldn't find a way to care about other teams.

So he and Brooke planned a dinner party. It would be their opportunity to make a contribution. As in theater, the dinner was simultaneously an act of generosity and a bid for admiration. Brooke bought game hens and fresh vegetables. Sheckley chose the liquor and beer and music. The table was small, but they made room for six places. There were new candles and cloth napkins and an ironed tablecloth. They opened all the windows that would open, and the breeze carried the scent of the city's firs.

"You come around that turn and the whole section of coast stretches out below you," Geary said. "It's like seeing it from the air, but you're on the road. And then it disappears when you start winding down, but you know where you're headed."

"There's a bookstore there," Lee said. "What's it called?"

"Cloud and Leaf." Geary announced the name as if invoking a revered password.

"It's tiny, but perfect. We always find things there."

"Next time we go to the coast, we should go there," Brooke told Sheckley.

Sheckley had a playful look in his eyes. He had planned something. "But do they carry *Harbinger*?" he asked.

"What is that?"

"They certainly don't," Geary said.

Sheckley stood, folded his napkin, and stepped into the living room, where he retrieved the book from atop the piano. He'd enjoyed the story—maybe because it was set in a time and place he knew, maybe because it was written by someone he knew, or maybe it stood on its own. The reason didn't matter. He raised book so everyone could see the cover. "A literary journal," he said. "May I read aloud from a story by Don Geary?"

"That's not necessary," Geary said.

"Just a short section I like, about the tape in the Walkman. You don't need to know anything, just that this is a list of things a high school basketball player packs in his duffel bag when he's on his way to a game. The whole list is good. I'm just going to read a part."

"It's too long," Geary said.

"I played basketball in high school," Lee said. "Let's hear it."

"This is item number eight in the list," Sheckley said. "Number seven was his warm-up jacket."

Lee laughed. "Warm-up jackets!"

"Okay," Sheckley said. "Item eight: One "Walkman" cassette player and assorted cassettes. Everyone used "Walkman" as a Kleenex-like general term for all portable cassette players. The boy's, a dull aluminum color with a row of black buttons along one side, wasn't an actual Sony Walkman, but an off-brand. The eject button was at the end of the row, and sometimes when the boy opened his bag to retrieve the Walkman, he would discover that the jostling and bumping a carried bag suffers had at some point resulted in the eject button being hit, which sprung the cover. The cassette that should have been clicked snugly into the player would have fallen out and the boy would have to rummage through the bag to find it blindly swimming through his clothes. It would be one of three cassettes he chose from for pre-game listening: Chicago's *Greatest Hits*, Simon & Garfunkel's *Greatest Hits*, or the eponymous Genesis album.'"

"I don't know any of those bands," Ana said.

"'He was aware these were nonstandard choices,'" Sheckley continued. "'Most of his teammates listened to the first Guns N' Roses album, recently released and all the rage then, or to Bon Jovi or AC/DC. The boy found Guns N' Roses to be comically bad, though, and was baffled not only by their popularity but by the fact that music critics seemed to consider them important. He had grown up listening to the pop, oldies, and soft rock radio stations his parents listened to, and though he realized the playlists of those stations also included plenty of embarrassing songs, a band as bad as Air Supply still struck him as superior to Guns N' Roses. He would not have been able to verbalize this and never tried, but his ears found the sounds of sappy earnestness less ridiculous than the sounds of sappily arrested development. He understood that music that managed to combine both sappy earnestness and sappily arrested development was for him entirely unlistenable, but for society in general somehow totally awesome. As a boy, his desire to verbalize these feelings amounted to nothing more than the urge, after having the Guns N' Roses song "Patience" inflicted upon him for the hundredth time, to shout, "This is exactly the same as an Air Supply song! This is Air Supply!"'"

Sheckley paused for laughter, but nobody laughed. Everyone but Geary was watching Sheckley attentively. Geary stared at the wall, hands in his lap. "That's probably enough," he said.

"Just a little more," Sheckley said. "'He was smart enough never to act upon this urge and thereby out himself as hating his own generation's pop culture deities, but he did not recognize that the appeal, to him, of the lonelier and older Simon & Garfunkel or Chicago songs versus his teammates' preference for Guns N' Roses pointed to two fundamentally different approaches to motivation. The players who listened to hard rock sought to amp up adrenaline and aggression in order to hit the floor ready to attack, essentially a biological motivation, in that it had to do with achieving physical dominance through superior speed, skill, or ferociousness in the same way any predator needs to be better, stronger, and faster than its prey. These are the athletes and fans who map predator/prey relationships onto athletics and end up screaming things like, "Kill 'em!" when they are ostensibly cheering. The listener of lonely music, on the other hand, seeks to enhance a sense of being isolated, overlooked, or unduly disrespected, an existential rather than biological motivation, in that its main goal is to make oneself seen or known. "Shock the world!" is often the slogan here, and the reason the boy could prepare for a game by listening to something as un-athletic as

"Kathy's Song" or "Wishing You Were Here" was roughly the same reason that caution should be taken with lost or wounded animals: they will attack as a form of self-defense. The boy's enjoyment of the Genesis album lay in the fact that the genius of Phil Collins's anthems in the years of the boy's youth, in fact the whole engine behind Collins's rise to superstardom, was that Collins bridged the gap between these modes. Later in the boy's life, when Collins's music had become fantastically and suspiciously out of fashion, he would read in a magazine that a top pro basketball player listed the über-Collins anthem "In the Air Tonight" as something he listened to before games. This news would come as a happy surprise, since the boy would by then have worked out a private theory that "In the Air Tonight" was possibly the most effective example of a song that starts in the existential mode, but builds the intensity of that mode until, when Collins hits the signature explosive drum fill, it shifts seamlessly into attack mode. In other words, the song revealed that existential motivations could easily blossom or morph into biological ones. A move in the opposite direction, from biological motivations to existential ones, was much more difficult. He had never, at least, encountered any examples.'"

"That seems right," Lee said.

"What is the story about? Is it about this boy?" Ana asked.

"No," Geary said. "Don't read any more. It's sentimental and not that funny and should be half as long."

"I liked it," Brooke said. "I could hear more."

"You have a captive audience," Sheckley said.

"No, there's no audience," Geary said. "The only people who buy *Harbinger* are writers trying to get something published in it, and they don't actually read it, they just skim it and read the author bios. They hate-skim it to confirm that the people who are in there shouldn't actually be in there. The only people reading that story are people reading it to hate it."

"We're not reading it to hate it," Sheckley said.

"But we don't count," Geary said. "No one reads literary journals. No one reads newspapers, either. Everything is either a Facebook post or nothing. When I was a kid I loved books, and that was it. It was just about the book and me. But everything is about the internet now, about being popular on the internet. There are publishers I used to admire. Their logos on the spine of the book, I used to admire *the logos*—they meant something. They all have Facebook accounts now. They were posting pictures of cats the other day. Major publishing houses were posting pictures of cats and puns about cats. I don't even recognize that. That's something a dumb, annoying person does."

"I posted pictures of our cat the other day," Brooke said.

"That's my point," Geary said. "Why are major American publishing houses behaving the same as a woman in Portland? Why are they posting bad puns on Facebook? And why are other publishers liking the shitty puns and adding their own? It's fucking childish. Nowhere in any of this did I sense that these people really knew or cared about literature."

"Those are just people in the marketing department," Lee said. "People in marketing are always annoying."

"So why are they handed the keys?" Geary said. "Why aren't they fired? The reason is that all of that annoying shit is what the publishers want. They want cat photos and stupid jokes, because they don't care. They don't care about literature, because there are no readers. Books are not a thing. There are internet users. That's it. There is no audience."

Sheckley had heard Geary hold forth on a number of topics over the years, but this was not familiar territory. The table was filled with dishes, glasses, candles, and flowers. There was nowhere for Sheckley to set his copy of *Harbinger*. He put it in his lap. "People will get tired of social media," he said.

"I doubt it," Geary said. "They'll get tired of Facebook, but they'll just move on to something new. There are already new ones, and all the supposedly literary people are already on there trying to be funny. There's no audience for actual books. Everything I cared about as a kid is over. It's dead."

"I'm still feeling bad about my cat photos," Brooke said.

"People think Bill Gates and Steve Jobs are geniuses," Geary said. "Bill Gates is an idiot and Steve Jobs is an asshole. One has Asperger's and the other's a sociopath. Our whole culture is socially retarded and dysfunctional because it's been designed by egomaniac assholes, and we have an asshole culture to show for it. They're obsessed with finding ways to do things through screens instead of with people. When we were growing up, if a new hire in a publishing company marketing department had suggested running ads with pictures of cats and puns about cats, that person would have been fired, because what the fuck does that have to do with books? That person would have been seen as a trivial idiot. Those people get promoted now. They're running everything."

"I'm not sure I'm an idiot just because I posted some pictures of my cat," Brooke said.

This had backfired in a way Sheckley didn't understand. He understood what Geary was saying, he just didn't understand why Geary was saying it, what the point was. All Sheckley had wanted to do was read part of a story. "Do you want another drink, Don?" he said.

"No. I probably need to leave."

"Okay," Sheckley said. He felt it was a good idea.

Geary folded his napkin and put it on the table. "Sorry. None of this was about any of you guys. This is about the fact that I hate the world we've made, and I hate contributing to it. It's a fucking dead world with dead people in it. This dinner was good. Sorry."

"It's okay," Sheckley said. "Let's talk sometime soon."

Geary stood, but hesitated. He hadn't worn a jacket, and he'd brought only some bread and a bottle of wine. There was nothing for him to collect. Sheckley crossed the room and opened the door. Geary followed and stepped out.

Everyone remained quiet until they felt Geary was safely out of earshot.

"I also post pictures of my cat," Ana said.

Three

1 | He sped past towns that seemed brick oven hamlets of helplessness boiling in the heat—Ashland, Yreka, Weed. The dashboard showed an outside temperature above a hundred degrees, but he didn't turn the air conditioning on, because he wanted to maximize gas mileage. He made it to Redding on a single tank. The road, coffee, energy drinks, and the constricted, apocalyptic tones of the men on the AM Christian radio stations had him feeling he was doing well. He could have been a contender, but he could also have been working at the Gas 'n Go in Shasta, listening to a warbling voice go on about God. He could have been in charge of placing the green highway sign that read "Mt. McLoughlin" beneath an arrow that extended up and to the left in the exact spot where, up and to the left indeed, Mount McLoughlin shimmered in the fading distance. Geary flew past the sign. The charms of Mount McLoughlin would have to wait for another life.

His mind spun. False thoughts, idle speculations. He

had long arguments in which he made excellent points. He defended the soundness of his way of life and relationships through ironclad proofs. He played both voices in the arguments, but his own points won every time. He could not detect anything rigged in the scenarios.

He developed comedy routines, laughed at his performances, and then immediately forgot the jokes. Halfway through the second tank he moved from I-505 to I-80 and descended into clouded San Francisco Bay. He listened to Sade at top volume, thrilled by a backing voice buried deep in the mix on one track. He couldn't believe he'd never noticed it before, that he continued to live in a fallen audio world of cheap speakers and a bad bookshelf system with the volume kept low at all times on account of the kids and neighbors. The crisp whirs and pings in the car seemed a revelation. He needed to play music loud, he told himself, he needed to hear it.

He went no more than nine miles per hour over the speed limit. The bands he listened to were not daring choices. But tracking the lights that spun past, inhaling the cool ocean air as he headed into San Francisco on a Friday night, he felt awake, alive. The mistakes he had made could not have been serious if he was here, now.

He drove down Balboa and found a place to park. The building's door was propped open. He climbed two carpeted flights of stairs, found the door, and knocked.

"Hello, soldier," Klein said when he opened the door. His khakis and collared shirt were rumpled, his thinning hair askew. In his youth he'd sung lead in a band and he still carried himself with an energy that suggested a show would start soon, or maybe had just finished. "What can I get you to drink? Did you find a place to park? They've figured out a thousand ways to give parking tickets."

Klein was shorter than Geary, moved quickly. He treated everyone like a friend he was pleased to have run into again, even if he didn't recall a name or had only met someone once. He was liked by neighbors, bartenders, and shopkeepers—happy to be recognized, they awakened in his presence and remembered him when he next stopped in to pick up his dry cleaning or get a drink.

"Was the traffic bad? It's always bad. I don't like driving here, I make CJ do it."

They crossed the bright hardwood floor of the main room. A folding screen hid two bicycles propped against the wall. Photos and cards lined the white mantel over the fireplace. The furniture was in front of the picture window at the other end of the room: a couch, bookshelves, a turntable, shelves of records, and a small desk. Beyond the window spread the roofs and backyards of the neighborhood. A few blocks away, the golden onion dome of a church rose like an island in the mist. The lights of the Golden Gate Bridge blinked in a languid rhythm in the distance. Klein grabbed a copy of the *Chronicle* from where it lay in disorder on the couch.

"I was trying to figure out what's going on this weekend," Klein said. "The de Young is right in the park, you can walk there in five minutes. They have the Impressionists right now, though—I don't know why. I mean I do know why, it's for money. It's just inconvenient to me personally."

"The Grouch is being mean!" a voice called from the bedroom.

"Tell him to cool it," Klein said.

"Did you hear that? You have to cool it."

The door opened. CJ was small, fine-featured, with curly brown hair and green eyes. "I told him to get off the bed," she said. "Then when I picked him up, he screeched at me."

"He's just a cranky old man," Klein said.

"It's lovely to see you, though," she told Geary as she hugged him. "I'm sorry you have to see this argument I'm having with my cat."

"It's fairly upsetting," he said.

"We'll stop. Grouch, let's stop, Don is here."

The cat appeared in the doorway. He was white with dark patches, the one above his lip the source of his name. After watching them for a moment, he walked toward the kitchen.

"Should you flip the record or are you running some kind of test?" CJ said. The stereo was playing the repeating static of a run-off groove.

"I didn't know you didn't like this track. You never said anything about it before, and I play it all the time," Klein said.

"Did you see the church on your way in?"

"I didn't come that way," Geary said. "What kind of church is it?"

"Russian Orthodox. This whole neighborhood was, originally. You should take a look at it when you go out tomorrow."

"Klein said the museum has Impressionist stuff," Geary said.

"The de Young? It seems like all the museums just pass the same paintings around. How are your kids?"

"Big. Mouthier."

"And are you still dating the same woman?"

"No. That recently ended."

"How recently?"

"A few weeks."

"A few weeks? Is it for real, or just a thing?"

"She said she had to make some life decisions."

"And the life decisions involved not dating you anymore? Have you talked to her?"

"She asked me not to."

"Was that in an argument, though? People say stuff like that in arguments. They don't necessarily mean it."

"He just got here," Klein complained.

"It wasn't an argument," Geary said. "She just told me. After dinner."

"What did you say?"

"I said okay. A life decision is a life decision. I'm not going to beg someone to stay with me."

"Well, you're a catch," CJ said. "I keep wanting to fix you up with someone, but it's tough now that we're not in Portland."

She went into the kitchen. They heard cat food being poured into a bowl.

"Do you want to move here so CJ can set you up with someone?" Klein said.

"Could I just visit occasionally to sleep with these women, then go back to Portland?"

"I know you're joking, but people do that," CJ called from the kitchen. "Marcus has a friend here who does that."

"Who?" Klein said.

"Isn't that what Toby does? When he goes to New York?"

Klein dropped the needle on a record. "That's a coworker, not a friend. And I'm not sure how much of that to believe. I'm sure the women would tell a different story."

Later they sat at the high metal table against the wall

in the kitchen, drinking beer and plucking from a plate of figs and prosciutto. The kitchen was built to the dimensions of the past. The sink had two shallow basins, there was a brief stretch of counter, and a small oven. The top of the refrigerator was even with Geary's chin.

"I think I already have a book by that guy," Klein was saying. "But it's not the book you're talking about. It had one of those really long titles they give the hip books nowadays. *What You Don't Know About Your Brand is It's the Story of Your Life*, or *What You Don't Know About Life is You're the Brand of Your Story*."

"*What You Don't Know About My Brand is I Want to Be the Story of Your Life*," Geary said.

"Yes, like that. It was just thoughts on advertising. I read it from start to finish in an afternoon. I'm sure it's here somewhere." He left the kitchen and they heard him strike up a conversation with the cat in the living room.

"Why are you researching this person?" CJ asked.

"He rebranded the Cascadia Arts Center—their website, logo, all that. I'm supposed to evaluate the project for them, just sign off on the idea that it was worth the money, I think. To satisfy their board."

"Was it?"

The calendar tacked to the wall featured a sand-colored image of a Frank Lloyd Wright sketch: an angular building in a desert. *Crater Resort at Meteor Arizona*, the faded lettering read.

"They haven't shown me how much they paid yet. The guy has a theory about the future of advertising, though, so I'm reading up on it. He says a brand isn't a company, it's a story. And that stories are best when they're in the service of a cause."

"A story that teaches? Like a fable?"

"Maybe. I'm not sure. It's not my theory."

"Don't ads always tell stories?"

"He says the brand itself is a story."

She looked at him blankly. "Isn't that what an ad campaign is?"

"He doesn't say things that way. He says things like, cause-centered brands existed in the past and are also the future."

She pulled a bottle of white wine from the refrigerator, opened and closed a cabinet, and then studied the jumble of plates, glasses, and silverware in the drying rack next to the sink. Geary could sense her parsing taxonomies, testing terminology, thinking it over.

CJ had grown up in a small town in southern Oregon, moved to Portland for school, and finished with a Ph.D. in biology. She worked at a research institute in Marin now, a property with gated entries and locked labs. She'd recently taken an extended absence from work, though. She'd started feeling bad in November—her stomach was upset, she couldn't eat. She thought she had a virus, but she continued to feel bad through the holidays, so she went to the doctor in January. At the doctor's office they took blood and ran tests, but couldn't find anything wrong. She felt worse and worse. She ate because she knew she needed to, but felt nauseous. She saw more doctors. Still, they found nothing wrong. February passed, March. Maybe she was lactose-intolerant, a doctor said. She and Klein used to host dinner parties with a group of friends they called "The Goat Cheese Society," but she felt so miserable that she agreed to stop eating dairy. It didn't help. The doctors suggested she stop gluten, too. She'd never been allergic to anything in her life, but she did it, she stopped gluten. She couldn't remember what it was like to feel normal. They were taking every food she liked. She understood she would never really enjoy life again.

It wasn't until June that a doctor said he wanted to do a scan of her entire abdomen. They did the scan in the morning and in the afternoon called and said they wanted her to come in again the next day. They did another scan and a doctor she'd never met before told her she had a tumor where her ovary was supposed to be—it was probably ovarian cancer. After that, she didn't have to make appointments anymore. They just told her what time to come in each day and what tests they were going to do. When they were satisfied with their diagnosis, they set her up with an oncological surgeon.

She had to wait a week to see the surgeon. She could find neither rhyme nor reason in the system. During the months she was feeling awful the doctors had been in no hurry. When they wanted to confirm their diagnosis, though, they ran scans and put needles in her every day, like people caught up in the excitement of placing the final pieces in a puzzle. When they decided she had a tumor where her ovary was supposed to be they returned to being in no hurry. They had completed the puzzle, seen the picture, and moved on. She waited a week to see the surgeon.

Her family was in Oregon and she talked to them on the phone, but it was just she and Klein who'd gone to all of the appointments. She'd lost twenty pounds and a stiff breeze could blow her over. Klein had lost fifteen pounds out of stress and sympathy, he too was thin as a rail. Was his wife slowly dying in their apartment, or did she just have an upset stomach? They went back and forth. They didn't know.

When she went to her appointment with the surgeon, he introduced himself and said, "I'm going to go in and take out this tumor, but I don't think it's cancer. I'd bet a thousand dollars it's not. I'd bet ten thousand dollars."

He was looking at the same pictures and numbers the other doctors had looked at. CJ hadn't the slightest idea what he saw or didn't see in them. His opinion was not particularly comforting, though. He wasn't expressing a belief she would be well, he was expressing a belief the other doctors were inferior.

Before the surgery she had to sign a wide-ranging release form. It said that once the surgeon opened her up, he could remove whatever he felt should be removed. *Allowed to remove the left ovary*, it read, *and if in the opinion of the surgical team it is necessary, the right ovary, and if in the opinion of the surgical team it is necessary, the spleen, and if in the opinion of the surgical team...* It went on like that.

"Jesus, everything is on here except my heart and lungs," she'd said to Klein.

"They probably just forgot those. Don't say anything," he said.

Jens, their friend from Portland, came down to San Francisco for the surgery. He pretended to be CJ's brother so he could stay in her hospital room and help take care of her. Jens was six-two and Scandinavian, CJ was five-three and Irish. The nurses did not believe he was her brother but said nothing, and Klein and Jens were waiting together in CJ's room when she came in after the surgery.

It was just a few hours after she'd regained consciousness that the surgeon stopped by. He'd taken out her ovary and her appendix—the appendix as a courtesy, he said—and he was pleased. He'd been right: it was endometriosis. The tissue had devoured her ovary and was growing into her abdomen, that was what had been poisoning her. He'd removed the ovary, scraped the tissue out of some other areas it was starting to grow, closed her up, and that was it. She would be fine, he said, there was nothing more that needed to be done. After an awkward pat on her leg and before anyone had a chance to say anything beyond thank you, he left. They never saw him again. A different doctor came in later to ask if they had any questions. He didn't mention the surgeon's name. Perhaps he was the one who'd lost the thousand or ten thousand dollar bet.

CJ had returned to work just a week ago. Snacking with Klein and Geary, feeling fine while chatting, listening to music and walking around the apartment on a Friday evening with no doctor's appointments ahead of her and nothing to brace for, it was still a revelation, all of it. Everything precious had been returned to her. She was almost dizzy with it.

"There are some glasses on the end of the counter," Geary said.

She snapped to. "Yes, because that's where glasses go, randomly on the end of the counter," she said. "Has something happened that requires all this new vocabulary? Did the entire advertising industry suddenly change?"

"Facebook, I guess."

"This guy doesn't want people to think a company's social media account is advertising? Wait, is he one of these guys who thinks corporations are people?"

"He said traditional advertising is dead. That was in a TED talk."

"Well, if it was in a TED talk," Klein said, returning to

the kitchen to hand Geary a book. It was Kelly green and read: *The Story of a Brand is a Search for Purpose by David Hulme*. The title was white, Hulme's name orange. "It's odd," Klein said. "I thought this book was *about* advertising. There's stuff in here about companies, brands, and famous ads, at least. About him playing basketball, too."

"About David Hulme playing basketball?"

"Yep. And stuff about Charles and Ray Eames, Buckminster Fuller, other famous people. They were doing that play about Buckminster Fuller in Portland at the time. If you'd asked me what the book was about, I would have said advertising."

Geary flipped through it. "I haven't seen this book referenced anywhere. Where did you get it?"

"CJ's friend Tamra did a program with him, she got the book as part of it. She left it here when she was visiting."

"Did she like the program?"

"She said there was useful stuff, but she didn't particularly like him as a person. She doesn't like most people, though."

"She took the class to meet people professionally, but I think there were a couple guys there who were interested in her unprofessionally," CJ said. "That kind of ruined it."

"She also wanted to learn some stuff, which I think she said she did," Klein said.

"Professional stuff, though. Not unprofessional stuff."

"Yes, I doubt Tamra has any unprofessional stuff to learn," Klein said.

"How would you know that?" CJ said.

"I certainly would not. I'm just speculating."

"On what Tamra does in bed?"

"Don, chime in anytime here."

"What else is in the book?" Geary asked.

"Quotes. Factoids," Klein said. "It alternates sections of quotes with anecdotes about his life. I thought it was about advertising and just had some other stuff in there to keep it interesting. I had no idea advertising was dead. I didn't get that."

"His Wikipedia entry says he's interested in cause and motive, not advertising."

"That sounds like one of those Wikipedia entries where a guy writes his own entry," CJ said.

"Look, we're just out here in the sticks," Klein said. "We don't understand a lot of the sophisticated things you fancy advertising people do. Like being interested in motive."

They'd finished the figs and prosciutto and moved back to the main room. Fog drifted past the window, pinpoints of mist collecting on the glass. The bridge had disappeared. Books were stacked on the end tables, haphazardly filled the shelves. Geary admitted he'd been watching CJ a bit, and that she seemed herself. He wondered how she felt.

"Compared to how I felt for eight months? Amazing. I'm probably only eighty percent, but eighty percent feels like a miracle."

"Which week was worse for you?" Klein said. "The week before the surgery was the worst for me, because we were confused about whether or not you had cancer, and I was also nervous about the surgery itself. I don't think I ate even our lactose-free, gluten-free food that week. I ate nothing."

"The week before the surgery was better for me," CJ said. "Because there was at least someone who said he thought I didn't have cancer. Though I did have to sit there and think, Okay, maybe I'm going to die. Not in the surgery, but I thought that if the cancer had already gotten the ovary, that meant it was advanced. And of course I looked up all sorts of stuff about ovarian cancer, and it kills women every day."

Certain rooms vibrate at a tranquil frequency. One enters and is quieted. Geary's father's den, the dark bookshelves lined with the volumes of *Encyclopedia Britannica*, the green-headed mallard stuffed and mounted on the wall, its tiny yellow glass eyes. The studio apartment he'd rented after college, with everything—a futon, a desk, a lamp—arranged exactly as he wished. His grandparents' living room with its long yellow sofa, metal ashtray in a stand, cabinet television, and the cherry sideboard that held a miniature statue of Venus and a book with the predictions of Nostradamus. That tranquility suffused Klein and CJ's living room. A photograph would depict only a flat section of these rooms, a meaningless instant. Memory alone can hold rooms. They are beyond the power of any other medium.

"You know when you're a teenager and your hormones or emotions are all weird, and you think things like, *I want to die*?" CJ said. "Or when you're kind of depressed in the winter and you think everything is gray and pointless and it wouldn't matter that much if you weren't around anymore?"

"Nihilism chic," Klein said.

"When I thought I actually was going to die, I found out I don't actually believe any of those things," CJ said. "I really did not want to die. I so wanted to stay alive it's not even funny."

Klein put on a Tindersticks album, the volume low. He and CJ had fought a battle that was over now. The walls were bare save for a few small paintings done by friends. A house. An orange candle on a green background. A boat in a blue sky.

2 | Saturday evening they took the bus to Union Square and slipped in among the crowd. Ivory mannequins modeled shirts and slacks in department store windows. There were dark doorways to bars, bright entries to boutiques, and signs and references to San Fancisco lore: Levi's, the gold rush, Chinatown. A sign in a gallery's plate glass window announced Picassos for sale. Geary assumed it was a ruse or half-truth until he remembered Picasso produced art every day of his life—in restaurants he would sketch on a napkin and leave it as payment for his bill. Stacks of Picasso sketches floated through the galleries of the world.

They weaved past groups stalled on the sidewalk, caught the arguments and indecisions. "Did you still want to take the cable car? It runs right through here." "I don't know, maybe it's touristy. Did you want to?" "Come on, kids! Kids, come on!"

He looked up at the widely spaced letters on a street sign: G e a r y. When he was a boy, his family drove from Colorado to San Francisco on summer vacation. He and his sister read for hours in the back seat while the car shot through the dusty red West. A green plastic cooler held soda, chocolate bars, and sandwiches his mother had made. They had a Rand McNally road atlas and a booklet that listed the location of every Holiday Inn in the United States. These were their guides and Geary studied them intently, the quirks of the interstates, which cities had Holidomes. When they made it to San Francisco and he saw the street sign, he sat up. Were they related to the Geary the street was named for? His father said no, not that he knew of.

"But everyone with the last name Geary is probably related in some way," his mother said.

Her point seemed abstract, unrelated. Geary's father had been just ten when his own father had died. Doctors had decided the man needed some kind of heart surgery. Geary's father was never clear why—no one told him what was wrong, or maybe no one knew. He remembered the phone ringing early in the morning and his sister coming into his bedroom to tell him Daddy had died during surgery. This was Tampa, Florida, 1955. His mother moved them to rural Kentucky after that, to live with an aunt and cousins. The house was small, he, his sister, and his four cousins shared two bedrooms, two to a bed. His mother slept on the couch in the living room. The first few years they were there the kitchen had a dirt floor—it was an accomplishment when they put in the linoleum. After high school, he joined the Air Force. He had an aptitude for fixing things, for systems and mechanics, so the Air Force sent him to the Azores to fix airplanes and peel potatoes. He left the island just once: when his mother died. He hadn't been told she was ill until the final weeks. The Azores were too far away and she didn't want to trouble him. He flew to Kentucky for the funeral. His sister was married and on her own by then. There was no estate, nothing to take care of. He spent a week with aunts and uncles and cousins in dimly lit sitting rooms, some with black and white televisions, many without. Joining up had been good, everyone said—the Air Force would take care of him. He flew back to the Azores and went back under the planes. He was on his own.

After he was discharged he went to the University of Illinois on the GI Bill. Geary's mother saw him playing basketball in the gym. One of her friends knew one of his, and they all went to a dance together. He didn't know how to dance, he just made it up as he went along. The result was not impressive. He was nice, though, and respectful. In her freshman composition class, no matter what Geary's mother wrote, the professor handed it back with a "C" at the top of the first page. No comments. She didn't understand. She liked books, had done well in English at Taft High in Chicago. The professor was old, his coat worn. He smoked a pipe in class and his beard was unkempt and tobacco-stained. When she received a C for the course she decided college wasn't for her. It wouldn't occur to her until years later that there was possibly something wrong with the professor.

She moved back home and took a job in a Capitol Records distribution facility, checking records coming off the line to make sure the covers were right and the shrink-wrap sealed. Geary's father drove to Chicago from Champaign every other Saturday to take her out. He slept on the couch in the living room and on Sunday drove back to Champaign. They got married the next summer, in one of the biggest Catholic churches in Chicago. Her father was a mechanic—he'd saved up enough to buy a Sinclair station a few years before. He told the family he was unhappy with the station's location, though, so he sold the Sinclair station and bought a Texaco station five blocks away. When his wife asked what difference the five blocks made, he told her it had to do with traffic, that she wouldn't understand because she didn't drive. The Texaco station, it turned out, was also cheaper. He used the difference to pay for the wedding, but said nothing about this. He was a World War II veteran and friendly with people but did not speak about money, even with his wife. For groceries and her daily expenses he left cash in a Folger's can in the kitchen cabinet. He paid all other bills.

At the wedding the bridesmaids wore powder blue dresses and the groomsmen powder blue tuxedos. Everyone drank and danced, including the priest. The newlyweds moved into married student housing in Champaign: a university-owned apartment. When Geary's father finished his electrical engineering degree, Hewlett-Packard offered him two positions: one in Stanford, California, and one in Loveland, Colorado. He and Geary's mother visited Stanford. The home prices stunned them. The numbers didn't seem real. Loveland was a small town in Northern Colorado, and houses there cost less than houses in Chicago or Champaign. It was simple math. When her father sold the Texaco station a few years later, Geary's mother was in Colorado, bouncing a baby on her knee and trying to adjust to life in a small town at the footstep of the Rockies. She thought it was funny her dad had bought the old Sinclair station back. She'd always liked the green dinosaur logo.

"Should we steal one of the signs with our name on it?" she asked on their San Francisco vacation years later. "We could take it home and put it on the wall."

"You want to get arrested in San Francisco? Spend some

time in jail with the hippies and the druggies?" Geary's father said.

"Groovy, man," his mother said.

Now, Geary, Klein, and CJ found themselves trapped behind a couple stopped in the middle of the sidewalk. Despite the heat, the man wore dark slacks and a sport coat. The pained expression he raised to the sky featured wild gray eyebrows beneath a sunburned forehead. The woman looked down, studying something, her face hidden by gray curls.

"Please don't open the map again," the man said. "We just need to keep walking up the hill here. It will be right over the hill!"

They didn't move. People on the crowded sidewalk kept approaching from either side, and Geary was stalled. There was no way past this couple.

Klein grabbed him by the sleeve and pointed behind them, to where CJ was headed through the doors of a large store they had passed. Geary looked up at the red awning: BORDERS.

Instead of the layout Geary was familiar with, in which the store sprawled into various sections on a single level, the Union Square Borders occupied a tight footprint that rose through four floors. The entrance level held only cash registers and select new titles stacked on honey-colored tables.

"I'm sorry, it was just too gnarly out there," CJ said. "And also maybe I'm starving."

An escalator carried them up through a shadowed corridor and deposited them in the fiction section, which CJ immediately left in search of the café. Multiple tables were stacked high with books surrounding signs announcing "New Fiction." To Geary, the covers blurred together, each like the next, even the titles, type, and author photos. He noted three different titles that each featured the phrase "Further Thoughts!" above a small icon on the cover's bottom corner: the silhouette of a gender-neutral head, index finger on temple.

"It's amazing to think what percentage of these books were all produced in the same neighborhood in Manhattan," Klein said.

"If a book requires further thoughts, why are the thoughts not in the book?" Geary said.

"Who was it that said in late capitalism every section is the children's section? I want to say Zizek, but it's too economical for him. Maybe I just read it in *Entertainment Weekly*."

Geary moved to the bookcases that lined the walls and floor space, looking for older titles, test cases. Each title he pulled had been given a new cover design to make it look as if it had only recently been conceived, written, and published. The stock photo on the cover of Chekhov's stories was an over-the-shoulder shot of a bearded man on a bicycle with a wire basket. It suggested Chekhov maybe wrote a witty blog and held forth at parties in his apartment in Park Slope. Geary turned the book over.

"Chekhov has a website," he told Klein.

"In English or Russian?"

"It doesn't say."

"I'm only interested if he has an Instagram."

Geary assumed the site featured the stock photo covers of other Chekhov books and further thoughts on how to read them. He'd designed some book covers for a small press in Portland. They were fun to make, and he knew covers were fun for shoppers to look at, which was why he was doing it at that very moment. Every generation of designers worked with the same technologies, though. There was something inescapable in the results, an unavoidable sameness. The new cover on Chekhov's stories was similar to the new covers on Willa Cather's novels, which featured design details repeated on the cover of a new story collection on a nearby table, a cover that reminded Geary of the new cover he'd just seen on *In Cold Blood*. That cover had carried a blurb from a writer of popular non-fiction who had probably been no more than two years old when Truman Capote was dying of liver failure in Bel Air. Geary assumed the non-fiction writer hadn't found it rude that Capote didn't email to thank him for the new blurb, since Capote had been dead for thirty years. The business seemed strangely bent on making all books indistinct. Same size, same paper, same covers. It made for efficiencies in shipping. These were the kinds of thoughts that had caused him to abandon filmmaking after film school, to stop writing after grad school. He was aware of this.

Klein had disappeared. Geary found the stairs and went up. The fourth floor was full of open space. There were compact discs in some bins, but no customers. A lone employee sat behind a desk near the escalator, watching a movie playing on a screen on the wall as Geary moved past. The employee didn't turn from the screen. Beyond the compact disc bins stretched an expanse of empty green carpet. The space did not seem arranged for the public, but the employee said nothing, so Geary walked through the empty space to the far end of the floor, where another group of bins stood in what appeared to be their proper rows. The DVDs in those bins weren't infused with any more energy or magic than the compact discs had been. Bad movies priced cheaply in ugly plastic cases. This is what becomes of a movie, he thought, this is what a movie is.

When he went back down to the café he found CJ alone at a table, a half-eaten package of apple slices in front of her. Only her eyes moved when she looked up at him.

"Do you know where Marcus is?" she asked.

"I can find him. Is there anything I can do?"

"No, I just got weak. I'm sorry, I don't have any reserves. You could carry me home, I guess."

"I'm willing to do that."

"I'm just kidding. That's Marcus's job."

Geary found him in the magazine section, flipping through *Baseball Digest*. "Can you believe they don't think the Mets are going to turn it around?" he said.

"CJ's not feeling well. She's in the café staring at some apple slices."

Klein put the magazine down. "She should be staring at steak and potatoes, something filling."

They sat with her in the café for ten minutes, but it became clear she wasn't going to feel any better. It had been months since she'd been out at night, months since she'd walked in a crowd. She apologized again and said she could take the bus home herself.

"I don't think so," Klein said. "If you fall asleep, you'll end up on the beach."

"It doesn't go all the way to the beach, does it?" she said.

"I just assume they carry unconscious people to the sand. I don't think you can leave people on the sidewalk."

"That sounds kind of lovely right now," she said. "The sand, not the sidewalk."

"Don, you're on your own," Klein said. "There are bars and various houses of ill repute. Do you need a bus map?"

"I can figure it out. I'll avoid the houses of ill repute."

"Okay, but that's supposedly where the important people are. They keep finding politicians in them, at least. You have your key."

He did. He lingered in the bookstore after they left. The store had two copies of *Harbinger* in the literary journal section of the magazine stand. He opened a copy to check his name in the table of contents, as if it might not appear in all copies. There it was, though. He turned to his story and imagined what he might think if he were a reader opening *Harbinger* at random, trying it out:

> Ian's basement was finished, tiled, well lit, with an area exactly the size of and permanently inhabited by the table. They were equally matched and sometimes played for hours, matches intended to be best-of-five agreeably extended to best-of-seven, best-of-nine, minds and bodies attuned only to the velocities of the game. The repetitions brought winnowed focus, refined techniques. An hour in, each could blister a topspin crosscourt forehand at any moment, but knew the other could return it at the wailed velocity of pure reflex. The roar and raised fist that followed a winner was the mind approving of having been dismissed, pleased not only by the body's skill but also its autonomy, the discovery that the horse knows the way.

He had expended unnecessary effort to describe a game

of ping-pong. The paragraph should have been half as long. Maybe never written.

It was after ten o'clock when he walked out. There were still people on the street, but he'd lost interest in their conversations. He caught the bus and headed back across town on the street with which he shared a name. It was too early to go back to Klein and CJ's apartment—he didn't want to impose. When the bus reached their stop he stayed in his seat. The vehicle continued on, swaying and rattling. The riders were silent, alone with their thoughts. A couple stops down the line an orange neon sign flashed past: *Pizza*. He pulled the cord.

Inside the restaurant, two men worked with no particular urgency in the galley kitchen that ran from behind the register to the back of the store. One placed pepperoni on a pizza while, nearly back to back with him, the other made a sweeping pass with a rag over a stretch of counter, tossed the rag into a bucket, and flipped a switch that killed the lights on that side. Geary was the only customer. He asked if they were still serving and one of the men nodded. "We've still got slices," he said.

Geary ordered a slice of pepperoni and carried the triangular box to a table by the wall. The local news played on a television mounted high in the opposite corner. An electronic fanfare announced the appearance of the sports anchor who delivered the updates: the A's had won, the Giants had lost. The three of them watched a montage of the Giants young, longhaired ace, Tim Lincecum, giving up hit after hit.

"Goddammit, fucking Giants," the man at the register said, waving his hand in disgust. "Sorry. They're driving me nuts."

"Lincecum's lost his stuff?"

"He hasn't won in a month," the man said.

"What's wrong with him?"

The man mimed smoking a joint. "He's a fucking kid is what's wrong. He doesn't take it seriously."

"He'll get it together," the other man said.

"He better," the first said. "If he doesn't, he'll be out of the league before he knows what the fuck happened. He'll be making pizzas with us."

3 | Klein stood near the curb, smoking a cigarette. One could not tell whether his narrowed eyes and unmoving gaze indicated he found the world lacking or enchanted. His hair was tousled, his t-shirt dirty. He looked as if he might have slept a few feet from where he was standing. His face was long, there was something noble in the features. It was the heavy lids, perhaps, or the mole on his cheek.

"Am I naïve to be stunned by that?" Geary said. "He told them this was his reduced rate, because they were a nonprofit and he liked the kind of work they did. It makes me feel stupid, like I'm doing everything wrong. If that's his reduced rate, I can't imagine what his standard rate is."

"Of course you can," Klein said. "Double or triple that number. Maybe he has multiple rates."

"Have you seen the website he designed for them as the central component of the whole rebrand? It has six thin columns that run from the top of the page to the bottom. The first column just has a search bar and their logo squeezed in, lo-res and blurry. The other five are filled with small type on a pale yellow background. It's like he was inspired by a 1970s issue of *The Wall Street Journal*. It's entirely unreadable, it actually repels the eyes."

Klein said nothing. In addition to his cigarette he held a cup of coffee. They were in front of the apartment building and there was no traffic on this stretch of Balboa in the morning. The buildings and sidewalks were the color of stone and sand, the sky was gray. Geary had just seen an email from Elizabeth Barrow that included David Hulme's invoices for rebranding the Cascadia Arts Council. He was not usually a person impressed by numbers, but the figure at the bottom of the invoice had made an impact.

"The site is beyond bad," he said. "It's unprofessional. I don't care that I didn't go to design school, I can still tell it's unprofessional—anyone can see that. The font is tiny. The images are tiny. I'd be embarrassed to have made it. They actually paid the invoice, though."

"But their budget is from grants, right? In some ways they're just passing grant money along," Klein said. "And this guy passed it along to whoever he paid to write the code. They may even have gotten a grant that's specifically for web development. You can't get a grant and then not spend the money."

"But you can get a grant and use it to get a decent website."

Klein tapped his cigarette so the ashes fell in the gutter. His coffee mug bore the logo of a Portland coffeehouse. In a few minutes he would be off to his own job. He spent half his day working the register at a high-end coffeehouse in the Mission District, the other half in the place's upstairs office, writing copy for the company's website and returning calls from shops that carried their beans. "You know what I like most about the internet?" he said.

"What?"

"Hating it. Before the internet, what did people hate?"

"Newspapers," Geary said. "The government."

"People still hate the government. Or they hate Obama, at least."

"Do they still hate him because he was born in Africa, or is there a new reason?"

"I think they said also because he's black."

"They finally said it straight out like that?"

"They may have said *African-American*."

"The bin Laden thing has maybe thrown a wrench in the hatred."

"Oh, that was fake. Didn't you hear? It wasn't bin Laden, or he was already dead. Or those weren't Navy SEALs. I can't remember. Fake, though."

"But newspapers have gotten off. No one hates newspapers anymore."

Klein tried to make it through his workdays without a second cigarette. If a morning was stressful, though, he allowed himself one at lunch. He wasn't trying to quit, it was just about moderation.

"It's hard to hate things that don't exist anymore," he said. "*The Chronicle* has been reduced to covering high school sports in-depth. Print newspapers are too slow to cover the pros, everyone already knows the scores."

"That has to warp high school kids, being in *The Chronicle*," Geary said.

"I'm sure they don't mind."

They were studying the empty street. They may have

looked, from a distance, like they shared a delusion of managerial authority over the concrete.

"I saw my high school basketball coach last year," Geary said. "It was strange, I was in the airport in Denver, with my kids. We got off the plane and were walking away from the gate and I heard someone say, 'Don.' There was no reason for there to be anyone there who knew me, though—I assumed someone was calling some other Don. But then a few steps later I heard it again: 'Don!' I looked back and there was this man in a baseball hat maybe fifteen feet away, smiling. I didn't recognize him, though, which must have been clear, because he took his hat off, like he was trying to help me out. And then I recognized him."

"Where was he going?"

"I don't think he was traveling. He didn't have a bag, at least."

"I thought if you're not traveling you can't go to the gates."

"Exactly. It was weird. I'd seen him a few times when I was home from college, but that's almost twenty years ago now. But when I recognized him I just felt this instant happiness. I shook his hand, I introduced the kids and told them who he was. We chatted for a minute, but I was distracted because Emily had to go to the bathroom. I just remember he told me he wasn't teaching or coaching anymore, he was a principal at a high school somewhere in Wyoming. As I was walking away I turned and told him I think about basketball all the time, every day."

"Is that true?"

"Not the game as much as the discipline, working toward something with other people, believing in yourself. All the clichés."

"What did he say?"

"Nothing. We were already a ways off by the time I said it. I kind of just shouted it at him on impulse. After Emily used the bathroom we were supposed to get on the train that takes you to the terminal, but I led the kids back to the gate to look for him again. He wasn't there, though. I don't know where he went."

"What were you going to tell him?"

"I don't know."

The garage door on the next building rolled up. A woman carried a green hose and a tin bucket onto the sidewalk and began filling the bucket with water.

"You have to see this," Klein said.

"What is it?"

"Just wait."

"My parents have a couple of my old high school basketball games on video," Geary said. "They're awful, we look like idiots. That's not what I miss. Don't go to a high school basketball game, they're train wrecks."

"Everything you're saying also applies to the New York Mets."

The woman led a golden retriever out to the sidewalk. It's muzzle was white, its eyes sleepy. It settled itself next to the bucket.

"Class and character," Geary said. "He used to talk about that all the time. The way we played and carried ourselves was supposed to be about class and character. We were supposed to play the right way, treat each other the right way."

"He helped you grow up."

"He tried. It didn't entirely work."

"What do you mean? You're stable. You take care of your kids."

"The second thing is true."

"You're more stable than I am."

"I'm not sure class and character actually get you anywhere."

"Look how far they've gotten me," Klein said. "I rent a one-bedroom apartment and make some pretty good coffee."

The woman helped the dog into the bucket. Water spilled over the sides as she poured soap on the bristles of a wooden brush and began scrubbing the dog's coat in rapid, vigorous strokes. He was soon covered in thick, frothing suds. He raised his snout as if appraising the morning air.

"That's pretty cute," Klein called to the neighbor. "If you don't watch it, someone's going to take a picture and turn it into a postcard."

"If you could smell this dog you would know it's not cute," she said.

"That's the key," Klein said. "Buy the postcard, but never smell the dog."

4 | Paula Holt sat behind a large birch desk, the hint of a smile on her face, a sketchpad open before her. Three coffee mugs sat at various points on the desk, each of them empty. Her hair was straight, blonde, dark at the roots. When she looked up, her smile disappeared. Geary was struck by her pale green eyes.

"Ms. Holt? I'm Don Geary. Your assistant told me to go ahead and come in."

She put her pen down with a degree of ceremony. "She did?"

Hers was a refined stillness. She did not have to move. People appeared before her, they sought an audience.

"Is this still an okay time to talk?"

"It must be, if it's on my schedule," she said. "I'm going to be honest with you, though, Don. I don't know who you are."

"Peter Larsen put me in touch with you."

"Peter Larsen."

"In Portland? I'm from—"

"Ah! Yes." She clapped her hands, closed the sketchpad. Her tan jacket was soft, with loose sleeves. She smiled, but it was a professional smile now, a courtesy. She wore no makeup. "You should have said Portland as soon as you stepped in the door. So you're working for Peter."

"As a freelancer, yes. He said the kind of work I was doing reminded him of what you do. I was coming to San Francisco anyway, so that's why I sent my portfolio."

"You sent a portfolio? I didn't see it. Did you bring a copy with you?"

"Sure, I have it right here…" It was the most important thing in his bag, but he still had difficulty finding and extracting it.

"Sit down," she said.

"Thank you. I'm looking for something more permanent than freelancing, an opportunity to work more closely with other people. To advance my skills."

"Peter doesn't have any openings?"

"I guess not. Not right now, at least."

"But he's happy to keep you around as a freelancer," she said, nodding in a way that indicated everything was understood. "Well, show me what you've got."

"Just across the desk here?"

"Sure. You have my attention."

He opened the folder, unfolded spreads, and put them on the desk. Outside of their original contexts, the pieces appeared different to him. It was like vivisection—he'd cut these things from a body and was carrying them around with him. It was grotesque. "These were for print."

She fanned them out, scanning until her gaze stopped. "These fabric patterns aren't digital. That's from a photo, right?"

"Yes."

"Same with the type. You printed it and then worked with the paper? Then scanned it?"

"Photographed it."

"The focus is a little soft." She leaned over the pages as if they were wet and should not be touched. "I see why Peter sent you. But we already have people that do this. If he knows we already do this kind of thing, then he knows we already have people that do it—so then why is he sending another person? You see what I'm saying? There's something blinkered about that. I'm not talking about your work, I'm talking about him. Is there something else?"

"Something else?"

"You're showing me things we already do. What do you have that's different?"

He didn't hesitate. "I designed a website. Literary."

"Literary? What's the address?"

"It's not on the internet, the project folded. I have it on a drive."

"Let's see it."

He disliked the little plastic drive. The things could have viruses, they were carriers of disease. "Should I pull it up on my laptop? I can—"

"No, just give it."

She extended her hand and he dropped it into her palm. "You have kids."

"Why do you say that?"

"The way you held out your palm," he said. "That's for a kid to drop his gum into."

She smiled. It was neither the thoughtful smile nor the professional smile, it was new. She plugged the drive into the side of her keyboard. "Do you have kids, then?"

"I have two. They're on a camping trip with their mom and stepdad this week. I'll be interested to hear how they slept."

"Whether they slept. The file I'm opening is?"

"Gielgud."

"Gielgud?"

"It's a long story."

She clicked through the menus, leaned back in her chair. Her monitor was angled across the corner of the desk—he could see the home page on it. There it was, on a screen. It had a reader.

"Any particular place?" she said.

"No. You can look at anything you want."

She went to the author list, clicked an entry, frowned. "Did the book's shadow move?"

"It shifts slightly, just an A-angle to a B-angle. It's a little piece of code."

Long moments of silence. He did not know what he wanted. He was trying to be open, purposeless. Maybe this was an interview, maybe it was just tourism. He'd seen the interior of Ad Astra, how the office was arranged, how the staff dressed and talked. He'd worked since he was thirteen, riding his bike four miles to the baseball fields in town to umpire nine- and ten-year-old little league games. At sixteen his parents bought him a 1971 Chevelle, gold with black vinyl interior. It cost three thousand dollars and was his mother's idea—Geary had never heard of a Chevelle. His mother was sure he would be in an accident as soon as he got his license. The weight of an old muscle car would protect him, she decided. No research into vehicle safety, collision physics, or the value of shoulder straps—the Chevelle had only waist belts—informed her theories. She simply believed.

Though his parents bought the car, he had to pay for his gas and insurance, so he got a job as a busboy at a Perkins restaurant. He carried a black bus bin around the dining room, clearing and wiping tables. He rolled silverware, stacked racks of glasses, took out the trash, and did whatever else was asked of him that didn't fall to the dishwashers. They occupied their own space at the end of the kitchen, surrounded on one side by stainless steel sinks over which hung high-powered sprayers, on the other by a wall of chugging dishwashing machines from which they pulled steaming racks of plates, glasses, silverware, and coffee cups. They stacked the green plastic racks on the steel counter that separated them from the swinging doors to the dining room. Geary's "bus station," as everyone called it, was in a nook just outside the plastic doors, hidden from customers' view. It was his job to grab the racks of clean glasses from the counter and carry them to the bus station, where he kept them stacked six or seven high. After he cleared and cleaned a table, he set it with silverware packets—pale green gum adhesed the strip of brown paper that banded the silverware in its paper napkin package—and placed clean coffee cups upside down on the table.

Though he set dirty dishes in the sink and took away racks of clean glasses, he rarely talked to the dishwashers. A lone dishwasher worked each weeknight shift, and two shared the space on Saturdays and Sundays. Each handled the job similarly, entering through the kitchen's back door, never leaving except to eat a meal in the break room or to step out back to smoke, and listening to classic rock on a portable radio the entire time. The radio's volume was a bone of contention between the dishwashers and the manager, who wanted diners' enjoyment of the soft rock Muzak in the dining room undiminished by stray or muted strains of thumping drums, wailing guitars, or operatic howls from the kitchen. The kitchen doors were made of heavy brown plastic lined with strips of thick black rubber, though, so the dining room's own tumult of conversation, Muzak, and plate and glass noise, combined with the effectiveness of the doors, meant that diners seated just fifteen physical feet from the dishwashers rarely heard anything at all from them, even when a dishwasher sang along while air drumming or shredding on air guitar to "Whole Lotta' Love." Geary never saw a dishwasher go through the double doors into the dining room. There were dishwashers who worked, sang, made jokes, and ate at Perkins for months without ever seeing a customer.

Dishwashers were also notorious for missing shifts or quitting with no notice. When a dishwasher didn't show up, the busboy was expected to cover. The strategy was to do dishes until the machines were chugging away and there was a supply of clean tableware, at which point the busboy thew off the dishwashing smock and headed into the dining room. Geary didn't mind these occasions. They turned the shift into a game of task management, and washing dishes was work he could do in a silent, meditative state. He enjoyed solitary work enough that he might have chosen to be a dishwasher full time, except for the other, significant ways in which he didn't fit dishwashing culture. Being a full time dishwasher would mean sharing space with another dishwasher on weekends, which would have been difficult for Geary, since he didn't curse in creative ways, smoke, allude to drug use, or tell stories like the one a dishwasher named Cory told him after waiting for a particular waitress to leave the kitchen one evening.

"Hey. Dave, Dean, whatever your name is, come over here," Cory had whispered. "Do you think she's hot? Would you fuck her? I would. I would totally fuck her. Want to know something I know about her?" He then relayed a rambling anecdote about a "kegger up at Chasteen's" during which the waitress had disappeared with a football player from the rival high school in town. They were discovered "behind some trees" by other party members, it seemed, engaged in a sex act Cory referred to by a slang term then in fashion. "That is truth, friend," he told Geary. "She's good to go, if you want her. You just have to be bold." He then raised his hand and cocked his ear, halting the conversation to listen to the radio. "Kashmir!" he announced, turning up the volume.

Geary was still a virgin, the extent of his experience consisting of having kissed some girls during games of spin the bottle. He hadn't seen much in the way of pornography beyond a few copies of *Playboy* or *Penthouse* at friends' houses, passed on from an older brother or cousin and stored with great secrecy in the back of a closet, but he'd read a couple of his mother's Sidney Sheldon novels, as well as some science fiction books from the library that turned out to feature the robots on the cover only marginally, and centered much more on a halting, soft-core, in-the-future-women-will-wear-latex kind of erotica. He had read enough, in other words, to know that any variety of sex acts seemed to be fairly standard between human beings. He wasn't scandalized by Cory's claim about what the waitress had done up at Chasteen's, but neither did he have enough experience to evaluate whether these kinds of stories were even true. He didn't know what kinds of things happened at Chasteen's. He'd never been to Chasteen's. He didn't totally understand what Chasteen's was, wasn't sure whether he was even saying it correctly. Kids had a word they said, and it sounded like "Chasteen's." It was a dam up in the canyon, or an area by a dam, or some kind of field or forest where scandalous events occurred until they were broken up by the police, though it seemed unlikely to Geary that the police would be driving all the way up the canyon so often just to see if teenagers were assembled at Chasteen's. A Chasteen's story was really just a genre of narrative that, like Dicken's London, Geary understood the conventions of despite lacking direct experience. The waitress was going to pass along ten or fifteen percent of her tips to Geary at the end of the evening, and all of the high school or college aged waitresses at Perkins were nice to him, so it struck him as poor form to encourage Cory. It wasn't as if he could respond with honesty, though, either. He couldn't say, "Are you claiming there is really a scenario in which that girl, who will be a popular senior next year, is going to be giving me, a not-on-the-social-radar junior, an opportunity to have sex with her? Let me tell you something, Cory. If that waitress, who is popular and hot, were to take her shirt off in some bedroom at some party and say to me, 'Don,'—my name is Don, by the way, Cory—'Don, I saw you score fifteen points in that sophomore basketball game against Longmont last winter, the one that started at four o'clock and was attended by twenty people. You went seven for eight from the line, including those crucial two at the end, which was totally clutch, and I want you to tear my clothes off and fuck me like the man you are, right here, right now,' I would probably just quietly back out of the bedroom, Cory. That's my answer to your question about whether or not I would fuck that waitress: I don't know how to fuck waitresses, Cory. So I would just avoid the situation. I need to go bus some tables now."

He couldn't say that. The kitchen at Perkins was not a site of emotional honesty. Instead he said, "I don't know, man. Probably out of my league?" And then he went to bus some tables. During the five months he worked at Perkins he grew no closer to Cory or to any of the other dishwashers. In every job he'd had afterward he'd sensed the presence of Cory-like figures: aggressive people, people who had inside information, who used talk to propel themselves.

Paula Holt clicked again. A shadow shifted and settled behind the photo of a different book cover. Geary was aware of the sound of his breathing, of his shoes against the floor when he shifted his feet. It would have been better if he were invisible, or not there at all.

"There are a lot of words here," she said.

"I guess it's the nature of the site."

"It's good, it's professional. Who wrote the copy?"

"I did."

She looked at him. "That's a lot of work. Don't get me wrong, I love books, but we don't design books. We communicate through design, not words. Our clients want sites with minimal language."

"This was just a contrast from the print layouts. You said—"

"Jesus, Philip Roth." She was looking at the screen again, leaning forward. "This is *a lot* of copy. Have you ever thought of getting in somewhere through writing? You clearly have the ability."

"No. I mean yes, I do, but no. I kind of already did the writing thing."

"I can see that. I've never heard of this person. How do you say this?"

"Casares."

"Tell me again why this isn't on the internet?"

"They decided there wasn't an audience."

It was June. The sunlight beyond the window was clean and bright, shot through with the rose and orange tones that make California sunlight seem a film of sunlight. It was polished sunlight. Sunlight as nostalgic reference to sunlight.

"There isn't an audience for modern art, either, but there are websites for it. I know people who would devour this."

"It wasn't my decision."

"Well, yes. That happens." She closed the site, handed him the drive. "It's great you came in. But we don't have openings right now for anyone doing what you're doing.

I like it, it's interesting. But this is a pretty saturated market."

"I understand."

She studied him, frowning. There was something wrong with him, it seemed, or something wrong with what he was doing. "Being able to write, though…" she said. "I don't like to give advice. But you should think about marketing yourself as a writer."

"Sure. That makes sense," he said. "Thank you so much for your time, Ms. Holt."

Thirteen hours later it was night and he was spinning over the Markham Bridge. The elevated concrete superstructure rendered downtown Portland's modest high rises and bridges a kind of carefully lit tabletop model below. The moon was up and Mt. Hood's snowcap shone ghostlike on the eastern horizon. The freeway dropped as quickly as it had risen, though, and after the glimpse of the city and the mountain he was exiting to the surface streets. Homeless people lined a brick sidestreet beneath the freeway, their faces, carts, and bicycles flashing past. Geary's back hurt, his right knee hurt, his shoulders were sore, but he was satisfied: he had again made the drive in a day. His travel expenses, sandwiches and coffee included, came to less than eighty dollars round trip.

The car's headlights formed bright circles on the cedar fence at the back of his drive. He cut the engine and unfolded himself from the driver's seat, pressing the door closed quietly so as not to wake his neighbor, Michael, a quiet man who lived alone in the small house—a duplicate of Geary's—on the other side of the drive.

The back porch light was on, as well as a light in the

kitchen. Unlocking the back door, Geary felt he would find someone inside the house. All was silent, though. A glass of water stood exactly where he'd left it on the kitchen counter. A black t-shirt he'd left behind lay folded on the coffee table. He'd been gone four days, but time had not passed here. The highway's vibrations continued in his muscles and nerves as he pulled a beer from the refrigerator. He felt he could drink the whole thing in an instant but restrained himself. In the basement, clothes lay strewn across his bed, the detritus of hurried packing. He had no desire to sleep.

He opened the back door and stepped into the yard. The firs towered beyond the back fence, their silhouettes stretching into the night. He had an odd sensation of the yard having grown somehow. Then he saw the mass of white vinyl on the grass—the pool, fallen and flat. In the faint illumination from the porch light he could see the stone steps that led to the lower level of the yard were caked in swirls of dried mud. He walked down and found, beneath the back fence, the rough channels left by the mass of water that must have rushed down and out of the yard when the pool collapsed. The water would have continued down the steep slope behind the back fence before spilling into the weeded, trash-strewn area behind the apartment building on the street below.

The television news had been repeating infrared footage of soldiers on the other side of the world, ghosts of green heat moving together through the night, searching and destroying. Settling into his bed in the basement, Geary wondered what his own home would look like through a satellite's heat-reading lens. A mass of darkness, probably. Maybe a faint blue shape, barely detectable. As his breathing slowed and his body cooled, the blue would fade further. In sleep, eventually, he might disappear.

5 | Mornings were bright. People awoke to birdsong, to the voices of dogwalkers encouraging their charges. Steam rose from the cup of coffee on Louise's desk. She was trying to get some writing done before work. Her phone chimed.

Are you going to two page Tuesdays? the text read. It was Elizabeth.

I forgot it's today. Are you going? Louise wrote.

You have to go so I can see you after work. I'm not in the office today but I want to tell you a story and ask advice.

After work, Louise walked to the restaurant. The sidewalks were bright white and west-facing windows bounced dazzling sunlight. The door swung open at Louise's touch, the restaurant's name immaculately lettered on the glass.

"Here, sit next to me, I'm having...what is it?" Elizabeth said. She was at the bar. "A Moscow Mule. Do you want one? It's vodka, ginger ale, and some other things I didn't understand."

"If you didn't understand it, then yes, I think I have to have one."

Elizabeth looked for the bartender, but she was busy at the other end of the counter. "So Toby is about to get kicked out of computer camp," she said.

"What?"

"That's why I want to ask your advice. I know we're here for the writing thing. Do you have pages for today?"

"They're in my purse. Do you?"

"No, I didn't get anything done." Elizabeth seemed enthusiastic, almost excited in her responses. "Wait, I'm sorry, did you need to talk to someone else? I just grabbed you as soon as you walked in."

Louise took the stool next to Elizabeth. The floor was white hexagon tile, the chairs and tables dark maple. The restaurant was new, she'd never even heard of it.

Elizabeth raised her mug. "Could we have another one of these, for her?" she asked the bartender.

They'd known each other for a decade. Elizabeth had moved from Eugene to Portland to take the job as editor of *Cascadia Arts* magazine. Louise had shown up because her husband wanted to build a forestry career and she wanted to live in a city friendly to writers and artists that was not New York. Their jobs were in different programs, not in any kind of hierarchical relationship. Elizabeth's longer tenure meant wider knowledge of the city's non-profit pecking order. Her kids were younger, though—a nine-year-old girl with the refined features of her husband and a six-year-old boy with the same dark eyes as his mother—so Louise was the authority on the city's schools and camps, the realpolitik of parenting. They'd both crossed forty now, and saw in each other a likeminded woman fighting the same fight.

"What do you mean Toby got kicked out of camp?" Louise said.

"I'm so glad you're here. I kept thinking of you last night, I kept thinking, *Don't do anything until you ask Louise.*"

"What happened?"

"It's a parks and rec camp. I guess they make their own little games on the computer and then play them, I don't know. He loves computers. He sits next to his dad on the couch all the time, playing little games on the phone or the laptop. But when I went to pick him up at the end of the day yesterday, the teacher told me she doesn't think he's 'ready for the camp.' She said he kept getting up from his chair, he didn't finish the steps of some project, something like that."

"He's six. What age is the camp for?"

"It said six through ten."

"Six-year-olds get up from chairs. They walk around."

"I told her I understood he wasn't finishing steps, but was he causing a problem? She said he was distracting the other kids."

"It's a camp where six-to-ten-year-olds are supposed to sit at a computer all day? During summer?"

"Maybe I chose a bad camp. There are other six-year-old boys in it, though. Toby was just standing there, embarrassed, while this woman told me she didn't think he could do it. She said she warned him about walking around a few times and I guess he didn't listen. It seems ridiculous now that I'm saying it out loud, like I should just laugh."

"Was he upset?"

"He didn't understand she was saying he shouldn't come back. In the car on the way home I had to explain to him that maybe the camp wasn't right for him, and he wouldn't be going back. Of course he started crying. I guess it turned out he'd been having a great time, he loved it. He had no idea the teacher didn't like him."

"What did he do today?"

"Mark took a sick day and stayed home with him. I guess

he kept asking Mark if there was a way he could go back and say he was sorry. He wanted to get back in the camp."

"Oh, no. The poor little guy."

Another woman entered the bar and walked over to them. She was small, with a business-like way about her. She'd published a true-crime book about a woman murdered by her husband and was at work on another. "Are we sitting at the bar today?" she said.

"Oh, I don't think so. I was just telling Louise a quick story. I think we're sitting at those pushed-together tables over there."

"Right. I see some of us are there already."

"Will you save us a seat? We'll be there in a minute."

"Fair enough," the woman said.

Louise was content to continue sitting at the bar. She could make out a John Coltrane tune beneath the din of conversation, from an album she and her husband had listened to often when they were first married. This group had been meeting once a month for almost a year. Louise was glad to have been invited and always considered skipping. She could be on her way home for a drink and dinner in the backyard with her husband and boys right now, comfortable in her old jeans and favorite t-shirt. Meeting in a bar to listen to women take turns reading two pages from a current project, trading tips and encouraging each other—it was inconvenient. And yet she was always glad she'd gone, she always learned something or met someone new. One part of her was in no hurry to sit down at the table and take out her pages. Another part of her looked forward to her turn.

"When the teacher was giving me this little condescending speech about how Toby shouldn't come back, I almost couldn't process it. I didn't understand what she was saying," Elizabeth said. "I can send Lyla to any camp and I know she'll make friends right away. Maybe Toby's not normal, maybe I can't leave him with people."

"Of course you can. He's a wonderful boy."

"I love my kids, but I can't just sit at home with them. I have a job. They'd be bored, anyway. We didn't have these problems in Hawaii, we just wandered around during the summer. No one watched us, no one cared. There weren't any camps, there wasn't any enrichment. We were dumb and we liked it."

It was mysterious, Elizabeth's childhood. Louise couldn't piece together the details, or perhaps Elizabeth never quite offered them. Her husband was an urban planner. He'd personally redesigned and remodeled the kitchen and dining room in their house. The appliances were stainless steel, the dining table was reclaimed wood. The fixtures were stylish and modern and the walls were pale blues and yellows and greens. Elizabeth was smart, confident, she knew everyone. She seemed so comfortable in Portland, so of the place, that it was a surprise to remember how far she had traveled. She'd told a story once about a garbage strike in Honolulu. Her parents had just thrown the garbage in the backyard for weeks, she'd said. This had become Louise's primary image of Elizabeth's childhood. She pictured run-down houses in the shade of palm trees, garbage-strewn backyards, a beach somehow at the end of the road. The images couldn't be accurate—they were strange, dream images—but they stuck.

"Maybe this is just a bad week," Elizabeth said. "Maybe there's nothing I have to think about here. I suppose we should join them at the table. I don't even have any pages, I don't know why I'm here. Parenting is awful."

"Yes."

"I don't know what boys need, I don't know what to do."

"You're already doing everything." Was Boston to Portland as strange as Hawaii to Portland? Was East Coast Irish Catholic to Oregon the same as Pacific Polynesian to Oregon? "What did Mark say?"

"He said it's not a big deal, Toby will be fine."

"That's true. Toby will be fine."

"His sister is just so different."

"It's been too long since we had you guys over. Come over for dinner this weekend. We'll figure it all out."

"I just wanted to punch that woman in the face," Elizabeth cried. "I know my son, he's smart and funny and he just wants to make people happy. He's not a distraction. He doesn't disrupt anyone."

"It was just a misunderstanding. It's not a real teacher."

"They only get to be kids once. The stakes seem so high. Why do the stakes always have to seem so high?"

6 | Some leave a self as a sea creature abandons a shell. There is no renunciation, because no mistake has been made—the construction has simply become obsolete. The move begins with neither warning nor urgency.

Some of Arden's possessions began to strike him as odd. The movies that lined the shelves in his living room, for whom were they displayed? His apartment seemed filled with suggestion, with advertisements for a personality that wasn't his. Over lunch recently, Larsen had told Arden he was going to divorce his wife, and that this would probably mean a difficult period for Polymath, since his attention would be elsewhere. Arden took the news as both a confirmation and an omen: he had been right to leave Polymath, but could he expect to keep getting work from Larsen as a freelancer? The currents were shifting.

In only a few weeks, Reina had changed. Where once Arden had noted a striver, a sharp jawline, a woman who interrupted too often and whose laugh seemed practiced, now he saw none of these. They had their own conversational rhythms. She had goals and was pursuing them. Her laugh was her laugh, her smile was her smile. His jokes did not always entertain her. She sometimes responded with serious questions when he expected further riffs. She hid neither boredom nor disagreement with him, in fact seemed at times to employ them as stratagems. He knew the curve of her hips, the press of her nipples beneath his fingertips. She straddled him on the couch, her hands in his hair. She was demanding in her desire and he buried himself in her.

Sunday morning, she stayed. In those first waking minutes all acts were allowed, everything was encouraged. Afterward they walked to breakfast. Paying the bill, Arden felt like a king who might settle the account with a wave of his jeweled fingers. He had known women before, but this sense of himself as a patriarch deeply satisfied was new.

On the walk home he looked at a house being remodeled and shook his head.

"What?" she said. "Are they doing it wrong? Are you also a critic of architecture?"

"See that area where there's no siding? Where there's just that fabric? Look at the name printed on it."

"*Arden,*" she read, squinting. "Is that your family?"

"It used to be my dad's company. I'm not sure I consider my dad family, though."

"What do you mean?"

"He didn't raise me. My mom raised me and my brother. My dad doesn't even own that company anymore, anyway. And that's a shitty font."

"Is your brother older or younger? Where does he live?"

"Younger. He's still in Montana. He likes to get in trouble."

"What kind of trouble?"

"His specialty was drunk driving. He's probably still selling pot and working construction."

"When was the last time you talked to him?"

He didn't discuss family issues, didn't turn conversation toward his childhood. He had walked or driven past houses with exposed Arden housewrap dozens of times over the years and never said a thing to anyone. Hundreds of structures in the city, maybe thousands, carried his last name beneath the siding. Hearing himself point it out to Reina was unsettling. His orientation toward her was dangerous. He was betraying himself.

"Maybe a year. No, I saw him at Christmas. Half a year."

"Where does your dad live?"

"Las Vegas."

"Is he a gambler?"

"Just a con artist. It doesn't matter. Everyone has family issues."

"I don't. My parents live together in the same house I grew up in. My youngest sister is still in high school. I go home to see them all the time."

"You have a sister in high school?"

"This surprises you?"

"Considering the adult nature of some of the things we've been doing, yes."

"Don't be gross."

"I'm not being gross, I'm sharing my surprise with you. This is a very sharing conversation."

"It was, but now you're ruining it."

"I'm not ruining anything. I'm just talking."

She had a way of raising her chin when displeased, but he couldn't tell whether it was sincere or playacting. Maybe she didn't know, either, maybe it was neither here nor there. He'd tried guessing at women's feelings in the past but had been unsuccessful. The struggle led to an increasing desire to please, but this had caused women to lose respect for him. He wanted to be a man who could make a woman happy but he did not want to be a man who tried too hard to do so. He could not solve the contradiction. Perhaps he was just not that kind of man.

He was older now, though, and Reina was not a friend or peer. She was younger, known by no one. She wore sweaters in the summer, high-heeled sandals, a floral fragrance he couldn't place. She did not own a bicycle, did not know or care about the Portland Trail Blazers, did not try to fit into the local culture. He could not anticipate her. He watched her closely and asked questions. Beyond that, she was a mystery.

"Why don't you have any movies directed by women?" she asked later. They were reading the *Times* and drinking coffee.

"Don't I? I guess they don't let women direct very often. It's not a progressive industry. Which ones do you think I should have?"

"I don't know. Do you know who Louise Brooks is?"

"Did she direct movies?"

"No, she was the original It Girl. They ruined her career, though."

"Was she a lesbian?"

"No. That was the rumor they used to ruin her career."

Arden sat on the floor, his back against the chair, Kira curled against him. Reina lay on the couch, refolding the newspaper as she read from page to page.

"Are there agencies in town run by women?" she asked.

He frowned, studying the dark television screen.

"I take it that's a no."

"I don't know every agency in town."

"I want to run my own agency," she said. "I don't want to answer to another man who wears tennis shoes and has Saul Bass posters on the wall."

Arden looked over his shoulder. "Is my Kurosawa poster okay?"

"I'm just saying I don't want to work for you. Or for someone like you."

"I don't think there's any danger of that. Working for me, I mean."

"Larsen is the same kind of man, though. You're all the same. You have the same aesthetics, that's why you get along so well."

"I thought I stopped working for Larsen specifically because his aesthetics were different."

"How is freelancing not still working for him? You have lunch together, you make jokes, you have a good time. I was there. Remember, when we met?"

It was this, being at sea in conversation, that he feared most. He wanted a quiet afternoon with the newspaper, to take Kira for a long walk, maybe to the reservoir. Everything should have been steady, everything should have been fine. He'd been thinking about renting a movie later but now worried he would have to rent a movie directed by a woman. "What's the article you're reading?" he said.

"It's about how men want to control everything."

"I thought it was about Louise Brooks."

She frowned. Kira stood and trotted to the kitchen and they heard him slurp from the water dish. The shades were up, the windows open. From where he sat on the floor Arden could see the sky. A car drove past, a hip-hop song playing on its stereo. The song faded into the distance.

"Don't you think it's funny men think the original It Girl was a lesbian?" Reina said.

They sat at a long table at the Goodfoot, a DJ at the front of the room playing music before a small, empty dance floor. "Is this not something people do here?" Reina asked Park's wife. She did not just mean dancing. The room was uncrowded, the music subdued. It was nothing like the clubs she went to in Los Angeles, with huge front windows thrown open to the street and all kinds of people on the dance floor from early in the evening until the small hours of the morning. People danced on the sidewalk, they moved in and out. The borders were loose, alive.

"Someone has to be first," Park's wife said. She was tall, with a wide smile and a friendly, open expression. Reina hadn't caught her name.

"Are there other places? This seems small," Reina said.

"There are some places downtown. Aren't there some clubs downtown?"

"I don't know," Park said.

"I was in a club downtown once," Geary said. "It was in the main level of an office building. It probably used to be a bank. They had velvet paintings of jaguars on the walls."

"Jaguars?"

"It was a kind of Miles Davis vibe, like the cover of *Bitches Brew.*"

"Are you sure you weren't under the influence of some other brew?" Arden said.

"Pretty sure."

Park was quiet, calm. Geary was like a cop or a criminal, always turning conversation away from himself. These friends of Arden's were smart and polite and Reina liked them, but there was also something docile about them. There was some shared defeat in their past, it seemed— something for which they felt accountable. She'd been in Portland for a month, in the grocery store alone, in the bookstore alone, walking around, and not a man in the city had spoken to her. The men in the grocery store studied food labels and looked at their phones. Was she not desirable here? Men in Los Angeles approached her. In clubs late at night, sweating on the dance floor, it wasn't unusual for a man to ask where he might take a woman. The first time it had happened, Reina had looked at the man, confused. He had leaned close to her. "I want to fuck you!" he'd shouted, the throbbing music and crowd making the explanation private, intimate. It had been a new kind of power, this choice she had. The men of Portland had robbed her of this power by ignoring her, by never once asking.

"How long have you been in Portland?" Park's wife asked.

"Just a month."

"How do you like it?"

"It seems like everything closes at nine o'clock."

"It really is the sleepiest city."

"I asked Lem, where do people go dancing? Is this it?"

The DJ started a new track. He turned the volume up, trying to lure people to the floor. He concentrated on his turntables, headphones over his ears. She should walk over and console him, she thought. She should tell him it wasn't his fault.

"You met with Paula Holt?" Arden was saying. "*The* Paula Holt? What was she like?"

"Busy," Geary said.

"How did it go?"

"I don't think I'm in their league."

"I'm not sure you want to be."

"You interviewed with a woman?" Reina said.

"It wasn't really an interview. Just a chat."

"The woman runs the agency?"

"Yes."

"You didn't mention this," she said to Arden.

"It's in San Francisco," he said.

"Are you moving to San Francisco?" Reina asked.

"No. It was just a meeting," Geary said.

She couldn't tell if she'd missed a part of the conversation or if these men were just impenetrable. No one was dancing. She had come to Portland hoping to find new possibilities but what she felt so far was something folded in on itself, tightly bound.

"Come on," she said to Arden. "Let's dance."

"I'm not sure I'm—"

"I don't care what you're about to say, you have to dance."

She pulled him out to the floor and began to dance. Arden responded with a stylized shuffle, elbows at his sides. It was serviceable, she decided. A start.

7 | Nathan was light as a sparrow. Geary could lift him off the ground with one arm, he could throw him over his shoulder and flip him upside down. He could still toss his boy in the air.

"Come on, Dad. You have to give me a chance."

"I am giving you a chance. Look, I'm just standing here."

Nathan rushed him, head down. Geary caught him under the arms and flipped him onto the bed. Before Nathan could collect himself, Geary pinned him. Nathan struggled, grunting and laughing at the same time, until Geary let him escape. Nathan clambered onto Geary's back and Geary stepped away from the bed. Geary bent at the waist, his head toward the bed so that Nathan was directly on top of him. Then he bent a bit more. "No..." Nathan said. Geary bucked, Nathan flew onto the bed, and Geary pinned him again.

"Dad, you've got to give me a chance!" Nathan said.

"I am giving you a chance," Geary whispered. "I'm giving you a chance over and over."

He watched his daughter, curious. A high window—it was small, unshaded, did not open—revealed a liquid square of night. They understood he had been to San Francisco, but they had never been there. To them, the words were like the name of a planet: a luminous sphere, swirling vapors. Emily looked up from the page and nodded impatiently. He continued.

"Everything was going great," he read. "Charlie slept in my big-girl bed, and Saturday morning I took him to see me do ballet. It was ballerific! Here I am getting ready to dance."

She pointed to the photo taped to the page. "Why am I sticking my stomach out?"

"I don't know, you were being goofy. Do you still have that dance outfit?"

"Yes. It's too small now."

He turned the page. "The trouble started when we sat down for lunch. My dad poured me a glass of chocolate milk, and he poured another for my brother, Nathan. 'What about me?' Charlie asked. 'Do I get chocolate milk?' 'No chocolate for animals,' my dad said. 'Hmph!' Charlie said. 'I've never had chocolate milk.' 'That's because you are a turtle,' my dad said."

It was two years ago he had taken these photos of Emily and a stuffed animal turtle. He printed the photos, pasted them into an empty white notebook, and wrote a story around them. The turtle had returned to its shelf in the preschool classroom the next morning so that another child could take it home, and the children had all looked at Emily's book about her weekend with the turtle. Reading it now, Geary felt the hastily assembled book was ideal—nothing more and nothing less was required of it. The turtle's comically large brown glass eyes peered into the camera above text that described how Charlie the Turtle, when the father leaves the room to do some laundry, convinces Emily and Nathan to let him have some chocolate milk. Then he goes crazy.

"Woop woop!" Geary read in Charlie's voice. "That chock-a-dockle mock-a-lock has gone straight to my head! That lock-a-chocka milla-killa makes me feel all buzzy!"

Beneath a photo of Emily looking into the camera, Emily-the-narrator implored the reader never to let Charlie look directly into your eyes. "He can be very convincing," the narrator warns above a close-up of Charlie's eye. When the father returns, the children blame each other for Charlie's state, and the father says Charlie needs some quiet time. Emily-the-narrator tells the reader she will never let Charlie drink chocolate milk again, because it's not good for him. "And I'm sure, now that I've told you this story, that you won't give him any chocolate milk, either. And that you'll never, ever let him look into your eyes. So the problem is solved. The end," Geary read.

He turned the page. The final spread featured a wordless photo of Charlie looking directly at the reader. Emily curled her fingers around Geary's arm. "I love this book," she said.

H'd written it with a ballpoint pen in the space of an hour. He worried it was better than anything else he'd ever made.

The men didn't bother to introduce themselves before turning to face their opponents. Geary already knew who he wanted to cover: a quiet young man, maybe nineteen or twenty, in red Jordan shorts. He'd been firing shots from beyond the three-point line when everyone had been warming up, and Geary had noticed a decent percentage go in. He moved in that direction while the other players milled around. *Let's go*, he thought. It had been two weeks since he'd played.

"Let me handle the ball," a short kid with a buzz cut and a Franklin High jersey told Geary. "These guys are quick, just stay between your man and the basket and I'll try to help."

Geary understood that to the young, the gray in his hair

and his male-pattern baldness were stigma. While they'd been shooting for teams, he'd noticed the kid brought the ball to his forehead in a labored semicircle motion before shooting.

"All right," the Franklin kid said, turning around as if they required formal warning. "Ball's in."

Geary put his hand in the passing lane. In his peripheral vision he could see players massed near the basket struggling through action that didn't involve him. He looked down at a spot on the court that allowed him to see his man in one side of his peripheral vision and the ball in the other.

"Shoot that!" someone shouted. Geary's man relaxed and looked toward the basket. Geary turned, saw how the shot would come off, and gathered the rebound. The feeling of the ball in his hands settled him. It was like old math, the realization that one could still solve the equation.

The Franklin kid immediately called for the ball. Geary flipped it to him and the kid took off down the court. Their teammates were a bearded man in a Trail Blazers t-shirt and a gangly, uncoordinated man, both of whom sprinted to keep up with the Franklin kid. They collected in a mass on the right side of the court. Geary jogged down the opposite side. "Move! Move! Set picks!" the Franklin kid shouted while dribbling. Geary raised his hand and the kid passed him the ball. The young man in Jordan shorts had set himself to force Geary left, so Geary caught the pass and immediately went left for a lay-up. "He's left-handed!" someone shouted.

Geary positioned himself on defense as he had been taught, denying his man the ball. The Franklin kid got burned for a layup. "Someone has to help me on that!"

he yelled. On offense, there was a progression of moves available to Geary in a first game against strangers. When the ball came to him on the right side, his defender dramatically overplayed to force him right. His right-handed drive was not as sure as it had once been, but he shielded his defender with his body and put the lay-up in. His defender cursed. "That's an old guy," one of his teammates said, laughing. "You can't let an old guy do that."

At the other end, the young man moved under the basket, leaned his shoulder into Geary's chest, and popped out to the wing to receive the ball. Geary tried to make him drive left but collided with someone setting a pick, and was left watching his man drive for a graceful, uncontested layup. He caught the Franklin kid looking at him with the same exasperated expression as before, so when Geary next got the ball he fired it immediately to the Franklin kid and set a pick on the kid's defender. The result was an open look, but the Franklin kid's shot was off. Geary gathered the rebound and dribbled out before passing to the bearded man. It was a game at the park, he decided—everyone would touch the ball. As soon as the bearded man began the motions of an odd hook, Geary circled to the basket and gathered the wild miss. The young man in Jordan shorts was quietly enraged, but this was incidental. Geary drove in order to draw the Franklin kid's defender into the lane and then fired a pass to the kid, whose shot was off again. "Fuck!" the Franklin kid shouted. Geary's man snatched the rebound with a degree of satisfaction.

Amid the shouted instructions, warnings, and frustrations, Geary anticipated the movements of his teammates and opponents and cycled from one end of the court to the other. He rebounded, set picks, and moved the ball. The Franklin kid couldn't shoot, so Geary made sure to keep getting him open shots. The kid wanted to play point guard, so Geary got a defensive rebound and brought the ball up the court himself. When a shot was blocked out of bounds, Geary and his defender watched the Franklin kid race after the ball.

"You really don't like that guy," the young man said.

"I don't know what you're talking about," Geary said.

A player dribbled the ball off his foot, another slipped and fell. There were awkward fouls. Geary's man hit a jumper and Geary was frustrated to have allowed it. He sailed a pass out of bounds when a teammate cut an unexpected direction and he was frustrated to have made a mistake. He remained silent, though, expressionless. He caught his defender off balance and spun to the basket and was fouled from behind. "I got him," the young man said. The ball was passed to him and in the same motion with which he caught it he moved into a jumper that was good.

The difference between offense and defense became less important than the nature of his passage up and down the court, a serpentine language of movement through which he and the young man guarding him came to understand one another. Geary drove and jumped and turned in the air to lay the ball in from the other side of the rim, a pet shot from childhood. Somebody laughed and he felt as if he were in an old, familiar dream. The young man was much quicker than Geary was, though—he had to keep backpedaling, trying to get the young man to shoot jumpers from odd distances. Everyone was breathing hard and soaked in sweat. Some seemed in pain, others played with grim resolve. Geary experienced the game as a single, convulsing entity. There were moments of balance and imbalance, seams that appeared and then disappeared. "Keep shooting, keep shooting," the bearded man told him. He held contradictory thoughts. There was the reality that they were three behind and the other team only needed one point to win. There was also the fantasy in which perhaps they could get defensive stops and he could score four straight on offense. When Geary crossed over between his legs, his defender stuck his hand out and caught Geary on the chin. Geary laughed and the young man smiled and they didn't bother to call a foul, they kept playing. When Geary hit a jumper the young man laughed again.

When they headed back to the other end and the Franklin kid called out the score, a kid on the other team disagreed. The game stopped as they traded divergent summaries of recent baskets. Geary and the young man stood near the basket, listening as the debate escalated. "They do this every time," the young man said.

"How many do you have?" the Franklin kid asked Geary.

"I don't know, I can't remember," Geary said.

"He has at least five," the Franklin kid said, unfazed.

"I don't care how many he has individually," the other kid said. "Your team has eight."

Geary looked at the young man. "Are you going to score on me to end the game here?" he asked.

"Oh, definitely," the young man said.

8 | His parents visited. His father was sixty-six, his mother sixty-one. His father's hair was thin and white but his mother kept hers the strawberry blonde of her youth. They both wore bifocals and a particular brand of slip-on shoes. His mother brought tea bags in a ziplock bag. His father's phone showed how many steps he had taken that day, the previous day, every day before that. "This is the day I played golf," he said. "This is the day we were watching your sister's kids and they had us running all over the place. This day, I don't know—obviously we didn't do much that day."

They were visiting for two days before continuing to Vancouver to board a cruise ship that would take them to Alaska. They were going to see glaciers and tundra, grizzly bears and wolves.

They took the kids to the bookstore, they took them for ice cream. "What do you want for dinner?" they asked.

"Hamburgers from the barbecue," Nathan said.

"What about you?" they asked Emily. "Do you like hamburgers from the barbecue?"

"They're good, but I have…I can't have a normal bun."

"Yes, we heard about that. We'll figure that out," his mother said.

They bought meat and cheese, potato chips, standard hamburger buns, gluten-free hamburger buns, barbecue briquettes, everything that was necessary. They bought pickles, mayonnaise, apples, and bananas. "I noticed your kettle was scorched, so I bought you a new one," his mother said. "I wasn't sure what color to get. I know red with a black handle is Loveland High School colors. Are you okay with that?"

"I don't know. Did they have yellow kettles with black handles?"

"No, they don't make kettles in your high school's colors."

"I'll do my best not to think about it."

In the backyard he knelt to stack coals in the barbecue grill. He'd picked the cheapest model the day he bought it, a small grill meant to be used when camping or at the beach. It was fine when he was alone or with the kids but in front of his parents he sensed how ridiculous it looked—the aluminum feet raised the grill only eight inches off the ground. He wore his torn jeans, a stained t-shirt, and old tennis shoes with soles that flopped loose at the back.

"There are three high schools now, you know, not just the two," his mother said. "I don't know what the new school's colors are, though. What are the colors for the new high school?" she asked.

His father was setting plates and glasses on the table they'd carried out from the basement. "What color is the new high school?"

"No, what are the school colors? The uniforms, not the building!"

"I have no idea."

"Purple, I think."

"Yes, purple."

"Why would I care what color the building is?" she said. "Whatever. You have a red kettle."

"Thank you," Geary said.

"Have you bought one of these yet?" his father asked that evening. He sat on the futon in the living room, checking his email.

Geary sat on a cheap canvas chair he'd bought and put

together that morning. His mother was in the kitchen wiping down counters and putting things away. Geary had told her he would clean up, but she had shooed him away.

"I just use my laptop," Geary said.

"I figured out I can keep track of everything with the iPad," his father said. He propped his feet on the oak coffee table they had built together the summer before Geary's last year in college. Geary had discovered mission furniture and Miles Davis albums and red wine and wanted to live a certain way. He could afford the albums and wine but not the furniture. His father had helped him draw up some plans, they'd bought oak at the lumberyard, and they spent weekend afternoons in the basement, ripping and cutting and joining the pieces.

"You can do almost everything, it's just a little different on here," his father said. "I don't know if it's something people really have to have. It's a lot lighter than my laptop, though."

When Geary was a child his father could often be found at his desk in the small den off the entryway, paying bills or filing paperwork related to the accounts, investments, and policies that described the material life of the family. Filing cabinets held years of credit card statements, mutual fund reports, children's report cards, checkbook ledgers, and budget spreadsheets. He also crafted his own charts and graphs of their financial life. The oldest were hand drawn on graph paper, but newer copies were made on the computer and printed out on the plotter, a device with small red, green, and yellow pens that moved over a piece of paper, stopped, and then bounced, piston-like, on the page, producing axis lines, colored bars, dates, and percentages. The sound of the plotter's guttural scream meant the family's finances had again been squared and documents filed. Geary would sometimes stand over the plotter while it was at work, watching the pens produce the story of their family's life.

Now, a quarter century later, he sat on a cheap chair in a dim room with dusty bookshelves. He was upbeat, he made his parents laugh, and was silently embarrassed. He wished he could show them Gielgud, but it would look different to them. He'd found a new understanding of literature and design and living, but on the screen it just looked like an incomplete, self-indulgent jumble. He'd gotten straight A's in high school, he'd helped with yard work, shoveled snow, hadn't caused trouble. But that boy had been replaced by this single father for whom everything seemed temporary, as if he were still hammering together the backdrop to a play to be performed later. He had not yet written the play, or maybe he was just an actor in it, awaiting his lines.

"You can really do everything on there?" he asked his father.

"Absolutely. This is how I read now. I've got dozens of books on here, a number by this guy I like, Robert Crais. I've got all of his, I think. And we pay all of our bills on here while we're traveling."

"When it works right," his mother said from the kitchen. "It doesn't always work right."

"That was just one time," his father said. "There was a snafu once, but I got it ironed out."

"Until it happens again," his mother said.

"Okay. Until it happens again."

"I know we're only here two days, but will we get to meet the woman you've been dating?" his mother asked.

"Oh. Well—that's over."

"What do you mean? Hadn't you been dating for a couple years?"

"Three."

"What happened?"

He pictured her crying, telling him she had to make decisions about her life, they didn't have the same priorities, she couldn't be with him anymore. When she finished her speech she'd said she had to go, she couldn't stay a last night with him, she couldn't even stay for the evening. She had to get some distance or she would fall back, she had said. He didn't understand exactly what she meant by "fall back."

"It just gets complicated when there are kids involved," he said.

"Wasn't her son friends with Emily?"

"They were in the same preschool class."

"So does this affect her friendship with him?"

"She hasn't asked about him. He goes to a different elementary school," he said. "She has new friends now, at her own school."

"Well. As long as the kids are okay," his mother said.

9 | He continued to work. He finished materials on time and had a particular talent for typography. He turned in redesigned stationery and business cards for a local credit union and the manager thanked him profusely

and assured him she would pass his name to others. At home he sat in front of the computer, books on his desk open to striking page spreads, particular color combinations. When he realized the record on the turntable had been spinning silently for thirty minutes he would flip it, and then the next side would finish and spin silently for an hour. Absorbed in problem solving, he failed to notice.

He met Nick Bouros at a coffeehouse in Northeast Portland. Bouros had emailed from his personal address and said the end of Gielgud still bothered him, and he wanted to check in. The room was crowded and loud. Freelancers worked on laptops, took calls on their cell phones. Someone was working on a screenplay near two mothers who talked while their babies slept in strollers next to their chairs.

"It was my project. Ed never wanted to do it. He was just indulging me," Bouros said.

"He didn't strike me as particularly interested," Geary admitted.

"He uses the word *culture* a lot," Bouros said. "He believes he's interested in it. He thinks he even knows where it's headed."

"Why would culture be headed somewhere? It's not a rocketship."

"*The* culture. He thinks he knows where *the* culture is headed."

"I don't know what that means."

Bouros shrugged. The gesture suggested semantics were of little importance. "An MFA in fiction writing," he said. "Film school for your undergrad. USC is supposed to be the best, right?"

"That's what they claim. Are you thinking about applying?"

"No. Are you? You're a designer without a degree in design. I've worked with some creatives who have four, five, half a dozen degrees."

"I'm not a 'creative.' That's not a real word. It's baby talk."

"Whatever you want to call it."

"Did my work seem like the work of someone who needs to go to design school?"

"No."

"School is a trap."

A dark afternoon in Northeast Portland. Geary sat against the wall, Bouros facing him across a small table that wobbled each time Geary set his cup down. A mother and her toddler waited at the register. The employees were busy pulling pies from the oven. They had mitts on their hands, argued about which case to put the pies in. Outside it was raining and then not raining, raining and then not raining.

"That's smart," Bouros said. "I don't agree with Ed about a lot of things, but there is something he likes to say that's true: Makers are a dime a dozen."

"Makers?"

"Designers, writers, actors, whatever—there are ten times as many as anyone needs. People like Ed see makers as a resource. You use the resource, and when it's exhausted, you get another. It's like the pyramids. The slaves that built the pyramids died, they were disposable. If you don't want to be disposable, you can't be someone who just makes bricks."

"So what is it that you're doing? You're going to find a better way to get rid of dead slaves?"

Bouros sighed. Geary was a disruptive student purposely saying something coarse, it seemed.

"It's your metaphor," Geary said.

"Okay, yes," Bouros said. "And you're just going to keep making websites, making little posters for concerts in local clubs? In a market where your competition is people with degrees from Parsons, from RISD?"

In this small coffeehouse, in a trivial afternoon hour on a gray day, Bouros was saying the things Geary did not want to hear. He knew these things the way an athlete knows the moves an opponent might make. Even when prepared for them, they are still moves one must block or evade.

"I don't care about degrees," Geary said. "I'm good at what I do. Work leads to work."

"Work leads to work? That's the philosophy that inspires you, that gets you going in the morning?"

"Work leads to work."

"You don't want to make more money? You don't want to get rewarded for all that work?"

He heard the discussion the employees were having, he heard the man at the register apologize to the woman who had been waiting. He'd believed in something he'd made. Bouros had helped kill it. He needed not to be a victim in this conversation, he needed to betray no particular feeling. The only way to remain himself—confident, productive—was to pretend he was someone unaffected, clear of purpose.

"What's the reward?" he said. "A huge house I have to take care of? Private school for the kids, reservations at the hottest new restaurant for me and my girlfriend? Are these the rewards you enjoy?"

Bouros laughed. "My rewards are being the VC equivalent of middle management, getting to spend my days listening to Ed Norman pontificate as if he's some kind of world market futurist sage while we actually just fund the same equation over and over. Or worse, listening to him talk about Jerry Lee Lewis. He's a big Jerry Lee Lewis fan, and I have to hear that stuff. My reward is I have to pretend to be interested in this long enough to make the money I want to make. Yes, I have a nice house. My kids go to private school. Yes, I'm interested in movies. But to make what you want to make, you have to have control. And you can only have control if you have money."

The rest of the room disappeared. His attention was now entirely on Bouros. Had Bouros just said he wanted to make movies? Did he believe he was secretly creative, secretly intellectual? It was like suddenly seeing the gap in the armor, the tender spot around which everything else has been constructed. "Here's a not very original piece of wisdom," Geary said. "We are what we pretend to be."

"We are what we pretend to be. That's your response?"

"There's a couple at my kids' school who've made a few independent movies. They don't live in a big house, and I doubt they eat at the best restaurants, but they've made some movies. Do you really think you're going to reach some magic amount of personal net worth that will make you suddenly able to write a screenplay? To know where to put the camera?"

"Money opens up opportunities. You don't care about money? You don't want to take your girlfriend out to eat? You don't want to build a future in which things grow and get better?"

"I took my girlfriend out to eat. She asked me some of these things. I told her I'm taking care of my kids and working to become who I want to become. That's it. I'm on a path."

"Your girlfriend wanted to talk about the future and you

said you're on a path? Was that a satisfying answer for her?"

"Not really."

Bouros smiled. Something had leveled between them. Bouros, too, had been pulled from something he once wanted. Or worse, moved away from it under his own power. "You know it wouldn't have mattered anyway, right?" he said. "With Gielgud?"

"What wouldn't have mattered?" Geary said.

"At most, you might have worked three, four more months. Even if we'd taken it forward."

"You think it would have failed?"

"I think it would have succeeded. But you wouldn't have been there. They don't use the same people who built something to manage something, Don. Creative people are service workers. You can hope you'll be invited to do more, but the odds are against it."

Geary nodded, smiled. There is nothing that makes him more calm than this last phrase. He noted that Bouros' goatee was perfect—there was a degree of vanity in the time put in. He studied the scratched surface of the table, the pattern where his coffee had stained the inside of the cup. "There's something I did when I was a kid that has always stuck with me," he said. "In geography class, in junior high, we were learning the countries and capitals of Europe. To help us review for the test, our teacher said we could divide the class into two teams, and the next day we would have a quiz—the winning team got extra credit points. One of the kids asked how we'd decide the teams, and the teacher said maybe we could just have two captains pick them. She said I could be one captain, and my friend could be the other. My friend goes first, and of course he picks the smartest kid in the class. I go second and pick another smart kid. We'd been picking teams for games on the playground for years, right? So I'm sitting there and I realize what's going to happen. We're going to reveal, through a process of elimination, who we think is the stupidest kid in class."

"That teacher should be fired."

"She was actually a good teacher, she just made a mistake here. But I realize what's going to happen, and I just know what to do. It's not a decision, it's just a reflex. I pick the most checked-out kid in class. He had long hair, wore a jean jacket with the name of some metal band drawn on it in black sharpie—that kind of kid. I was actually scared of this guy, but I picked him anyway. Everyone was confused, and when it was my friend's turn, he just picked a smart kid again."

"He wasn't going along with what you were doing."

"I didn't want him to. I picked another misfit. It was maybe just a shy girl, I don't remember. But it goes on this way—my friend picks the smart kids, I pick the others. We end up with teams that are essentially smart and popular kids versus misfits."

"What were you?"

"Smart, but also played sports. Not popular. I don't know. The point is that the next day, when we're all back in class and the teacher starts asking questions, no one misses any. Throughout the entire class, as she moves from student to student, team to team, Liechtenstein, Andorra, the Scandinavian countries, it doesn't matter—every student has everything memorized. Everyone is absolutely desperate to win. The popular kids don't want to be embarrassed by losing to the misfits, and the misfits finally have a clear shot at taking down the popular kids. It was only at the very end of class, when we were going through all of the questions a second time, that one of the kids on my team got confused and missed a question. We lost by a point. When the bell rang I didn't wait for the teacher to dismiss us, I just walked out. We'd been so close."

"I get it," Bouros said. "You don't like the game, and you want to break it."

"I'm not going to break anything. I'm just saying that I've always remembered that geography class. I think I did the right thing."

"We're not in seventh grade, Don. Even public elementary schools have fundraising foundations now. They have to raise money so they can have the fucking geography quiz in the first place. You can't just pick a team of screwed up kids and believe that if you win a quiz then everyone will be free."

"I'm not picking a team. There is no team. There's just me. And I won't be a monkey that dances every time you play your music."

"And you enjoy what you're doing, working alone? Ed was amazed that you lived on what we paid you, that you accepted that. You told your girlfriend you're on a path. What's on the path?"

"I don't get to know that."

"So you're involved in a mystical experience? And you move forward on what? On faith?"

"What's on your path?" Geary said. "Spending your life with Ed Norman, listening to 'Great Balls of Fire'?"

"Oh, I've learned that Jerry Lee Lewis is actually much deeper than 'Great Balls of Fire.'"

"Aren't we all," Geary said.

10 | The moon rose without color, an arc that implied but did not reveal its full shape. Crickets sang in the grass and gardens, a sprinkler churred in the distance. Geary sat on the back stairs, the window above him aglow. The laurels along the fence on the other side of the yard had grown into a high wall that plunged the yard into deep darkness. The breeze was warm, almost tropical. Silver wisps of cloud hung in the night sky. They disappeared when Geary looked directly at them, but when he looked elsewhere he saw them again, ghosts at the edge of his vision.

He sensed some aspect of himself had disappeared. He did not know when, or where it might be found, only that he was calm now. It was not the calm of peace, but of waiting. Life lasts a moment and one is redundant from the beginning—all struggles begin with and return to this fact. He tried to imagine himself, tried to see the man sitting in the dark and to name who that man was, but he could not. The part of him he wanted to name had slipped away.

He had finished his analysis of David Hulme. He turned in hard copies—three of them—in person, because he had carefully written and designed the document and printed it on high quality paper. It had a sober, text-only cover, was folded and saddle-stitched. There were images throughout, carefully identified and captioned, and commentary set in Garamond. The cover featured the same font used on the cover of *Cascadia Arts* magazine. The title read *Cascadia Arts Brand and Identity: An Analysis*. He'd slipped the copies into a manila envelope and rode his bike downtown to the CAC office. He stood in the reception area for a minute, but no one appeared. A dozen copies of *Cascadia Arts* magazine sat on the reception desk, neatly stacked. The cover was a blurred image of dancing ballerinas, hands entwined. The word COMMUNITY ran above the dancers, bright white, all-caps. *What does it mean here, now?* the subhead read. There was a plant behind the desk. Geary studied the leaves, trying to decide if it was real.

A man came around the corner at the back of the long room and walked toward the front. "Can I help you?" he asked. He was thin, older, with glasses and the kind of white-collared blue dress shirt Geary associated with men who worked in finance in the 1980s.

"I just need to drop something off," Geary said. "It's for the board meeting, I guess. Is Elizabeth in?"

The man opened the envelope and looked at the documents. "She's out of the office today. Is this your report?"

"Yes. Is Kevin Sheckley here?"

"Everyone's gone today. They're at a team-building thing—a ropes course, I think." The man scanned a page of the report. He tilted his head to look at something more closely. Geary knew which page he was looking at.

"Why aren't you there?" Geary asked.

"Oh, I'm not full-time," the man said. "I do accounting for CAC part-time, mostly as a favor."

"Maybe you can answer the question I was going to ask Elizabeth. I was…are you able to pay me today?"

The man smiled. "You get paid after you present."

"After I present?"

"At the board meeting. You present your evaluation, answer some questions, that's it. It's simple. We cut you a check the next day."

The contents of Geary's report shifted, changed meaning. He had pictured himself handing the report to Elizabeth and that she would quietly read it at some later point. Nothing beyond that. "Elizabeth never said anything about a presentation."

"Oh, I'm sure it's in the contract. We do it the same way every year."

"When would this presentation be?"

"Tuesday evening."

"Shoot. I have my kids Tuesday evening."

The man's attention had returned to the report. He flipped a page, nodded, and flipped another. Geary mentally reviewed his kids' schedule, their friends, places they might go for a couple hours. "Is it absolutely necessary I be at this meeting?"

"The meeting is where the board hears the summaries and evaluations of the programs," he said. "It's the whole point."

"Why did I have to write and design this huge report, then? The report is the evaluation, it presents everything more clearly than I could talking about it. Can't the board just read the report?"

"The board members don't have time to read all of this. That's why you present."

"For someone who only works here part time, you seem to know a lot about the operations."

"That's because I'm one of the people you'll be presenting to. I'm on the board. Randy Alston," he said, shaking Geary's hand as if the act were a test of strength.

"Don Geary," Geary said.

"Yes, that's what it says right here," Alston said, pointing to the report. "Don Geary.'"

Someone was walking through the house. Geary heard the footsteps from outside and was on his feet and headed up to the back door, which he had left open. He stepped into the kitchen to find Nathan standing at the other end. He was shirtless but wore long pajama pants. The hair on one side of his head was flattened in a swirl and he squinted against the overhead kitchen light, peering at Geary as if uncertain whether he was dreaming or awake.

"What are you doing up, bud?" Geary asked.

"I don't know."

"I think maybe you're still asleep. You're walking around asleep."

"I'm not asleep," Nathan said.

Geary ruffled the boy's hair and led him back to his room. He helped him into bed, pulled the sheet and blanket up, and rubbed Nathan's back through the blanket. The boy's body was warm, pliant.

"You need to get your sleep," Geary said. "It's late at night. No time for a boy to be wandering around the house."

Nathan sighed. He shifted his legs, adjusted his head on the pillow.

"You want to have energy for tomorrow, so you can have fun and have a good day," Geary said.

"What am I doing tomorrow?"

"Going to the Vermont Hills camp, just like today. You said you liked the other boys there, didn't you?"

There was a long silence. "Yes," he said finally.

"It's going to be a good day. Sleep well now. Have good dreams. Do fun things in your dreams."

Geary spoke to both of his children as if he knew the future, had seen that it held warmth and comfort and happiness. The image of a blue rocketship glowed on a plastic disc over the nightlight in the corner of the room. Bins of Legos were stacked in another corner, near a Nerf gun and Nerf darts. Even in the dark, Geary knew every book on his son's shelf. They were about dragons and dinosaurs, battles from other times, wars in other worlds.

He believed and did not believe in his suggestion that dreams could be managed, thought mastered. If so, what were the dreams of the creature that managed dreams? What thoughts troubled the self that mastered thought?

To raise a child is to fall into the well of illusion. The fantasy of total protection, the rage for total control—the belief that one can say not only what is happening now, but what will happen tomorrow, the day after, all days beyond. The illusion that there is no end, there will never be an end. A lie one believes during the telling.

The weekend before, a woman at a barbecue party had expressed confusion over the fact that her eight-year-old son became angry during his soccer games and cried if his team lost, but he also wanted to play soccer every day and would love nothing more than to have a game every evening, even though the game would just be annother opportunity to become angry and cry.

"I played a lot of sports when I was a kid, and I cried when I lost," Geary said. "I was ashamed of losing, but that was actually one of the things I was addicted to."

"Losing?" she said.

"The fear. When I played a game, I was scared to lose. But I wanted to go into that fear, and from somewhere inside it—from being scared of losing—I wanted to find a way to *not* lose."

Immediately upon using the phrase, he realized he would be misunderstood. Competitors were supposed to remain aggressive and play to win, not play not to lose.

Geary had had his struggles with playing to win instead of playing not to lose, but it was also true that even when he had played to win, he had sometimes lost. He had practiced correctly and intensely for hours and hours, years and years. His teammates had worked together and played as a team, exactly the way they had planned. Still, they sometimes lost. It was a simple fact that he might, despite everything, not only lose, but lose in front of everyone. He had reconciled himself to this by denying that a loss was losing. If he practiced with focus, took care of himself, and played the right way, then even if he lost, he had at least faced public failure and responded. What he had loved about sports was the struggle not necessarily to win, but to not be—to quote a term in vogue when he was a boy—"a loser."

By the time Geary heard himself say "to not lose," however, and recognized the internal connections that had led him to use that phrase, the woman he'd been speaking to was saying something about the sheer cost, in fees and equipment, of youth sports. His personal distinctions were not only irrelevant, but beyond the depth of analysis appropriate to casual conversation.

Geary asked the woman what sports her son played in addition to soccer.

"Basketball and Tae Kwan Do," she said. "Though I'm not sure Tae Kwan Do is a sport. Is choreographed kicking a sport?"

"A discipline, maybe," he said.

"It costs a lot of money, there's a uniform, and the kids fight each other. So maybe it's a sport."

"They really fight each other?"

"They're not supposed to touch when they spar, but they

smash into each other accidentally all the time. They get hurt and then they get mad at each other."

"It's a semantic issue, probably."

"You know, my son has cried at Tae Kwan Do, too," the woman said. "So maybe it qualifies."

11 | Hulme complimented Bermea on the warehouse, the energy he sensed there, the way Bermea's office was located in the middle of things. Bermea was accustomed to hurried conversation with men who looked elsewhere, but Hulme maintained constant eye contact. It was unnerving at first, then merely odd. Eventually it became something else, something Bermea couldn't name.

"Do you see how dynamic this is?" Bermea was saying. "I just want something like this, something that moves."

"It's about energy," Hulme said. "And energy is about life. You're about more than just plumbing and fixtures."

"Yes, I'm about much more than that. *We're* about more than that, I mean. The company."

"The company is a journey. What the company sells is part of that journey, but the journey itself is bigger than that. The journey is about values."

"Yes. You get it," Bermea said. "But how would you do that?"

"The question is, how would *you* do that? What do you value?"

Bermea hadn't thought about this. Didn't everybody

value the same things? He was in his office, sitting in his comfortable chair. Hulme was looking at him. His eyes were blue. He seemed fascinated by Bermea, awaiting his answer.

The office door opened and a man in a Broadway Plumbing shirt poked his head into the room. "You said you wanted to know when that Adirondack shipment showed up?"

"Oh, yes. Thank you," Bermea said.

The man disappeared. Bermea spun his computer monitor back to where only he could see it. He clicked his mouse, studied the results.

"I'm sorry," Bermea said. "This will just take a minute." He clicked once more, stood, and walked out of the office. Hulme pulled out his mobile phone and began swiping between screens. The fan in Bermea's computer kicked on. The room was silent.

A minute later, the door opened and Bermea walked back to his desk. "Sorry. They always ship the wrong stuff, so I have to check. Where were we? Wait, what I value. Right. First, family."

"That's good," Hulme said. "This is a family journey."

"And community," Bermea said. "I grew up here. This is my community. I care about it."

"A lot of powerful narratives are about the long relationship between a family and a community. It's meaningful."

Bermea had read a document suggesting Hulme overcharged, but he felt what he was getting right now—a listener, interest, actual understanding—was well worth the price.

"It *is* meaningful," Bermea said. "It's the whole way I got in touch with you. I'm on the CAC board because I'm interested in the community. I want to be part of it, it's important to me."

"It's important to you because it's important, period. It's everything."

The document Bermea had read questioned Hulme's design skills. It suggested that though Hulme claimed he was an expert in designing logos, websites, brands, and corporate identities, he was not actually skilled at those things. It questioned the user experience of a website and claimed a logo Hulme had developed was pedestrian. The document suggested a cult of personality surrounded Hulme and that his value was largely a fantasy of his clients.

The Hulme sitting before Bermea, though, was attentive, thoughtful, and engaged. Bermea felt enlarged in his presence. He felt filled with potential, part of a life and community that were dynamic, poised to grow. This was about more than just Broadway Plumbing, it was about life. He felt excited, he felt real. He felt a connection.

"Do you know someone by the name of Don Geary?" he asked.

"No," Hulme said. "Should I?"

12 | "It needs to be more personal," Lana Luft-Castillo said.

Sheckley sat in one fabric chair, Elizabeth in another. Luft-Castillo's office was glass. Behind her was her diploma from Brown, a framed photo of the Liberty Bell, and a LeRoy Neiman print of horses mid-race, the jockeys leaning forward in their goggles and silks, the horses' nostrils flared, turf flying.

"How so?" Sheckley said.

"This reads like a typical mass-mailed letter," Luft-Castillo said. "I want a letter that reads like it was written to each donor individually."

Sheckley looked at Elizabeth. She was his immediate supervisor.

"Something they won't just toss aside," she said.

"Something that reads as if it's from me," Luft-Castillo said. "This is good, Kevin, don't get me wrong. But it reads like it's from Cascadia Arts. I want something that reads like it's from me."

It was ten thirty and Sheckley had a number of things to get done that day. He returned to his desk, keyboard before him, a hard copy of the letter next to it. The letter was a variation on the donor letter that had been sent out the previous year. Elizabeth had composed that letter. Sheckley had assumed a simple update would be fine. He read it again. It was clean, clear, and direct. He set to work.

"This is an intermediate step," Luft-Castillo said. "Some of this is a bit clunky, but I see where it's headed." She had three small white boxes of Thai food on her desk. Steam rose from two of them, but the third was inert, a mystery. She ate with a white plastic fork.

"Which parts are clunky?" Sheckley said.

Elizabeth wasn't there this time. There was no one for Sheckley to look to.

"'Though my duties as Executive Director may have kept me busy at an event and prevented me from saying hello or chatting with you, I was always glad to see you there,'" Luft-Castillo read. "It sounds a bit fake."

"It is fake," Sheckley said.

"Let's not be fake."

"There's no reason to be fake."

"Let's find a way to make this personal that isn't fake," Luft-Castillo said.

CAC was an open office, the desks arranged in order of hierarchy. Luft-Castillo's office was at the back of the room, behind glass walls. Elizabeth's desk was the first outside of Luft-Castillo's office. Sheckley's desk was at the other end of the room, just behind the receptionist's area. He wore headphones when he needed to concentrate, because otherwise he heard every interaction at the reception desk. Jen answered the phone with the same phrase at least thirty times a day.

Sheckley tried to rewrite the letter. He felt a hand on his shoulder and looked up to find Louise standing behind him.

"Is that it?" she whispered.

He nodded.

"What draft is this?"

He held up his hand, fingers spread.

"Oh, Sheck," Louise said. "Poor, poor Sheck."

The CAC's offices were at street level, behind a single long pane of glass. People walking past saw Jen sitting at the reception desk. If the light was right and they looked carefully, they could also see deeper, to where Sheckley sat at his desk and stared at his screen.

Later in the afternoon they had a staff meeting. Luft-Castillo projected draft six onto the wall. "Sheckley needs help with the donor letter," she said.

Sheckley sat still, chin propped on his fist, eyes on the screen.

"We need something that connects with people, that is personal," Luft-Castillo said. "Cascadia Arts is about connecting with the community, so I want this letter to feel like a personal connection."

"It is a mass mailing though, right?" Louise said. "These are not unique letters."

"No, they're not unique letters," Luft-Castillo said carefully. "But I don't want them to feel like form letters, either. I don't want them to feel impersonal."

"This is a language challenge," Elizabeth said.

"What kind of letter did we send last year?" Louise said. She looked at Sheckley, but his gaze stayed on the screen.

"I don't want to use last year's letter as a model," Luft-Castillo said. "I want us to brainstorm some language here, some phrases that are fresh, that feel personal."

The group was silent. A few people nodded.

"Sheck, I assume you'll take notes? Jot down some of our ideas?" Luft-Castillo said.

"Of course," Sheckley said.

A pedestrian walking past would have seen, in the middle depths of the office, the staff seated around a long wooden table. Everyone other than Sheckley looked at the screen on the wall. Sheckley walked to his desk to retrieve a yellow legal pad. There was a curious lack of expression on his face.

Later, he moved quietly about his apartment. One of Brooke's friends had rented a storefront on Alberta Street in which she was going to open a vintage dress shop, and Brooke was spending the evening there helping set up the store. Sheckley made himself a sandwich. When he finished eating it, he washed his dish and a knife and set them in the dishdrain.

He thought he might read for a bit, but none of the magazines in the apartment appealed to him, and he didn't want to open a book. He put on a record, but halfway through the first song he changed his mind and turned it off. He looked out the window into the evening. Cars slipped past, each with the rising whir of a door closing against a draft. He picked up his phone.

Your analysis is accurate. I'll be happy to second it at the meeting, he texted.

Geary's reply arrived a minute later: *I'm not making many friends.*

Making friends is overrated, Sheckley wrote back.

Four

1 | "Paul Alexander is someone you would like," Louise said.

"The guy by the wine?"

"With his back to us. He's an architect. A real architect, not apartment buildings or anything like that. He's brilliant."

The Cascadia Arts event space was a long, dark chamber with wine and candles. Geary recognized some people, but most were strangers. The men wore starched shirts with silk ties, the women black dresses and expensive sandals.

"He reads fiction, too," Louise said. "Unlike most men."

Elizabeth stood at the back of the room. She was in black slacks and a beige silk blouse—usually she wore tortoiseshell glasses, but not now. She laughed at something someone had said, and Geary realized she was talking to Hal Bermea. He hadn't heard from Bermea since he and Sheckley had met with him. Geary recalled the dusty metal shelves, the pieces of hardware on the floor. Bermea was gesturing emphatically, index finger stabbing the air.

The room was ringed by orange lights set chest-high in the concrete walls, each light covered by a glass panel with a black line drawing etched in it: a dancer mid-leap, an actor gesticulating, a paintbrush trailing a thick line. The light nearest the door featured "The Thinker," chin on fist.

"Seems dark in here for a board meeting," Louise said. "It feels like we're out to dinner."

"There isn't a picture for writing," Geary noted.

"On the lights? It's probably too hard to make writing seem interesting. I guess they could have done typewriter keys."

"There's not an architecture picture, either. So the brilliant architect is also left out."

"No, we have architecture. There's a drawing of Fallingwater, over by the bookshelf."

"I see," Geary said. "I'm going to get some food."

"Could you get me a glass of wine?"

He sidestepped one group and slipped behind another, taking care not to pass between people in conversation. Louise chatted with a group nearby. She was tall, her smile relaxed. She looked people in the eye and nodded, encouraging them. People felt relieved to find her in a crowd, they opened up to her.

"Hal Bermea is already talking about David Hulme," Elizabeth told Louise.

"Is there a way I can avoid him tonight?" Louise said.

"Don't go near the wine."

Bermea remained by the table with open bottles and clean glasses. He was speaking to Lana Luft-Castillo, who listened with an expression of great seriousness.

"I don't think I've ever met his wife," Louise said. "He's at a lot of events, but he never brings her."

"It's suspicious," Elizabeth said.

"Maybe she doesn't exist."

"He's upset about the review. He says we have to address it. I should have known Don would do something like that."

"I think it's funny," Louise said.

"I did too, at first. But it has become unfunny—especially after the meeting with Kevin this afternoon."

Louise looked at her. "She did not."

"She did."

"Are you kidding me?"

Lust-Castillo had made her way to them. She wore the same red dress she'd worn to previous board meetings. Her wine glass held water. "I think it's time," she said. "Where's the rest of the staff?"

"Most are already in the office," Louise said.

"We should get started before people start having second glasses of wine."

"Anyone in particular?" Elizabeth said.

"Of course not," Luft-Castillo said. She surveyed the room. "We should have done this on a Saturday morning, like usual."

"An evening board meeting was your idea," Elizabeth said.

"I wondered how long it would take before you pointed that out."

"I think we've mentioned it every week for a month."

"Always graciously," Luft-Castillo said. "Here's Mr. Alston."

"We should start the board-only meeting before—"

"I was just saying that," Luft-Castillo said.

"Otherwise we're going to be here until midnight," Alston said.

Alston was efficient in the manner of men who have called meetings to order across multiple decades. Though he was semi-retired now, it was not for lack of energy. He moved through the room, offering directives to everyone he passed. He knew more about the actual health and viability of the Cascadia Arts Council than anyone scheduled to speak that evening.

"We're going to go ahead and start," he said. "Ladies, if you could head over to the office for a bit while we begin with board members only…If you could take your seats, please…Let's go ahead and close the doors, and if everyone but the board could step into the other room…"

"Can we bring wine to the office?" Jen asked. As receptionist, she was free to be direct about certain issues.

"Is there any left?"

"There better be. Lana had us buy ten extra bottles."

"We don't go into the meeting?" Geary asked.

"The board has a discussion without us first," Elizabeth said. She did not quite turn to him, did not quite look him in the eye.

Louise took him by the arm and led him toward the reception desk. "There are probably some things we should explain," she said. "Wait, have you met Sheila? She runs the grants and fellowships programs. Sheila, this is Don Geary. He wrote the identity report."

Sheila had the faint mustache of a woman who has a bad light in the bathroom, or perhaps has freed herself from caring what others think. She wore a pilled gray sweater with jeans and boots, as if the season too did not matter. "Is the report as brutal as I hear?" she said.

"Brutal? It's honest," Louise said. "It's also the best looking report I've ever seen."

"It's the honesty people are talking about," Sheila said.

"Sheila has been here longer than anyone else. She's probably seen dozens of CAC identities over the years," Louise said.

"We didn't call them identities. We put our logo on stationery. That was it."

"I think some honesty is good for these things," Louise said.

"What things do you mean?"

"Sometimes you have to say what you think."

Geary scanned the office area, looking for Sheckley. He hadn't seen him yet.

"What do you hope to get by saying what you think?" Sheila asked.

"Learning. Improvement," Louise said.

"Do you think we've been improving? I think we've just been getting bigger. Other organizations used to do a lot of the things we do now, but we crowded them out. Some we took over directly. It's mostly a matter of having money."

It wasn't like Sheckley to be late. Geary knew he could text Sheckley, but he was in the middle of this conversation, and Sheila had turned to him.

"Can you think of an arts organization whose health isn't a function of how much money it has?"

"That probably depends on how you define health," Geary said.

"You can define it however you want. I'm just asking if you can think of one."

"I don't think Godard had access to much. At least not in the beginning."

"What?" She looked at him as if he'd said something

in a foreign language, but then her eyes widened in delight. "The French New Wave. I'm not sure that's an organization. But when I saw those movies in college, they changed my life."

Events can often be read by noting who is absent rather than who is present. Sheila was saying something about how in the nineties the CAC had given screenwriting fellowships. None of the screenplays had ever been produced, though—the money had just disappeared. No one had been able to decide if they'd funded bad screenwriters or if it was that screenwriters of creativity and conviction were precisely the ones who never got anything produced. Alston had closed the doors to the events room. All of the staff members were on the office side now, and Geary wasn't sure where to sit. Everyone else worked there, they had a place. People settled on desks, moved chairs. The conversations were about work, donors, which food carts were the best, issues Geary knew nothing about and which did not involve him. At events he usually looked for other outsiders, people there due to an actual interest in the topic and therefore somewhat embarrassed or abashed. He avoided anyone working a room, anyone who walked up and started speaking too confidently. This was not a place where he could make that distinction. One of the staff members knocked over a cup of water and laughed. She used her palm to sweep the liquid over the edge of the desk and said she would get the rest of it later.

Elizabeth was talking to Luft-Castillo at the opposite end of the room. She had not spoken to Geary about his report other than a brief email to thank him for delivering it. He couldn't tell if she was angry or if he was imagining it. If she had come to him and said, Listen, you criticized something we spent a lot of money on, someone we've featured at more than one event, this is a problem—he would have been able to talk about it with her. If you just wanted me to sign off on something and take a check, you should have told me, he might have said. I thought I was supposed to be analytical, I thought that's what you wanted. You called me and pitched this, I don't even want to be here this evening. She was involved in a conversation with Luft-Castillo, though, at the far back of the room. He wasn't even sure she cared. Maybe she was just busy.

"Could you ask Lana and Elizabeth to come in?" Alston said. He had opened the door from the event space just wide enough to poke his head out. Luft-Castillo and Elizabeth nodded and left the office area through a door at the back of the room, some second way into the event space.

The staff ate hors d'oeuvres on paper plates. Sheila complained about the film society, how it was run by kids in their twenties. Someone was playing a video on a computer. Geary couldn't hear the audio, but the three people huddled around the screen laughed. Two other staffers—women Geary didn't know—had gone back into Luft-Castillo's office and closed the door. Sheila looked at the printed agenda and said the board-only part of the meeting was supposed to last just ten minutes, but it had already gone twenty.

They finished their food and drinks. Jen snuck into the small kitchen behind the event space and retrieve a baguette and a bottle of sparkling water. She carried them to the reception desk like a hero, offering chunks of bread and filling people's glasses as if she were a waitress. Her coworkers laughed, asked whether they would have to tip her at the end of the evening.

"Did they forget about us?" Louise said. "Sheila, tell them we're coming in whether they like it or not."

Sheila was standing by the glass door to the event space, peering through. "Hal just keeps talking," she said.

"They just never get tired of hearing themselves."

Louise had also moved toward the door when Alston appeared and opened it.

"Did you have the whole meeting without us, Randy?"

"I'm sorry about the delay," he said. "Everyone, come in. Please come in."

Geary let everyone else move ahead of him. "Randy, when I present the report…" he said.

"Yes?"

"Does everyone have a copy? Do I have to explain from the beginning?"

"Oh, you don't need to worry about that. We've already been discussing it."

Louise had pulled out the chair next to her and was gesturing to Geary to take it.

"You'll be entering the middle of a conversation," Alston said.

"A conversation about what?"

"Don." Alston took him by the arm. "You don't need to do much here."

"The other day you said this was the whole point."

"Well. Other issues have arisen."

Louise stood by her chair, waiting for him. The room looked larger now that everyone was seated. When Geary and Andrea had first moved to Portland, CAC's offices had been somewhere else. The room he was now entering had been a dry cleaner's—he had carried shirts and slacks through the front door more than once. There had been a low, paneled ceiling. The space had been filled with steaming machines and clothing on racks.

"Randy said we're entering the middle of a conversation," Geary told Louise. "He told me there's not much I need to do."

"We should have kept the meeting on a Saturday morning."

"I had tickets to a play tonight," Sheila said.

People continued chatting after the staff members found seats. Hal Bermea sat at the head of the table. He cleared his throat once, then again. Elizabeth was seated next to Luft-Castillo on the other side of the table, far from Geary. They sat silently, waiting. Geary was pleased to understand little would be asked of him. Like a horse with blinders, he was aware only of his desire to run well. His own position, the betting interests, what became of the injured, these were mysteries.

"I'm willing to skip discussion of my program entirely if it gets us back on schedule," Sheila whispered.

The meeting resumed. The orderliness of the procedure, the way in which Roberts' Rules were carefully followed, approval of old minutes dutifully moved and seconded and voted upon, struck Geary as a bizarre affectation.

"You can probably sneak out of here after your presentation," Louise said.

Sheila wrote something in a small notebook. Geary could see it was a grocery list. He sat straight, uncertain if he was being observed, unclear of the connection between his report and whatever conversation had occurred before the staff's entrance. In an hour he would be home. Tomorrow morning he would deposit the check he would receive for his report and would use the money to buy groceries.

Attention turned to the head of the table, where Hal Bermea sat smiling.

"Don, we've met," Bermea said. "Though I imagine it's surprising to you that someone like me is on the Cascadia Arts board."

"Not surprising at all," Geary said. "Kevin Sheckley told me that some time ago."

"Yes, I know. Honestly, Don, we don't really need much more from you."

He left forty-five minutes later, during a lull while Sheila and Jen struggled to set up a video projector. The sun had slipped behind the West Hills. Geary drove east across the river, the first stars showing like pin pricks in a soft sky. The kids were with Andrea—he'd traded nights with her. When he walked into the house, their plastic cups were in the kitchen sink. Nathan's Nerf gun lay on the coffee table. Emily's blue blanket was abandoned on the couch.

Hal Bermea is a deeply weird person, he texted Sheckley. *The meeting was only halfway over when I left. Why weren't you there?*

He turned on the television and flipped through the channels that played old television shows or pan-and-scan versions of movies. When he found Bob Newhart holding a group counseling session, he stopped, pleased. Sheckley didn't text back.

2 | The morning was golden. Birds sang from sunrise on, tireless. Trees fluttered in the breeze. Sheckley was at home, taking a day off.

Stop by if you have time today, he texted.

Have to run an errand later this moring. Could stop by then if that works, Geary wrote.

I have a funny story to tell you, Sheckley wrote.

Geary arrived at eleven. The flowers out front were wilting in the heat. The brick apartments looked baked, dusty. The sunsoaked neighborhood lay silent.

"I'm going to have a beer," Sheckley said. "Want one? It's some kind of summer thing."

"Absolutely."

Sheckley pried the cap off. "Lana gave me two months notice," he said. "There's another after that if you want it. She said I'm not the right fit for Cascadia Arts, which is fine. A month is a lot of time."

"What?"

"Sorry, I just put these in the fridge," he said. "I guess they're not all the way cold. I'm going to put mine in the freezer for a few minutes. Want me to put yours in, too?"

"I'm okay either way."

"Freezer," Sheckley said. He grabbed Geary's beer and went into the apartment. Geary sat patiently. Scheckley had set two chairs in the small shaded space behind the apartment. A rusted silver air conditioning unit sat amid ferns that bordered the narrow concrete path.

"I'll grab those in a few minutes," Sheckley said.

"What's going on?"

Sheckley sat, offered a weak smile. "Your text about Hal Bermea made me laugh. It's true. He's even weirder than you know."

"How so?"

"He sent me a two-line email a few days ago to tell me he decided to go with someone else to redesign his website. Can you think of someone in town who would actually indulge his fantasy to have a plumbing company version of the ESPN site? Someone who would charge him a ton of money for a weird vanity project?"

"One of the big ad agencies?"

"I'll give you a hint: it's someone we've been talking about."

"No. David Hulme."

"Yes."

"David Hulme is going to redesign the Broadway Plumbing website? Wait, he doesn't do that. Hulme is going to develop a new identity for Hal Bermea's plumbing and heating company."

"I can't imagine how much Hal is paying."

"I bet I know exactly how much he's paying," Geary said. "I bet the number is right in the report I wrote. Hal is the chairman of the CAC board. I criticized Hulme in that report, and Hal just hired him?"

"Let me get those beers."

Geary studied the fronds of the ragged, sickly ferns. They were covered with tiny red spores, dots invisible to the eye if one wasn't looking for them.

"I don't know if that helped. They're maybe a little colder," Sheckley said.

"The board must have decided I was totally wrong. They must have trashed my entire report right before I walked into the meeting."

"Not necessarily. It's just Hal who didn't agree."

Geary looked at him. "Did my report get you fired?"

"No. Lana is an idiot is what got me fired. It's not possible to produce what she wants. The woman who had the position before me only lasted a year before she quit. I emailed her yesterday and she said getting out was the best thing she ever did. I'm going to have lunch with her next week. A month is a good amount of time to find something new."

"This isn't right."

"It's kind of cold back here in the shade. Should we go inside? There's sun there, at least."

While they were carrying their chairs in, Sheckley's phone rang. "Kevin Sheckley," he said. "Oh, that's not necessarily the case, I'm still doing some of that." He listened. "It's not an issue of time. I'm in Portland, Oregon. Where are you guys?"

Sheckley had a spider plant on a round wire stand in the corner of the living room, and another plant on a similar stand next to the fireplace. Classical guitar played on the stereo. Sheckley came back, held up his phone, and laughed. Like a magician before an audience, he made a show of pushing the button to silence it and the button to turn it off, then dropped it onto the couch. Geary recalled the Sheckley of the past, an analog man who biked everywhere, made his own bread, and sipped coffee from a mason jar while reading library books in a rented room. The business conversations, life in the city's cultural circles—Sheckley probably wished he was chopping firewood at a campsite, preparing to walk down to some quiet spot on a lake where he would try to catch some fish.

"I once said I would never own a cell phone," Sheckley said.

He could still write. And he was on good terms with people at other nonprofits in town, he said—it wasn't like he was going to pack it in and look for a job at a coffee-house. "I love coffeehouses, but I've already done that, a few times."

There were al sorts of opportunities for a writer in town, he said. He looked at his bookshelves, at the old typewriter—it worked, he'd had it repaired—currently beig used as a bookend. He was at home in sentences. He liked to consider different phrasings, the impact of certain words.

"I assume everything I'm saying is also being said by dozens of unemployed writers in town at this exact moment."

"I don't think so," Geary said.

"Only a few?"

"At this time of day most of them are napping."

"I have to stay in the mix," Sheckley said. "I have to maintain my contacts, check in with everyone, see what's out there."

The classical guitar piece had ended. A dulcet toned male voice discussed the fineness of the composition and its playing. It was the same male voice that had discussed classical music Geary's entire life, on every classical music station he'd ever heard.

"I'm going to find something better," Sheckley said.

A hummingbird appeared outside the window. It zipped toward the branches of a nearby tree, twitched its head, shifted three feet higher in the air, and hovered. Then it disappeared. It had maybe gone up over the roof of the apartment, but Geary wasn't sure, it had been too quick to see.

"I also kind of can't believe they got rid of me," Sheckley said.

"They're idiots."

"I thought the wandering around was over. No more trying to figure things out all the time."

"You'll find something better," Geary said. What am I talking about? he thought. Is there really anything to find? "You said you have a month. That's plenty of time."

"Brooke is working. That's good."

"I haven't talked to her since I left dinner that night."

"I thought this was who I was going to be," Sheckley said. "From the first day, I thought, This is the right place for me. I know how to do this."

"You do know how to do it."

"I can't believe I have to start again," he said. "How many times does a person have to start over?"

3 | On the hottest days he closes the windows, lowers the shades, and works in half-light. Emily's stuffed horse lays as if asleep, its reins worn and cracked where her fingers grasp the plastic. Clean clothes, not yet folded, sit in a pile on the futon.

In the basement, Geary lies on the bed. Unable to sleep, he arose before dawn and started work. Now, mid-morning, fatigue overcomes him. He lies on his back, arms at his side, palms up. He has an alarm set for twenty minutes—he doesn't want to fall too deeply asleep, lose too much of the day. Once, stuck in a grocery store parking lot on a weekday afternoon, he said to Nathan and Emily, "Never go to the grocery during the day."

"Why?" they asked.

"You think it will be faster because everyone is at work. But who's here? Old people, weird people, crazy people. Look how long we're waiting for this guy. He's just sitting there. Here we go. And this will be…a three-point turn to get out of a parking space. Now it's a five-point turn."

"Dad, you're being mean."

"You can just back out of a parking space and leave, there's no five-point turn necessary. Don't go to the grocery store during the day."

He knew he was no longer young, no longer someone professionals would speak of as having potential, whom they would see growing with their firm. He does not want to nap more than twenty minutes because he does not believe a man should nap at all. He does not believe a man should be in his basement on a weekday morning. A man should not be home at all on a workday.

His phone rang, but not the chime he expected, and he could not understand what the device was trying to tell him. He fumbled with it, stared at the strange number on the screen, and answered by saying his name.

"Don, this is Evan Craig," a voice said. "I work for Paula Holt at Ad Astra, in San Franciso. I understand you had a meeting with her recently."

"Yes."

"We just signed a couple new clients, and we had some people move on, and Paula suggested I might call and see if you'd be interested in a position. She said you do the kind of work that fits our aesthetic."

Geary was sitting on the edge of the bed now, studying the floorboards. "I'm definitely interested."

"We'd be looking for someone as soon as possible. How soon would you be available?"

"I'm available now."

There was a pause at the other end of the line. "I'm not talking about freelancing or working remotely. We work collaboratively here. Paula believes in the importance of being in the room together, of the value of conversation."

"Of course."

"I guess what I'm asking is if you'd be interested in moving. Our office is in San Francisco, as you know."

"Moving to San Francisco."

"Or somewhere nearby. But yes."

His mind was clearing, returning to normal speed. He stood and moved toward his desk.

"I know there are a lot of things you're going to want to consider," the man said.

"What kind of salary are you offering?"

"That would be one of the things to consider. But first we would want to know if relocating is even something you would be able to do. I know I've caught you by surprise, I expect you may want to think about this for a day or two. We are looking for someone soon, though."

He had three large bookshelves along the wall behind his desk. The books were carefully arranged, with gaps for framed photos of Nathan, of Emily, of a sunset over the Rocky Mountains, snapped in the 1980s from in front of his childhood home. The image was faded, grainy. He had put it on a shelf in every place he had ever lived.

He began his conversation with Louise casually. They joked about children, how they had a radar for detecting and interrupting any attempt at working at home. He and Louise had first met in a writing group, and Louise continued to speak to him as if he were a writer, though she was aware he spent his time on other things now.

"It makes me sick," she said. "I can't stand her."

They sat at the picnic table in Louise's backyard. A metal fire pit sat further up the slope of the yard. Berry bushes grew along the back fence. The raspberries were ripe, but the strawberries were still green.

"She didn't just make the decision on her own, though, right?" Geary said.

"Lana's not decisive enough to make a decision on her own."

"Was Elizabeth unhappy with him?"

"No. Elizabeth is the one who chose him in the first place. Hal Bermea went through the budget and said the staff was too big, he didn't see why Elizabeth couldn't handle the writing herself, or delegate it to other staff members. This is all according to Elizabeth. All of this is confidential."

Jeffrey stepped out the back door. There was sawdust in his hair, he'd been in the forest all day. He still had his battered denim overalls on over a long-sleeved shirt. They talked about the forest for a bit, how quiet it was up in the trees, how you understood the forest differently forty feet off the ground. Branches moved oddly in the breeze, Jeffrey said. They seemed alive, to have their own ideas.

"You're not scared of heights?" Geary said.

"No."

"I definitely like the idea of quiet. I usually look for it at ground level, though."

"I can't find it at ground level is the problem," Jeffrey said.

Louise put a plate in front of Jeffrey, passed him the chips and guacamole and raspberries and cheese. "Hal had to persuade the other board members, of course," Louise said, "but they didn't do the math. They just assumed he knew what he was talking about. Which he didn't."

Geary didn't say anything. He looked at the grass, but absently. Not really looking.

"We're talking about Sheckley," Louise said to Jeffrey.

"About…"

"Lana cutting his position."

He nodded. "It seems…not right," he said.

"It makes the board feel important to have demands," Louise said. "Like they're really smart and did something useful. And Lana has to keep the board happy so they don't accuse her of mismanaging the place and get rid of her. So because she doesn't have any backbone, she did what she thought was safest for herself. It's bizarre. Sheckley used to write copy for Hal's company. Hal knew the position that would be cut was Sheckley's."

"Hello, everyone," Louise's son Michael said as he came around the side of the house. He still had a basketball uniform on. He was bashful, quiet, like a sleepy animal. They put out a plate for him and he accepted food silently, with a smile and a nod.

At the top of the backyard was a hammock strung between two trees, the netting gray with age. Three large stumps sat in a semicircle near the hammock, rough seats Jeffrey had crafted with his chainsaw. An old yellow Frisbee sat in the grass, its label faded. The bowls that held the guacamole and berries were irregularly shaped school ceramics projects.

"What about David Hulme?" Geary said. "What's he going to be doing next for CAC?"

"David Hulme?" Louise said. "Don't waste any more energy on David Hulme."

"I'm not short of energy. I'm sure he had something to do with this."

"Why do you think that?"

"Why wouldn't I? I'd just be interested to know what the next inspiring David Hulme event is."

"I can look on the calendar at work—if you promise you're not going to do anything stupid."

"I'm not stupid," Geary said.

He had known Louise and Jeffrey for seven years now. He understood Jeffrey had only ever wanted to be a forester, that he'd worked years to build his business. Louise had only ever been interested in the arts, she'd worked temporary or part-time positions all over, trying to find something durable. Everything in their yard—the hammock, the bowls, the table, the Frisbee—was evidence of a paycheck they'd earned, a month they'd made it through, the life they had built and were able to offer their sons and each other.

The world frustrates our dreams and imagination, and we decide there is a reality separate from our desire. We become convinced of this. How do we come to accept it? When Geary asked about Hal Bermea and David Hulme, Louise answered, but she was watching him. She had known him long enough to know he sometimes tested boundaries. He held a quiet, carefully-nursed contempt for reality.

Later he was at home, picking up the kids' rooms, bringing order to the house. The sun had gone down and he played music loud on the stereo, old songs he would not have listened to with others in the room.

He picked up his phone and texted Park. *I have some dark web stuff I want to ask you about. Totally hypothetical.*

It was only two or three minutes before his phone buzzed. *I'm sure I don't know what you mean*, Park wrote.

4 | Bermea had played baseball when he was a child, and he never let go of the game. It had been years since he'd taken the field, but he could recall with great exactness the feel of his hand inside the leather glove, the pop of a well-thrown ball hitting the pocket. He suffered the frustration of watching boys outpace him in other sports for no reason other than that they were taller, or their frames more muscular. Bermea was short and stocky, but this had not affected his place in baseball. He played third base all the way through high school, knocking down lined grounders with his stomach and chest, the bruises a point of pride. He batted in the middle of the order, had a good eye, made contact. In the dugout he chewed sunflower seeds and cursed. Nothing in life had matched playing baseball.

He liked to start summer mornings with highlights. He was a Yankees man, though he followed the Mariners too, out of regional duty. He knew the players, which pitchers were having problems with their mechanics, which hitters were in a slump. He was watching Mark Teixeira hit a home run in Yankee Stadium when someone knocked on his office door. He studied the smooth swing, the way the ball rose into the sky.

"Are we running some kind of online promotion?" Roger asked, stepping into the office. "Are we doing something new?"

"What do you mean?"

"Everything on our website is a dollar."

Bermea looked at him. Roger didn't say anything more, he didn't move. "What do you mean everything on our website is a dollar?"

"I mean every product we have for sale on the site is currently priced a dollar. Hardware, fixtures, everything, it's all a dollar. We're getting a lot of orders."

Bermea pulled up the site. The home page looked normal. He clicked to product pages, to fixtures, to sinks. A grid opened up four columns wide and twelve rows long: forty-eight sinks. Each showed the same price. One dollar.

"I don't understand," Bermea said.

"Have we been hacked? Is it the Chinese?"

He clicked to pipes, PVC. A long grid again filled the page, each product showing the same price. He selected one, went to the cart, then to checkout. The pipe cost a dollar. Shipping was a dollar. His order total was two dollars.

"This can't be, I didn't do this. We didn't do this," Bermea said.

"Who's in charge of the site these days? Our web people can take it down, right?" Roger said.

Bermea couldn't think. He wanted to tear his hair, claw the skin from his face. "Fuck!" he yelled.

"What should we do about the orders we've gotten?"

He looked at Roger, breathing hard. "What the fuck do you expect me to say?" he said.

5 | In late June—it had been more than a month by then—she was stepping out of a deli after lunch and saw Kevin Sheckley headed toward her. The street's geometry

shifted, it seemed to tilt. The sun was on her face, but beyond the buildings across the street she saw dark clouds to the north.

"…but what if you have a serious kid who wants to kick ass?" Gavin was saying. "You have to look at a club's coaches, and that club's coaching is poor."

"Yes. I don't know much about that," she managed to say. Her hands had gone cold, she felt the urge to run. She knew this would happen at some point. She worked just a few blocks from CAC, saw Sheckley on the street every month or two. He'd shaved. Without his mustache and beard he looked younger. He wore jeans and a yellow t-shirt with a drawing of a tree on it—the tree's tangled roots formed the face of an old man. The man's eyes were closed, as if he were a forest spirit asleep and dreaming the tree. Or maybe the tree was dreaming him. The shirt made Sheckley seem a Tolkien fan from 1970 sent to the future to shame the people of the twenty-first century. She was in her best gray slacks and a new white blouse that hadn't even been washed yet. It was so bright it was practically glowing.

When she was a girl, her father had worn t-shirts like Sheckley's.

"How are you, Kevin?"

He smiled, hugged her. "I'm good. You?"

"This is my friend Gavin, he works in my building. We just got some lunch."

Gavin stood a step behind her. She was aware of his position, the exactness of the distance. She imagined him through Sheckley's eyes: the button-down shirt, the suit pants and leather shoes, the gold watch. The serious expression he wore as he stepped forward to shake Sheckley's hand, as if before to wrestling match.

There were things she wanted to ask Sheckley. It was impossible, though—not there, maybe not ever. She couldn't move from where she stood between Sheckley and the door, though. Everything about the timing of her life seemed off, and she couldn't get it back. She'd done nothing wrong but felt mortified. She couldn't be two different people at once on the sidewalk outside the deli.

Gavin had stationed himself a step behind and to her right, like a bodyguard.

"Are you going into the deli?" she said.

"Yes," Sheckley said. "I'm supposed to meet a friend to talk about a job."

"Are you not at the Arts Council anymore?"

"Just for a few more weeks. My time there has…come to an end."

She didn't understand. Getting the job at Cascadia Arts had been a huge success for Sheckley. He was one of the most guileless people she had ever met, and she couldn't imagine what he could do to get fired from a job. Neither could she imagine him quitting, though. "Lunch today is about your next job?" she said.

"No, just a freelancing thing. I'm not sure what I'm going to do for my next full-time job. If that even is a thing anymore."

"I'm sure you'll find something great. Have you seen Don lately?"

She looked him in the eye, trying to gauge what he knew, what he'd been told and what he hadn't. What could he possibly understand? Sheckley didn't have kids, he could do whatever he wanted. And Don had four evenings a week free from his own kids. She couldn't know what Don did, where he went and with whom. She had been able to see him one night a week, sometimes not even that. Now she knew even less. She wanted to grab Sheckley by the shirt and tell him he knew nothing, her son was in Seattle with her parents this week, it was the one week of the year she was free, and did Don even care?

Gavin stood behind her like a chaperone. Like a well-trained dog.

"Don had his own issue with Cascadia," Sheckley said. "They kind of went sideways on something he did for them. Then he also had a long-term project get canceled, so I think he's hustling now. That's kind of always the way, though."

"What project?"

"It was a website. A business concept, really."

"Not the one about books."

"Right. I didn't want to say too much, because I know there was some kind of confidentiality agreement. But I suppose it doesn't matter now."

She felt sick, as if lunch had been a mistake. Sheckley was describing a universe contrary to the one she lived in. She wanted to demand he tell her where Don was at that moment. She wanted never to have known of Don at all. She would be forty soon, she was thinking of moving to Seattle to be closer to her family. She needed to be in control of her life, she needed to make decisions. She could feel the thud of her own pulse.

She glanced at Gavin. He raised his eyebrows.

"But he worked on that forever," she said. "He put everything into that. Is he okay?"

"You know him, always even-keeled, always working on the next thing," Sheckley said. "I think my friend's waiting for me in there, I better go in. It was good to see you. Nice to meet you, Gavin."

"Yes, nice to meet you."

After Sheckley went through the door, Gavin asked how she knew him. He was a friend of a friend, she said. She made it maybe fifteen more steps until she told Gavin she would be right back, she'd forgotten to tell Sheckley something. She didn't wait for Gavin's response.

She found Sheckley sitting across from a woman with angular eyeglasses on a chain, like a nineteen-fifties librarian. He looked up at her, surprised.

"Kevin? Will you tell Don I said hello? Tell him I'm sorry the website got canceled. I didn't know."

"Of course."

"We haven't talked. Tell him he should call me. If he wants."

"Absolutely."

"Sorry to interrupt."

Gavin was waiting for her outside the door. A breeze had kicked up and the clouds to the north were almost black now. They walked past the movie theater, the bookstore, the sports bar, each building alive with people laughing and at leisure, many probably on vacation. Gavin made more points about kids' soccer, and she agreed with him.

She sat at her desk and concentrated on the numbers on the computer screen, the documents she needed to send. In college, she'd spent six months in Italy in a study abroad program. Florence. Uffizi. Rome. Historic cities, stone buildings that seemed avatars of ancient wisdom by day, and at night transformed into beacons of something supernatural, of the mysteries of life. She pictured herself walking those streets again, smarter now, more alive to what was at stake. That was who and where she was supposed to be. She needed to get back to the person she had been then, to the direction her life had been headed. She didn't know how to get there. The road had vanished.

At home that evening she made a pasta sauce from scratch, cookbook open on the kitchen counter, flour dust twisting in the air. She listened to the jazz station, the program on which they played the classic women singers crooning songs of heartbreak and loss. After she made herself dinner there were the dishes to do, then laundry. She took a long bath. She brought her book and stayed in the water for an hour. The time and silence were priceless, like delicacies. When she stood from the water she felt renewed, as if everything were possible. She dried herself, put on her shorts and t-shirt, and checked her phone. There was a text message photo of her son in his pajamas, giving her a thumbs up as he prepared for bed at her parents' house. He was smart, already he acted as if he didn't need her anymore, as if six was old enough to do it himself. She scrolled up and down, checking, but there were no other messages. She slipped into bed. She had made a decision. There would be more to make. They had parted on good terms. He'd even asked if she wanted to stay the night. She needed to keep her resolve, it was already hard enough. She couldn't imagine him not working on his books website, not planning for the unveiling of his great project. Everything had become something else. The world had changed its face, had become unknowable and strange.

She fell asleep with her book at her side, the lamp left on. At eleven o'clock her phone chimed and she woke with a start.

I had a great time at lunch today! Interested in dinner tomorrow? Gotta take advantage of your week of freedom!

It was Gavin.

6 | We prepare endlessly for the challenges we will face, but when they arrive they are of an entirely different character than we expected. And we are unprepared.

He went to a party at Arden's apartment. The rooms were full of people, most of whom he had never met. The men shook his hand formally, with firm grips. The women smiled. Reina wore a black dress with a scoop neck, stacked silver bracelets on her wrists. He realized he'd never seen her in a dress before. She seemed comfortable, settled. She introduced Geary to a man standing nearby. He was the creative director at the agency that had just hired Arden, she said. This was news to Geary. He stumbled through some questions and then noticed Arden at the kitchen counter.

"What do you want, Don?" Arden asked.

"It looks like you already have things set up. Whiskey, lemons—is there a house drink?"

"There is, but I have other things, too."

"The house drink is fine."

Arden opened a bottle of ginger ale and sliced more lemons. He wasn't making a single drink, he was mixing a pitcher. He poured whiskey in for what seemed an inordinate amount of time.

"I'm surprised," Geary said when he tried the drink Arden handed him. "I'm not even sure I can taste the liquor."

"If you drank ginger ale without the liquor you would know the difference. I can add more bourbon if you want, though—"

"No, no, that's not necessary," Geary said.

"There was a time I was doing stuff for one of the local distilleries and I decided I'd teach myself about whiskey,"

Arden said. "So I started drinking it neat. I was disciplined about it. I had whiskey every evening before bed. One day I was looking up at the ceiling and I said to myself, this can't continue."

"Did you have a favorite?" the creative director asked.

"The beauty of being a student is you can decide everything is worth your attention. My favorite was usually whichever one was in front of me. I could have earned a degree in it."

"I'd be careful about colleges granting degrees in whiskey," the creative director said.

"The materials get expensive, so I'd have to take out a loan," Arden said. "And I'm still paying my original student loans, so it's probably not in the cards."

"You'd probably learn more in whiskey conversations than I've learned in a lot of my grad school classes," Reina said.

Arden shook his head. "I think the content would devolve into loose political science. Or other people's problems."

"That's called psychology, I think."

"Conflict resolution," he said.

"I feel like we have plenty of those conversations anyway. Wouldn't you say that, Don? You spend time with him."

"Wait," Arden said. "Are you saying I'm the one who starts the discussion of personal problems?"

"No. Politics," she said.

"Well, someone has to acknowledge what a shit-show things have become."

"You have mentioned a certain disappointment in our current political system. Once or twice," Geary said.

More people arrived and squeezed into the apartment.

They began to gather outside, as well—on the concrete steps to the door, on the sidewalk below. Geary didn't like tight spaces. He drifted outside and fell into a discussion of movies. He was describing a French film whose title he couldn't remember.

"We were just talking about this the other day," a man said. "And I know this is wrong, that I'm wrong to feel this way, but are there any good movies made before, say, 1970? Every movie I look at that was made in the 1960s or earlier just seems awful. I know I'm wrong."

"Yes. You're wrong," Geary said. He was happy to say so. The man didn't care—he and the woman he was with were laughing. She had flowers woven into a bracelet on her right wrist.

"Maybe it's that I was born in the 1970s, so everything earlier seems prehistoric," the man said.

"*Butch Cassidy* is 1968," Geary said. "*2001* is also 1968."

"Okay, maybe 1968 is the dividing line. It's just—"

"What have you seen from before then?"

"I don't know. Charlie Chaplin."

"Charlie Chaplin?"

"The acting is always bad, the stories are so overdone, they're soap operas. The music in movies before—are we saying 1968?—the music is horrible."

Arden's apartment was on the corner, off the sloping street. They could look up and see most of the living room through the picture window. The brick and stucco building could have been built in any year and would have looked fine, no one would have questioned it.

Arden knew art, he knew film and whiskey. He knew which distilleries in town were less expensive but just as good. He knew the towns on the Oregon coast, the state parks, where to camp for a weekend, where for a full week. He stood in his kitchen, quartered lemons and limes stacking up, bottles of liquor, wine, and beer on the counter. He held a knife in his hand, still slicing citrus.

"Find the hotel you like best and ask them to set you up there for two months," he told Geary. "They can pay for your travel down there, all your moving expenses, a new computer, a new cell phone. They won't find that unusual, it's all part of relocating. They've definitely done it for other people."

"I'll need to fly up a couple weekends a month to be with my kids."

"Don't tell them that."

"Why?"

"It's personal stuff. You don't negotiate personal stuff."

The party had grown louder, the windows were wide open. They could see even more people had gathered outside on the sidewalk. Arden was looking in his refrigerator, searching for a can of cherries. "All of these jars look the same," he said. "Mustard, olives, chilis, cherries. The jars are all made by the same company, I think, they just put different labels on them. Wait, here it is."

"What kind of drinks are you making that require cherries?"

"All drinks I'm making now will have cherries."

The simplicity of his apartment, the carefully selected books, expertly framed posters, the single bedroom and bathroom and small kitchen with its small refrigerator. Now, during the party, it was a mess, but no children lived there, so the disorder was harmless and appropriate. Geary could imagine cleaning the entire place in half an hour. The only oddity was Arden's framed Kurosawa poster—it was down from the wall and propped in the corner. Geary asked why it had lost its place.

"I just got tired of it. You can't keep the same things up forever," Arden said.

"I'm going to have to leave early a couple Fridays a month to fly up here. Do I tell them that?"

"No. What you do on the weekend is your own business. There'll be a point where someone asks what you're doing for the weekend and you'll say you're going to Portland to spend the weekend with your kids. It's the same as if someone else says they're going to a baseball game. It doesn't matter, it's your own business." Arden seemed confident about this, though it was unclear whether it was a truth of negotiating or just a personal conviction. "Come up with a salary request you think is fair, then figure out the cost of two round-trip tickets a month for a year, and add that cost onto your salary request. Add what you think any hotels will cost, too. Just fold it all into the figure."

"I don't want to ask for something too high."

"It's San Francisco!" Arden said. "They're not going to think your salary request is too high. People burn cash for heat there. Ad Astra is a pretentious fucking high end firm, Don. I'd ask for six figures if I were you."

Geary was surprised. He'd been thinking half of that. He would need to start at the bottom and work his way up, he thought. His plan had been to add twenty percent to what he'd made on his own the previous year and ask for that.

Arden wasn't even looking at him, he was pouring vodka and juice into an oversized cocktail shaker. He didn't measure, his mixing was loose approximation. "They want what you do," he said. "You've been vetted by Peter, so they don't have to worry whether you're crazy. I bet Paula Holt called Peter before she ever had that guy call and offer you the job."

"I should ask for a low six figure, though, right?"

"If that's what makes you happy. Give me a call after you're done talking to them. I want to hear how they handle things."

"Do you want the job?"

"Me?" He shook the cocktail shaker with two hands. He was speaking loudly, over the din of the party and the ice rattling in the shaker. "The Bay Area makes me vomit. Tech bros, venture cap morons, they all think they're libertarians, with their little apps that turn people into slaves. Actual libertarians would beat the shit out of them. A modest Vermont libertarian who sells maple syrup and cuts his own firewood would physically and intellectually crush any tech billionaire."

"So then why am I moving there?"

"You're more mature than I am," Arden said. "You can handle things. And you have your kids to take care of."

The next day they came to him and asked if they could switch rooms. He thought, Perfect, let's go through all of the possessions. They pulled everything out, the dolls and guns and bells and books and folders and papers, they made piles in the living room, first in a kind of order but soon in chaos, things just thrown wherever there was a spot. They dragged pillows and blankets and bins from room to room, abandoning items along the eight foot journey, not bothering to acknowledge the things with a name, just saying I don't want this, I don't want that, this is too small, that's broken. Everything they had accrued in the years they'd lived there, everything he had given them, it was all spilled on the coffee table, the futon, every open inch of floorboard. He hid in the basement until they were ready and then he came back upstairs with his tools and took their beds apart and lugged them piece by piece from room to room and put them back together, sweating, caught up in their urgency. He remade the beds and told them putting their things away again was like school, it would be fun and free, but also mandatory.

He noticed how dirty their hands were, the grit under their nails. When Nathan asked to take a break, Geary called him into the bathroom. He grabbed the nail clippers and put them in Nathan's hand.

"Your fingernails are out of control. You guys need to start doing this kind of thing yourselves."

"Mom does it for us."

"Mom can't keep doing everything for you. You're old enough now that you can learn how to do this."

He showed Nathan how to hold the clippers, how to slip the blade under the nail, how the mechanism worked.

"I'm scared," Nathan said. "I don't know how to keep it under there."

"You just…"

"Can you do it?"

"No, you do it. That's the only way you'll learn."

Nathan struggled. He didn't have the dexterity. The clippers fell to the floor and Geary picked them up and put them back in Nathan's hand. They fell again and Geary picked them up and put them back in his hand again. Nathan bent over his hand, the clippers wobbling as he tried to find a decisive grip, the right moment. "I can't do it."

"You can. It just takes a little practice."

Nathan could not close the blade firmly, though. He made a weak attempt and then overcorrected and squeezed the lever as hard as he could. He cried out—a crooked slice appeared in the edge of his thumbnail.

"You didn't do anything," Geary said.

"It hurt!"

"It did not. It's out on the edge."

"It did, it hurts, how do you know what I feel?"

"Give me that."

Emily appeared at the bathroom door. She was carrying a pink bin of Legos. "What are you doing?" she asked.

"Nathan's learning to trim his fingernails. You're next."

She disappeared, Legos rattling away into the bedroom. "Give me your hand."

"You're shaking," Nathan said. "Why are you shaking?"

"I'm just tired, that's all. I'm super tired."

He braced the clippers against the thumbnail to steady himself and clipped cleanly, trimming Nathan's angled slice and then rounding the nail.

"I'm sorry I couldn't do it," Nathan said.

"It's my fault. You tried."

He moved to the index finger, working quickly. He wiped his eyes with the back of his hand.

"Are you crying?"

"I'm just tired. I'm super tired."

When he finished Nathan's nails and called Emily, she announced before even stepping into the bathroom that she couldn't do it by herself. She'd tried before, she said, but it didn't work, it was too hard, it was scary.

"I know," he said. "I was wrong. It's fine."

She stepped into the bathroom, put her hand in his, and looked up at him. Her little fingers, her tiny nails.

7 | He chopped down the laurels. He had a list of chores he needed to take care of around the house, including Kressler's complaint about the yard. Cutting the laurels was giving in to Kressler's manipulation, but when Geary was forced to do something against his will, he liked to do it thoroughly. He believed there was a way to do the wrong thing so well that it shamed the person who had asked for it. He knew this led to him spending significant time on tasks he despised, but it was the only way he knew to find pleasure in the joyless.

He hated that he had to cut the laurels. It was a spite job, he was cutting the laurels out of spite.

He'd gone into the basement, back beyond the washing machine to where he kept his tools, and grabbed his heavy gloves, the yellow-handled tree saw, the pruning shears, the metal garden rake, and the plastic leaf rake. He'd rubbed sunscreen into his face and neck and arms and put on his baseball hat. The point of executing the spite job was to show that one could enter the crucible and remain there as required. By allowing the enemy to choose the weapon, you suggested you could win any weapon. By suggesting you could win with any weapon, you implied the fight was not about the weapon. You were saying, essentially, that you were invulnerable. Kressler had decided to make an issue of the thirty laurels that lined the side of the yard and now stood fifteen feet tall. Geary decided he would end the issue by chopping the laurels, one by one, to six feet. He had work gloves and a tree saw and an iron will.

He stood before the fifth laurel now. He was working from the top of the yard down. He lopped off the branches that extended from the trunks, any foliage in the way, and then tossed the loppers aside and grabbed the saw and held the trunk of the laurel in his right hand while he sawed with his left. The wood was soft, white shavings flew from the blade. By doing this alone, methodically, he was proving he could accomplish great tasks alone and methodically. Four laurels already lay across the lawn. Sometimes the blade tried to cut at an angle rather than straight across, sometimes the teeth caught on something, some tough or twisted fiber in the wood, and he had to ease the pressure and recover the rhythm.

Success is not something that is handed to you. Doctors in residency work insane hours until they drop, young lawyers work sixty or eighty hour weeks. There is always a test of the will. It will be difficult to move to San Francisco. He knows this. There will be adversity. But being unemployed and broke in Portland wasn't a career. Moving to San Francisco to work for Ad Astra was the step forward. It was money, opportunity, and advancement. It was success.

He hadn't spoken to Andrea about it. He wasn't sure how to frame it, and he needed to wait until it was official, anyway. They could come to an arrangement—the kids could spend the summer in San Francisco. He could visit at the holidays, he could take them on trips to visit his parents. He would find ways to make it work.

He continued sawing. The laurels were soft, weak. When he reached the last few fibers he pulled the trunk toward him so that it fell into his yard rather than over the fence.

In three years of renting the house he had become less and less able to see it. The gray vinyl siding was lined by a shadow of faint gray moss. The backyard grass was half weeds, the lower level where no grass grew entirely weeds. The narrow passage between the side of the house and the fence: weeds. The house had been empty for a few months before he moved in, and he remembered the early months, pulling every weed, removing the overgrowth, cutting down and tearing out three trees in the front yard, keeping track of what he'd spent on supplies so he could write it off the rent. Kessler had been thrilled. Covered in dirt, building the dream, Geary had crafted a home.

He had cleaned the inside, too—Wednesday afternoons, before she came over for dinner. Every room dusted, the sheets clean, the bed made, a record on the turntable, a vodka tonic waiting for her. Now he was working even more, he was bathed in sweat in the backyard and considering the ways the climate wanted to take the house back. The pear tree's branches had grown onto the roof. Some animal—the raccoons? The squirrel?—had eaten his tomatoes off the vine. They were bloody nubs now, shriveled and torn. He recalled reading years ago that if you wanted to understand the state of a person's mind, you could just look at their home.

Others will think what they will. They'll see him as an absent father. But he loses either way. He'll either be the unemployed father who can't pay child support—a villain—or the father who lives in a different city, who isn't around—a villain. The latter, at least, was villainy with means. Villainy that provides, that is in town every other weekend.

His left arm was tired so he switched to his right. Back and forth, back and forth, and another laurel fell. The way the thing twisted as it gave, the crash of leaves and branches. He dragged it onto the pile.

It will be like death and rebirth. A few people might ask where he's been, others will tell them he got a job and moved to San Francisco. The house abandoned, the struggle abandoned, no longer would he add the cost of the groceries in his cart before approaching the checkstand, no longer would he drink two-dollar beers. It intrigued him, this death, it whispered to him, promised freedom. He would return every so often to haunt the city, to judge the living and the dead. His fallen self would be gone, people would see him in a new form, bright and shining.

The next laurel wasn't as easy. The blade caught, there was something different about it.

He thought about her. To move, to disappear, without a word? And yet what was he supposed to do? She didn't want to fall back.

It was smart to take a break. He put the saw down and dragged branches to the lower part of the yard. It was good to clear things up every so often, to stay organized.

Sweat rolled off his nose. He wiped his face with the back of his arm. He pulled his gloves off and couldn't find his glass of water and then found it over on the steps.

He continued to see her, more now than ever. When he was in the grocery store he caught her leaving the aisle he'd just turned into. When he moved to the next aisle it wasn't her, though, it was some other woman nothing like her. He sensed her in the night, too. Not only next to him but also her rhythm, the sense of her body, the way she closed her eyes or pressed against him. He saw her on the street, up ahead on the sidewalk, but it was a mirage, it wasn't her. She always arrived twenty minutes late, out of breath, and she set her alarm to be up early, because she had to be to work on time. She said when they called it the rat race she thought it was just about hurrying—she didn't know it was because work makes us feel like rodents. You have to aspire to be an admirable rodent, he'd said, maybe there are rodents that are gifted and noble, like a smart and savvy opossum. Pride in the spite chore. Shaming the landlord. It had been two years since the laurels had been cut, maybe three. He used the yellow-handled tree saw, moving through them one by one. Just a cold, methodical bastard. He liked the exactness of it, the spectacle of the chopped trunks.

She needed to make decisions about her future. She didn't want to fall back. Hulme would remake Bermea's plumbing company into an aspirational lifestyle brand. A couple weeks before, Geary was watching Letterman when Justin Bieber had appeared to read the Top Ten list. Letterman had said, "You have no idea who I am, do you?" Bieber had seemed confused, shook his head. It was hard to tell if he was admitting he didn't know or if perhaps from where he was standing he couldn't hear. Dave and Paul improvised some jokes—Letterman told Bieber to stop throwing the paper on the lawn, Shaffer said he was surprised the cameras were shooting him from the waist down—but nothing seemed to land. The audience was uncertain whether to laugh or let the kid read the list. Bieber stood there, waiting. He probably had no context for print newspapers and their traditional delivery by boys on bicycles, and neither would he have understood Shaffer's Elvis reference, how he was in the same theater. Or maybe it was just the bright lights, and Bieber standing there alone, waiting for a cue Dave and Paul seemed in no hurry to offer. Shaffer asked whether Bieber's fragrance was for men or ladies. Bieber told him it was for *women*, and the audience laughed at the correction. Justin Bieber reading a Top Ten list as a means of pushing a fragrance for women was hardly a novel horror. Geary had been struck for a number of years by the same outrage—not just that the new generation of internet celebrities didn't seem to know who David Letterman was, but that Letterman had agreed to let Bieber read a Top Ten list at all.

Geary looked at the stack of felled laurels. Something would have to be done with them, of course. They couldn't just be left there.

She'd said she had to make decisions about her future and of course he needed to do the same. Here was the opportunity. His future was San Francisco.

He began again to saw. A laurel fell and he threw it on the pile. The pile was growing again and he thought, It won't harm anything to drag them to the bottom of the yard where nothing grows anyway. He grabbed two of the felled laurels and dragged them down the stone steps, one in each gloved hand, to where the ruined vinyl pool lay in dirt and fir needles.

He would have to tell her. She had sent him those few text messages, brief and polite. She had established that this was how they communicated now, this was the space she needed. He would text her that he'd accepted a job in San Francisco but that he would be back every other weekend to see his kids, and he hoped she was well. Why mention the kids, what did that matter? He would text that he'd accepted a job in San Francisco and he hoped she was well.

He would ask for an advance on moving expenses and use the money to pay his last bills and would abandon all design work in Portland and spend a week packing. He would rent a storage unit and put his things there and put the kids' things there and give Andrea a key so that if the kids needed or wanted anything they could get it. He would find a unit in the cleanest, safest place, somewhere near her house. For everyone's convenience.

He wiped the sweat from his face. He dragged two more felled laurels to the bottom of the yard and surveyed his progress and saw he was almost halfway through the line.

A single mother. The phrase with all its pathos, the note of struggle in the face of male betrayal and irresponsibility. The single mother sacrifices her life for the life of her child. A religious figure, a saint, the Madonna in beatific light.

He felled two more laurels, he dragged them to the bottom of the yard.

She was not a woman who had made demands of him. She was only free on Wednesday evenings and he could not divine from that limited schedule what it was she wanted or expected of him, in what ways he had disappointed or become a person to whom she did not want to fall back.

He pulled his gloves off, opened his phone, and read the texts. Telling him he had her heart, wishing him a happy birthday. When he closed his eyes he could see her face. He saw her in the store, on the street. He stood there in the heat, the saws and rakes and laurels on the grass, and read the texts. Dark letters on a gray background, words in the technological void. All the messages, where will they go? What will become of them?

He drank some water. He cut laurels until there was a high pile of them at the bottom of the yard, until he was done.

8 | Nathan slipped. Anyone can take a wrong step.

Two counselors from his day camp herded kids onto a bus at lunchtime and took them to Keller Fountain. The upper level was a group of irregularly sized and spaced concrete troughs, water spilling over the walls between them. People waded in, and younger people walked the walls, hopping from trough to trough. Some sat on the last walls of the concrete Brutalist structure, from which water cascaded to a shallow pool fifteen feet below. The camp counselors were college students, Colin and Stephanie. Colin had never been to the fountain before and was surprised. What prevented someone falling from the edge? Fear? Self-preservation? They had brought third through fifth graders—coordinated, athletic kids. The boys, especially, fed on the fountain's energy. They splashed each other, they pushed, they jumped from wall to wall.

"Cool it, guys," Colin said. "This is a public place. Be respectful of others."

"We are being respectful," they complained.

"Be *more* respectful." His complaints were pointless. He was embarrassed by his own tone.

They dodged and leaped, pushed and pulled and shouted, exhilarated. Nathan wore a Day-Glo camp t-shirt that said "Fun in the City!" above a silhouette of black sunglasses. His swimming trunks had a shark on one leg. He had never experienced the city this way, as a place he could run through with a pack of new friends. He sometimes forgot the other boys' names, but they forgot his, too. It didn't matter.

Clouds had gathered, people had mostly left the pools. The boys were running unimpeded along the walls, jumping from perch to perch, playing a game of tag. Afterward people often say they sensed something, they knew it. The boys had run the walls a number of times, they knew the pattern now, the distances between. Nathan was chasing, he was close to catching someone, and he leaped, arm outstretched. It was a matter of an inch, maybe two. His toe hit but did not make the edge of the next wall. His upper body moved forward and down, a shift so sudden it seemed a violation of physics. People looked over, trying to identify the skip in their vision. Nathan's face hit the top of the wall so squarely the boys near him cried out and recoiled, fists to their foreheads.

He stood, mouth contorted. Blood flowed from his nose and mouth, it was stunning how quickly it appeared. It dripped from his chin, blosomed in bright spots on his shirt.

"Shit," Colin said.

"Get the first aid kit."

"I'm not sure where..."

"In the duffel bag," Stephanie told him. She was older, this was her fourth summer working for the program. The boys said she was the bossy one who didn't let them have fun. She was already moving toward Nathan.

He stood in the water, covering his face. He saw with great clarity the way the toe of his shoe had missed the top of the wall, his mind replayed it. He didn't know what to do. School and camp days had schedules, there were rules for classes and games. He knew no procedure for pain, for being broken. He was confused.

"Nathan, I need to see your face," Stephanie said. The water was above his waist but came only to her thighs, it darkened the hem of her shorts. "I need to see what happened."

If he moved his hands from his face, something bad

would happen. He felt this strongly. It required an effort of will.

There was nothing to see but blood. It flowed from his nose, from his lips, from inside of his mouth. "Okay," Stephanie said. "Let's go."

She lifted him from the water in one swift movement. He smelled of chlorine and sunscreen. A woman stood nearby with two small children stood nearby, hand over her mouth. The children stared.

"I tripped," Nathan mumbled.

"You absolutely did."

"I'm sorry."

"It's okay." She carried him like a rag doll. Colin was still rooting through the duffel bag. There was no first-aid kit, he couldn't believe it. He looked through the bag again and again as if it would appear, as if his eyes had deceived him.

Geary had watched the clouds roll in and wondered if Nathan would be cold at the fountain. He was leaving the grocery, a bag in either hand. The kids were tired at the end of camp days and complained if he stopped at the store on the way home. Then they asked if they could get candy or a toy. When he said no, they complained more, he snapped at them, and things went downhill. Things would go smoothly today. He already had food, he could take them straight home.

He put the bags down by his car before answering his phone and listening to Stephanie's breathless report. "I'll be there in five minutes," he said, though he was fifteen minutes away.

He drove at a deliberate pace, his mind on his destination and the importance of staying focused. He slipped over the bridge, descended into downtown, and parked three blocks from the fountain—he didn't want to risk not being able to find another spot. He didn't bother to pay the machine and began sidestepping pedestrians, assuming a pace that was urgent but unpanicked. An alarm sounded as a white van backed out of a garage. Geary waited for it to clear the sidewalk. The man in the passenger seat saluted him.

He moved along the parking lane to avoid the sidewalk tables of a coffeehouse. He was negotiating the route like an obstacle course. His phone rang.

"Do you have him yet?"

"Not yet. I'm almost there."

"Bring him straight to the emergency entrance."

He didn't see them at the lower pool. He jogged up the sidewalk that rose to the next street and was sweating when he found the counselors on a bench near the upper pools, a boy between them holding a towel to his face. The rest of the towel covered his head like a shroud.

"I was going to take him myself, but I remembered from last summer that you maybe worked near here," Stephanie said.

"Sometimes. What happened?"

"He was chasing other boys, jumping from one wall to another, and he missed and hit the wall."

"Nathan? Are you in there?"

The boy nodded. Blood had soaked the towel where his face would be.

"Can you talk?"

He shook his head. "There's too much blood in my mouth. It tastes gross. I might throw up."

"Let me see."

Nathan raised the towel and Geary peered beneath it.

"Do you need another towel?" Stephanie said.

"No, I keep some in my car. Let's go, bud."

He carried his son the same way the counselor had. He was conscious of their presence as spectacle, of the element of *Kramer vs. Kramer* in carrying an injured child.

"How far is the car?" Nathan asked, his voice muffled by the towel.

"A couple blocks."

"I can walk, Dad. Put me down."

They continued on foot, Nathan holding the towel to his nose and mouth, peering over it.

On the drive to the hospital he slumped in the back seat, eyes closed, a fresh towel to his face. Foliage lined the rising road, a jungle of green. Branches cast patterns that flowed up the windshield and disappeared. Geary parked in the emergency roundabout and Andrea came out.

"Let me see," she said.

Nathan lowered the towel. Geary watched her wince. She took a breath.

"Open your mouth."

"The blood tastes gross."

"You can spit it into the towel. Okay, let's get you in there. They know you're here."

She led him by the hand. The glass doors slid shut behind them and Geary saw a liquid version of himself in their reflection, his t-shirt and jeans, his rundown car. He wanted to go back in time and stop Nathan from being hurt, but how far back? There were so many links in the chain. They somehow included the fact that he didn't have health insurance for his own children. Andrea did.

When the doctor finished examining Nathan, she said he was lucky. "Nothing's broken," she said. "Some pretty good scrapes, definitely bruising and split lips, but that will heal. He didn't break any teeth. He didn't break his jaw or any bones in his face. The only scar will probably be on his tongue."

"His tongue?"

"He bit through it, in the middle."

"Through it?"

"Yes, but we don't do stitches in the middle of a tongue. We'll give you something to keep it clean. It will heal on its own."

"How do you keep a tongue clean?" Andrea asked.

"You chew on soap," the doctor said, patting Nathan on the knee. "No, I'm sorry, that's for bad language. We have an antibiotic mouthwash."

"Did you check for a concussion? I always worry about concussions."

"He has no idea what date it is or what day of the week it is, but kids usually don't in summer. I asked him who just won the NBA championship, but he said doesn't follow sports. He knows where he is, though, and everything that happened. Keep an eye on him, but he's probably fine. He can walk right out of here once Mom and Dad sign a couple things. Make sure you tell your friends they should see what the other guy looked like, Nathan."

"What do you mean?"

"She's pretending you were in a fight, like you beat up the other guy even worse," Andrea said.

"Everyone saw me fall."

"It's just a joke."

He lay on the futon that evening, watching a movie.

Emily was solicitous—she brought him cups of juice, broke cookies into pieces, gave him her extra pillow. She'd never been to that fountain, she didn't understand where or how this had happened. She understood only that she would need to help take care of her brother.

Geary watched them from the kitchen while he dried dishes. Later he went and sat between them. They watched a show together—a fake documentary about dinosaurs, a clever mix of props and digital effects. A triceratops had defecated in a steaming pile.

"Is this real?" Emily said.

"No."

"Dinosaurs did poop like that, though," Nathan mumbled.

"Okay, it might be somewhat accurate," Geary said. "But it's not real."

Emily nodded. "It's history," she said.

He walked down the street to the elementary school playground late each evening, laptop under his arm, to check email one last time. There could be something from Ad Astra—he needed to be responsive. He understood people from San Francisco were always connected, they emailed and chatted and posted at all hours, he saw them on Facebook and Twitter, the endless stream of wit and connection and outrage and power tumbling down the screen all evening and through the night.

He could check email one last time at the playground, at about nine thirty. That was it.

There was nothing from Ad Astra. But there was something from her. The sight of her name altered his breathing.

If you have a few hours on Sunday, please consider seeing Il Gattopardo at the Film Center. It is worth it for the color alone. I'm sure Criterion has done a great job with it, but the chance to see this particular film at this magnitude—it doesn't come along everyday.

He read it four times, five times, and then closed his laptop and carried it home. A bird whistled a few last lines in the twilight. It was odd, he could never locate singing birds. The songs just came from some airy overhead, from the ether.

9 | Dishes in the sink, a sweatshirt over the chair, a towel on the bathroom floor. The apartment was silent, forlorn. It was like a theater set that appears to be an apartment, but is obviously not a real apartment, clearly not an actual home.

Arden didn't care. He took Kira for his walks every morning and evening—the leash still hung by the door—but something had changed. There was nothing Kira could do about it. He lay by the door, head on his paws, watching his master. Arden treated the apartment like a hotel room, as if expecting the maid to straighten things. There was no maid.

He had walked to the Laurelhurst Theater one night because they were playing *The Third Man*. He sat alone in the dark, a slice of pizza and a beer on the counter before him. Reina's absence changed the film, though—he saw it differently, as if it were a taunt. Was he Holly Martins, telling everyone how the world worked, assuming he had a chance with the woman, blind to the fact that she was not in love with him at all? Was he too stupid to realize a Harry Lime lived somewhere in the margins—some other, more magnetic man, very much alive? His beer disappeared quickly, he was surprised to discover he'd finished it. Holly looked out the window while Anna looked at a photo of Lime. Well, that's the whole thing right there, he thought.

He studied the audience. It was mostly couples, older, eyes on the screen. A few had fallen asleep.

He could do nothing. Reina had announced she was going back to Los Angeles. She needed to make money, she said, and she could wait tables at a place she'd worked before. She could stay with her parents for the last six weeks of summer, save money on rent. Besides, she'd seen everything there was to see at Polymath. He'd been shocked, had asked the wrong questions. He was surprised the internship didn't pay. He'd asked why she couldn't get a job in Portland, what she was paying for rent. He'd replayed the conversation a number of times and went through it again during the movie. His questions had been foolish and pointless. He envied the others in the theater, their ability to enjoy the film as a fantasy. He had to watch Holly miss every clue, as if the film knew Arden, and was mocking him.

When it was over he walked out onto the sidewalk beneath the marquee with everyone else, one of many considering Lime's death and the last shot. He'd always found couples childish, saw in their handholding and kisses something desperate and needy, but he realized then he was no different. He wished Reina was with him, wanted to hold her hand and talk about the film, wanted to kiss her and take her home.

Now he stood in his shadowed apartment and looked into the afternoon sunlight at the bicyclists going past. A skateboarder slalomed lazily down the street. Where was Reina, what might she might be doing? She had escaped, but to what? An old boyfriend? A family home she preferred to being on her own? He could not shake the shame, the belief that there was something wrong with him. No one leaves a good lover. He doesn't know what other men do, though—it's a blind competition. There was pornography, but that was just anatomy, no information. A deeper mystery troubled him. The question of what it is to be someone else.

He forced himself to work, listlessly building layers in an image. He would start his new job soon, heading to an office in industrial Southeast Portland each morning. He would have a routine for where he locked his bike, where he got his coffee. He couldn't recall why he'd taken the job, what the advantage had been.

When his phone rang he grabbed it and looked at the screen, but it was just Don Geary. He answered and listened patiently to Geary's summary of his conversation with someone at Ad Astra.

"The package they're offering is more than fair," Arden said. "If you don't take it, I might. You're going to get paid to play."

"It's hard to believe."

"Only because you're used to our little servant economy here in Portland. We're all mediocre, so it's easy for everyone to undercut each other until nobody gets paid at all. And speaking of mediocre, did you notice your friend David Hulme is one of the keynote speakers at the design conference? With those pseudo-venture-cap dudes?"

"What? Where's that?"

"The art museum. Since advertising is art now, just like fashion. You're lucky you don't have to pay attention. You have a job in San Francisco and they don't care about little Portland conferences where people play grab-ass all afternoon and then go out for fucking kombucha. You're free, you don't have to deal with this."

"They're really the speakers? This afternoon?"

"Of course. Charlatans hang with charlatans. If there are enough of them in one place, they can convince each other they're real."

There was a long silence on the other end of the line. "That's insane," Geary said.

"It's the opposite of insane. It's totally predictable."

After he hung up with Geary he stared out the window for three minutes, for four minutes. He had already called Reina and he had texted her and it would be unseemly now to do more. He was playing a game badly, he felt. Every move he made further weakened his position. It wasn't true he would want the job Geary was taking at Ad Astra, but he believed what he'd said about Portland. The feelings left him nowhere, they left him stranded. He'd become a man whose next move would be to scratch a message onto the beach of his island. After that there was nothing to do but stare at the sky, waiting.

Geary considered it immediately. He couldn't help it, it was how his mind worked. He was stirred by feats of daring, by risks in the service of truth. If even just to witness the thing, to lay eyes on the dog and pony show.

"Who were you talking to?" Emily asked.

"It was just about work."

"All your phone calls are about work," she complained.

He let five minutes pass, ten. Emily pushed a plastic car around her room. It held a doll shoved into the front seat at an odd angle. There was a flaw in the doll's articulation or the car's size, possibly both.

The clock ticked, minutes like hours. He tried to clean the kitchen, to fold the laundry. The tasks took no time. He knew this because he checked the clock after each of them.

"Listen, I'm sorry, Em," he said finally. "There's something I forgot about that I have to take care of. I'm going to have to take you over to Mom's for a bit. You can spend some time helping her take care of Nathan."

"Okay. Will I see you again?"

"What do you mean will you see me again?" he said, alarmed.

"Am I staying at Mom's or coming back to your house?"

"Of course you'll see me again. You always see me again."

10 | He had been so many people in Portland. He'd written book and movie reviews for the weekly newspaper, he was a barista for eight months, in grad school he taught composition courses, he published short fiction, he published essays, he did web design, he did branding and evaluated branding and was now perhaps a failed evaluator of branding. Life was supposed to make sense in retrospect,

he'd heard. His last dozen years had all seemed natural, the move from one thing to another. It was in retrospect that it seemed nonsense, chaos, noise with no signal. The story of his life was there was no story.

People gathered in knots outside the museum, talked while checking their phones. A statue of Theodore Roosevelt stood in the middle of the park, but the conference attendees didn't drift that far. The park belonged to the homeless, their bags and backpacks next to them on benches. They gathered in their own knots, talking and laughing. The difference was that they did not check phones. The homeless looked each other in the eye.

A woman stood behind the desk at the entrance to the ballroom. It was the woman he'd seen at the art museum weeks before, the one by the door Hulme had come through. Her hair was the same, pulled tightly back, but today she wore a white pantsuit instead of black. A large piece of twisting red glass adorned the wall behind her. A fern next to the desk was so healthy it seemed artificially green. He nodded to her as he approached. He thought she might raise her hand or stop him, but she just smiled. She was older, stood with a regal formality, a dancer's posture. He made no attempt to affect any particular attitude. He did not pretend to have his conference badge in his pocket, did not stare at his cell phone to avoid her glance. He was scared. He recognized in her the presence of legitimate authority. He decided he would simply walk into the ballroom and when she asked if he had a badge or had paid for the conference he would apologize. He even rehearsed the apology in his head, rehearsed telling her the truth, that he wanted only to hear Hulme's speech. But she just nodded politely at him, seemed encouraging, even. And then he was past her and into the large ballroom filled with booths and tables, the mustard carpet and walls extending into the distance. The entire room felt suspended in a dusty haze. He felt more fear now, because no one was going to stop him. It would be up to him and he would learn something about himself he wasn't sure he wanted to learn.

Some booths were staffed by three or four people and others were staffed by lone individuals, but every table featuring carefully laid out materials, one-sheets and pamphlets and brochures and magazines. "Have you seen this? Take a look at this." Some booths had video monitors on stands. The monitors broadcast floating logos, cursors swiftly navigating websites, videos in which the camera floated smoothly through an office or a building or a forest and then gracefully up and out over everything. The tables with multiple staffers belonged to thriving agencies. Maybe some of the tables staffed by one person were also agencies, but many were just a lone soul trying to affect the appearance of an agency, acting as if he were a part of some larger entity although he—the lone souls were exclusively male—was not actually a part of anything. "Let me show you this, have you seen this?"

Near the end of the first aisle he went past a table where a middle-aged man with a long beard and a plain gray t-shirt was repeating, "Automated sites, beautiful design, anyone can do it. Automated sites, beautiful design, anyone can do it." At the end of the aisle Geary turned to head down the other side. "Automated sites, beautiful design, anyone can do it." No one stopped, people walked right past the man. It wasn't clear if he understood his chant might offend, or if that was in fact his intention.

"Automated sites, beautiful design, anyone can do it."
Maybe he liked offending these people, maybe he hated
designers. Automated websites, beautiful design. Who, after all, needed to be liberated from the imperatives of design more than designers themselves? Maybe design was
the problem. People walked past, some laughed and shook
their head, others just ignored him. No one approached,
no one asked him what he was selling. He had no video
monitor, just two stacks of paper. Geary could see they
were the same one-sheet, the man had just put them in
two different stacks. "Automated sites, beautiful design.
Anyone can do it."

In the auditorium Geary stood in the back and watched
the people assembling for the keynote. Every kind of
clothing, every kind of style. There were clean-cut men
in suits and men with long beards who wore shorts and
t-shirts. There were women in heels and skirts and ironed
blouses and women in sneakers and jeans. Again there was
a podium at the front of the room, again a large screen that
had been pulled down or more likely mechanically lowered
from some overhead device. The screen displayed Hulme's
name in large black Helvetica, and beneath Hulme's name
was Norman's name, and beneath Norman's name was
Bouros's name. Beneath Bouros's name was *Landscape
with the Fall of Icarus*, the horse and ploughman, the sea
and sky. Geary studied the auditorium, the stream of people finding seats, the way they looked into their phones
and looked up to laugh and then looked into their phones
again. This was what they called the "Creative Class." It
could easily turn out to be the same talk Hulme had given
at the art museum a month ago, but with Norman and
Bouros now serving as hype men. There could be others in

the audience like Geary, people who had already heard the talk. Geary knew he could listen again. He could listen a third or fourth time, even. He would study the timing of Hulme's jokes, when and where Hulme chose to look over his shoulder at the screen, when and where he searched the eyes of the audience.

A man seated at the front of the auditorium turned and looked up toward the back and his eyes came to rest on Geary. It was Hal Bermea, forty rows away—far enough that Geary felt no need to acknowledge him. Or maybe distance had nothing to do with it, maybe it was unnecessary regardless.

He could still hear the man. *Automated sites, beautiful design, anyone can do it.* His voice carried from the doors of the ballroom and through the breezeway to the auditorium, plain and clear. *Anyone can do it. Beautiful design.*

He did not want to sit, but felt conspicuous lurking behind everyone. He left the auditorium and walked down a section of hallway that curved along the back, toward the bathrooms. He had looked the woman at the front desk in the eye, but now he avoided all eyes—there was no one here he wanted to see. He kept thinking about the *Creative Class*, how the auditorium was filled with the *Creative Class*. Had the Creative Class named themselves, or had people not among the Creative Class named them? Was the term sincere or ironic? The hallway continued around the side of the auditorium. Through another set of double doors he saw the stairs along the side of the auditorium that led down to the stage. He was sideways to the screen here and could not see *Fall of Icarus*, saw only a pool of light rippling on the screen and the dark stage behind, where a bearded man in jeans and a red t-shirt was rapidly coiling a long black cable around his palm and elbow. The man leaned back, keeping his face away from the loose cable that danced before him as he wound it.

"There are times to start on time and there are times not to start on time," Norman said.

"We're in no hurry," Hulme said.

"This is a not-start-on-time time," Norman said.

Geary had almost stumbled into them as they came through a door just beyond the bathroom. They looked at him.

"Hello, Don," Bouros said.

"The keynoters," Geary said. "How was the green room?"

"It was...beige."

"Everything looks ready," Geary said. "You, the audience, actual art. You know a lot of people think that's a copy, though, right?"

"Think what's a copy?" Bouros said.

"*The Fall of Icarus*. We've probably never seen the real one."

"Interesting. I didn't know that. Are you here for the presentation?"

They were watching him closely. Or maybe he was projecting. "I'm not sure. Is it new material?"

"I don't know about us," Norman said. "David, at least, is always doing something new."

Geary couldn't tell if Hulme knew who he was. Even if he'd introduced himself, it seemed likely Hulme wouldn't have been able to place the name.

"I hope you're doing well, Don," Bouros said.

"Me? No, not really."

"I'm sorry to hear that."

"I don't mean to bother you, I know you have to go on. But what is it you've done, again?"

"What do you mean?" Bouros said.

"You know what I mean. Don't worry, you're safe, you'll coast through life. But you tell people how the world works, you pontificate, you are supposed *thought leaders*... but what have you actually done?"

"What have *you* done, Don?" Hulme said. He was looking at Geary as if fascinated.

Hal Bermea appeared in the doorway to the auditorium along with the man in the red t-shirt. Bermea was saying something to him as they stepped into the hall.

"Nothing," Geary said. "I'm still working on it."

"Don believes he's on a path," Bouros said.

Norman laughed. "A path to where?"

"Keep laughing, asshole," Geary said.

The man in the red shirt stepped toward them, Bermea a step behind. The man was larger up close, he seemed almost bored. "You can't be here, sir," he said.

"It's okay," Hulme said. "It's belief that's the crucial element, isn't it?"

"I like to think the path is the crucial element."

"No, he can't be here," the man said.

"It's not the destination, it's the journey?" Norman said. "You can't go out there with that, Don. That's a cliché."

"Shut the fuck up," Geary said.

The man in the red shirt took Geary by the elbow and hand and pulled Geary's thumb back toward his wrist. Geary grimaced and tried to twist away but could not.

"What are you doing?" Bouros said.

"I'm doing this to calm you down," the man told Geary.

"Let go of me," Geary said. He put his free hand under the man's chin, into the bristles of his beard, and tried to push the man's head back, but the man bent Geary's thumb further and Geary dropped to his knees.

"You need to leave."

"You're breaking my thumb."

"You don't need to do that," Hulme said.

"Are you going to leave?"

"Let go of me."

"And you will leave?"

"I will leave!" Geary said.

The man let go. Geary, kneeling, immediately began massaging the base of his thumb. He did not want to, did not want to appear weak, but he couldn't help it.

"That was not necessary," Hulme said.

"Unfortunately, it was," Bermea said.

Geary got to his feet and looked at the group of men assembled before him. He was breathing hard. "Have a great presentation," he said. "You do nothing."

He turned and walked away. He didn't look back to see if anyone was following, but no one stopped him. When he walked out past the entry podium, the woman who had been there was gone. No one had replaced her, the podium was empty.

He had a sense, while driving home, that he was not the one driving. When he turned right, he watched himself turn right. When he signaled and changed lanes, he watched himself signal and change lanes. He was following himself. And because he was being followed, he felt a desire to hide, to get away. To end something forever.

11 | He made the call mid-morning. Nathan had recovered enough to go to the tennis camp he and Emily were enrolled in that week. College kids had welcomed them, a young man and young woman in bright white t-shirts, rackets in hand, upbeat and energetic and calling the kids by name. Emily was already dropping a ball and swinging at it before Geary left. Nathan hung back, leaning against the chain-link fence, reluctant to be seen in an ungraceful moment. His lips and chin were scabbed, but the swelling was gone. When Geary waved goodbye, he had offered just a slight nod.

Geary settled at his desk. Three times he checked the envelope on which he had written the number, afraid he would transpose digits or otherwise fail, and would end up inconveniencing a stranger. He felt the embarrassment of dialing a wrong number just as keenly as an adult as he had as a child, when he'd first learned to use the phone that hung on the kitchen wall.

He managed the feat, though. A receptionist answered and put him through to Evan Craig, who said good morning and asked how he was, a question Geary did not know how to respond to and so ignored. "I'm sorry, but I'm going to have to turn down your job offer," he said. "Everything about it is generous and I would love to work for Ad Astra, but I can't relocate. I'm a single dad and moving… it just wouldn't work."

"I understand," Craig said, a slight reverberation in the audio suggesting he had Geary on speaker. "These kinds of decisions are difficult."

"And you're sure there's no chance of me working from Portland?"

"No, I'm sorry. We work collaboratively and communicate in person. We don't do distance."

"Yes. That's how I like to do things, too."

They traded expressions of mutual gratitude and goodwill. After the line went dead, Geary looked at the phone as if it might offer some final bit of information, but the screen was blank. He was shaking, he felt sick. He'd been offered a chance to change his life and had passed. He'd chosen some other future, headed toward some other life he might now never control or understand.

After dinner that night the kids watched a movie. They brought popsicles to the futon in little plastic bowls and ate the popsicles with great care and abandoned the bowls and sticks on the coffee table with no care at all. Their attention was on the animated heroes of the movie. Their eyes were wide and their arms and legs were like long toothpicks clothed in little shorts and t-shirts. They seemed to grow faster in the summer.

When the movie was over, Nathan found Geary at the kitchen table, laptop open before him. "What are you working on?"

"A new project," Geary said.

"What is it?" Nathan wore his serious expression. He could be very insistent.

"It's work."

"What's the work? More websites?"

Geary looked at him. It was too much to explain. And he was right, in a way—everything, eventually, was just a website.

"No. No websites this time," Geary said.

"Then what is it?"

"Words."

"A story?"

"I don't know if I'd call it that. Just words."

"Can I read it when you're done?"

Geary didn't know what to do, how to get there. He had only a great quiet. He knew he wanted to take a different path, but he didn't know how to start. Beyond the windows, the night was a dark void, as if the house were a ship drifting through space, he, Nathan, and Emily nested within. The night offers timeless moments, darkness a frame that sets off faces in the light. But then the frame dissolves. Another day arrives, the clock continues to tick. Nothing survives time.

Geary looked at his son. "Okay. You can read it when it's done." It seemed a safe thing to say, since he believed he would never be done.

12 | He decided to carry his dining table into the backyard. He gripped the opposing ends, tipped it toward himself, and when the edge settled against his thighs, he leaned back and cantilevered it off the ground.

No professional mover would condone this, no physical therapist would suggest it.

He shuffled forward, breathing hard, and made his way out the basement's French doors. There were the two concrete steps to the yard. He grunted up the first step, the edge of the table digging into his thighs. His stomach and back were tight, his palms on fire, and the one thumb was sore, but it was nothing. One more move and he'd be up the second step and onto the grass. He lurched forward, but again the table's leg clipped the step—again the thing jolted out of his grip. His reflex was not to allow the edge to hit him in the ribs again, but this resulted in him dropping the table while stumbling forward and over it as it rolled. One of the legs caught him just behind his hip, a kidney strike. He cried out and fell into the grass, cursing.

He lay on his back, eyes closed, waiting for the pain to ebb. He heard their footsteps, heard them call his name, and when he opened his eyes they were standing over him. Behind their faces was the sky, brilliant blue.

"Are you okay?" they asked.

"Yes."

"You're not dead, are you?"

"No. I'm immortal."

"What does that mean?"

"It means I can be hurt, but I can't be killed."

They laughed.

"I don't ever want you to die, though. For real," Nathan said.

"I won't. But can you do me a favor?"

"What?"

"Bring me my phone. It's on the table by my bed."

"To call the ambulance?" Emily said.

"No. Just a friend."

Nathan headed away on the task. Emily stayed, looking down at him. "You always get hurt," she said.

"I do not always get hurt."

"You get hurt a lot," she said.

Nathan returned, handed Geary the phone.

"Now go away. Go back in the house," Geary said.

"Why?"

"Because I want to have a private conversation. Not everything is for you."

They walked dutifully back into the basement and he listened to the thump of their footsteps heading up the stairs. Their voices faded as they returned to the living room, and he then heard the sound of animal cries carrying faintly from within the house. He could not place the source, what program they might be watching that would include those sounds. He was still in the grass. He opened his phone, scrolled to the name, and dialed. He had known for some time what he wanted, so he would try. He understood it was probably too late.

ABOUT THE AUTHOR

Dan DeWeese's novel *You Don't Love This Man* was nominated for an Oregon Book Award. He is also the author of the story collection *Disorder*, the novella *Soft Rock*, and the novels *Gielgud* and *Double Standard*. His fiction has appeared in publications including *Tin House*, *New England Review*, and *The Normal School*. He lives in Portland, Oregon.